'An SF Master
There can be few better examples of how
science fiction at its best can illuminate man
by taking parts of his physical and
psychological make-up and expanding them
almost to breaking point'
NEW SCIENTIST

'Strange Relations
The long overdue first assemblage of Philip
José Farmer's stories, turns out to be the
most exciting science fiction collection in at
least two years'
NEW YORK HERALD TRIBUNE

Philip José Farmer

Strange Relations

A Panther Book

Strange Relations
A Panther Book

First published in Great Britain
by Victor Gollancz Limited 1964

Panther edition published 1966

Copyright © Ballantine Books Inc. 1960

Printed by the permission of the author's agent,
stories first appeared in:
MOTHER: *Thrilling Wonder Stories*, April 1953.
DAUGHTER: *Thrilling Wonder Stories*, Winter 1954.
FATHER: *Magazine of Fantasy & Science Fiction*,
July 1955.
SON: (originally titled QUEEN OF THE DEEP) *Argosy*,
March 1954.
MY SISTER'S BROTHER: (originally titled THE
STRANGE BIRTH) *Satellite*, June 1959.

*Printed in Great Britain by Cox & Wyman Ltd.,
London, Reading and Fakenham, and published
by Panther Books Ltd.,
108 Brompton Road, London, S.W.3*

Contents

I

'LOOK, mother. The clock is running backwards.'
Eddie Fetts pointed to the hands on the pilot room dial.
Dr. Paula Fetts said, 'The crash must have reversed it.'
'How could it do that?'
'I can't tell you. I don't know everything, son.'
'Oh!'
'Well, don't look at me so disappointedly. I'm a pathologist, not an electronician.'
'Don't be so cross, mother. I can't stand it. Not now.'
He walked out of the pilot room. Anxiously, she followed him. The burial of the crew and her fellow scientists had been very trying for him. Spilled blood had always made him dizzy and sick; he could scarcely control his hands enough to help her sack the scattered bones and entrails.

He had wanted to put the corpses in the nuclear furnace, but she had forbidden that. The Geigers amidships were ticking loudly, warning that there was invisible death in the stern.

The meteor that struck the moment the ship came out of Translation into normal space had probably wrecked the engine-room. So she had understood from the incoherent high-pitched phrases of a colleague before he fled to the pilot room. She had hurried to find Eddie. She feared his cabin door would still be locked, as he had been making a tape of the aria 'Heavy Hangs the Albatross' from Gianelli's *Ancient Mariner*.

Fortunately, the emergency system had automatically thrown out the locking circuits. Entering, she had called out his name in fear he'd been hurt. He was lying half-unconscious on the floor, but it was not the accident that had thrown him there. The reason lay in the corner, released from his lax hand; a quart free-fall thermos, rubber-nippled. From Eddie's open mouth charged a breath of rye that not even Nodor pills had been able to conceal.

Sharply she had commanded him to get up and on to the

7

bed. Her voice, the first he had ever heard, pierced through the phalanx of Old Red Star. He struggled up, and she, though smaller, had thrown every ounce of her weight into getting him up and on to the bed.

There she had lain down with him and strapped them both in. She understood that the lifeboat had been wrecked also, and that it was up to the captain to bring the yacht down safely to the surface of this charted but unexplored planet, Baudelaire. Everybody else had gone to sit behind the captain, strapped in crashchairs, unable to help except with their silent backing.

Moral support had not been enough. The ship had come in on a shallow slant. Too fast. The wounded motors had not been able to hold her up. The prow had taken the brunt of the punishment. So had those seated in the nose.

Dr. Fetts had held her son's head on her bosom and prayed out loud to her God. Eddie had snored and muttered. Then there was a sound like the clashing of the gates of doom – a tremendous bong as if the ship were a clapper in a gargantuan bell tolling the most frightening message human ears may hear – a blinding blast of light – and darkness and silence.

A few moments later Eddie began crying out in a childish voice, 'Don't leave me to die, mother! Come back! Come back!'

Mother was unconscious by his side, but he did not know that. He wept for a while, then he lapsed back into his rye-fogged stupor – if he had ever been out of it – and slept. Again, darkness and silence.

It was the second day since the crash, if 'day' could describe that twilight state on Baudelaire. Dr. Fetts followed her son wherever he went. She knew he was very sensitive and easily upset. All his life she had known it and had tried to get between him and anything that would cause trouble. She had succeeded, she thought, fairly well until three months ago when Eddie had eloped.

The girl was Polina Fameux, the ash-blonde long-legged actress whose tridi image, taped, had been shipped to frontier stars where a small acting talent meant little and a large and shapely bosom much. Since Eddie was a well-known Metro tenor, the marriage made a big splash whose ripples ran around the civilized Galaxy.

Dr. Fetts had felt very bad about the elopement, but she had, she hoped, hidden her grief very well beneath a smiling mask. She didn't regret having to give him up; after all, he was a full-grown man, no longer her little boy. But, really, aside from the seasons at the Met and his tours, he had not been parted from her since he was eight.

That was when she went on a honeymoon with her second husband. And then she and Eddie had not been separated long, for Eddie had got very sick, and she'd had to hurry back and take care of him, as he had insisted she was the only one who could make him well.

Moreover, you couldn't count his days at the opera as a total loss, for he vised her every noon and they had a long talk – no matter how high the vise bills ran.

The ripples caused by her son's marriage were scarcely a week old before they were followed by even bigger ones. They bore the news of the separation of Eddie and his wife. A fortnight later, Polina applied for divorce on grounds of incompatibility. Eddie was handed the papers in his mother's apartment. He had come back to her the day he and Polina had agreed they 'couldn't make a go of it,' or, as he phrased it to his mother, 'couldn't get together.'

Dr. Fetts was, of course, very curious about the reason for their parting, but, as she explained to her friends, she 'respected' his silence. What she didn't say was that she had told herself the time would come when he would tell her all.

Eddie's 'nervous breakdown' started shortly afterwards. He had been very irritable, moody, and depressed, but he got worse the day a so-called friend told Eddie that whenever Polina heard his name mentioned, she laughed loud and long. The friend added that Polina had promised to tell someday the true story of their brief merger.

That night his mother had to call in a doctor.

In the days that followed, she thought of giving up her position as research pathologist at De Kruif and taking all her time to help him 'get back on his feet'. It was a sign of the struggle going on in her mind that she had not been able to decide within a week's time. Ordinarily given to swift consideration and resolution of a problem, she could not agree to surrender her beloved quest into tissue regeneration.

Just as she was on the verge of doing what was for her the incredible and the shameful, tossing a coin, she had been vised by her superior. He told her she had been chosen to go with a group of biologists on a research cruise to ten preselected planetary systems.

Joyfully, she had thrown away the papers that would turn Eddie over to a sanatorium. And, since he was quite famous, she had used her influence to get the government to allow him to go along. Ostensibly, he was to make a survey of the development of opera on planets colonized by Terrans. That the yacht was not visiting any colonized globes seemed to have been missed by the bureaus concerned. But it was not the first time in the history of a government that its left hand knew not what its right was doing.

Actually, he was to be 'rebuilt' by his mother, who thought herself much more capable of curing him than any of the prevalent A, F, J, R, S, K, or H therapies. True, some of her friends reported amazing results with some of the symbol-chasing techniques. On the other hand, two of her close companions had tried them all and had got no benefits from any of them. She was his mother; she could do more for him than any of those 'alphabatties'; he was flesh of her flesh, blood of her blood. Besides, he wasn't so sick. He just got awfully blue sometimes and made theatrical but insincere threats of suicide or else just sat and stared into space. But she could handle him.

II

So now it was that she followed him from the backward-running clock to his room. And saw him step inside, look for a second, and then turn to her with a twisted face.

'Neddie is ruined, mother. Absolutely ruined.'

She glanced at the piano. It had torn loose from the wall-racks at the moment of impact and smashed itself against the opposite wall. To Eddie it wasn't just a piano; it was Neddie. He had a pet name for everything he contacted for more than a brief time. It was as if he hopped from one appellation to the next, like an ancient sailor who felt lost unless he was close to the familiar and designated points of the shoreline. Otherwise, Eddie seemed to be drifting helplessly in a chaotic ocean, one that was anonymous and amorphous.

Or, analogy more typical of him, he was like the night-clubber who feels submerged, drowning, unless he hops from table to table, going from one well-known group of faces to the next, avoiding the featureless and unnamed dummies at the strangers' tables.

He did not cry over Neddie. She wished he would. He had been so apathetic during the voyage. Nothing, not even the unparalleled splendour of the naked stars nor the inexpressible alienness of strange planets had seemed to lift him very long. If he would only weep or laugh loudly or display some sign that he was reacting violently to what was happening. She would even have welcomed his striking her in anger or calling her 'bad' names.

But no, not even during the gathering of the mangled corpses, when he looked for a while as if he were going to vomit, would he give way to his body's demand for expression. She understood that if he were to throw up, he would be much better for it, would have got rid of much of the psychic disturbance along with the physical.

He would not. He had kept on raking flesh and bones into the large plastic bags and kept a fixed look of resentment and sullenness.

She hoped now that the loss of his piano would bring tears and shaking shoulders. Then she could take him in her arms and give him sympathy. He would be her little boy again, afraid of the dark, afraid of the dog killed by a car, seeking her arms for the sure safety, the sure love.

'Never mind, baby,' she said. 'When we're rescued, we'll get you a new one.'

'When—!'

He lifted his eyebrows and sat down on the bed's edge. 'What do we do now?'

She became very brisk and efficient.

'The ultrad automatically started working the moment the meteor struck. If it's survived the crash, it's still sending SOS's. If not, then there's nothing we can do about it. Neither of us knows how to repair it.

'However, it's possible that in the last five years since this planet was located, other expeditions may have landed here. Not from Earth but from some of the colonies. Or from non-human globes. Who knows? It's worth taking a chance. Let's see.'

A single glance was enough to wreck their hopes. The ultrad had been twisted and broken until it was no longer recognizable as the machine that sent swifter-than-light waves through the no-ether.

Dr. Fetts said with false cheeriness, 'Well, that's that! So what? It makes things too easy. Let's go into the storeroom and see what we can see.'

Eddie shrugged and followed her. There she insisted that each take a panrad. If they had to separate for any reason, they could always communicate and also, using the DF's – the built-in direction finders – locate each other. Having used them before, they knew the instruments' capabilities and how essential they were on scouting or camping trips.

The panrads were lightweight cylinders about two feet high and eight inches in diameter. Crampacked, they held the mechanisms of two dozen different utilities. Their batteries lasted a year without recharging, they were practically indestructible and worked under almost any conditions.

Keeping away from the inside of the ship that had the huge hole in it, they took the panrads outside. The long wave bands were searched by Eddie while his mother moved the dial that ranged up and down the shortwaves. Neither really expected to hear anything, but to search was better than doing nothing.

Finding the modulated wave-frequencies empty of any significant noises, he switched to the continuous waves. He was startled by a dot-dashing.

'Hey, mom! Something in the 1000 kilocycles! Unmodulated!'

'Naturally, son,' she said with some exasperation in the midst of her elation. 'What would you expect from a radio-telegraphic signal?'

She found the band on her own cylinder. He looked blankly at her. 'I know nothing about radio, but that's not Morse.'

'What? You must be mistaken!'

'I – I don't think so.'

'Is it or isn't it? Good God, son, can't you be certain of *anything*!'

She turned the amplifier up. As both of them had learned Galacto-Morse through sleeplearn techniques, she checked him at once.

'You're right. What do you make of it?'

His quick ear sorted out the pulses.

'No simple dot and dash. Four different time-lengths.'

He listened some more.

'They've got a certain rhythm, all right. I can make out definite groupings. Ah! That's the sixth time I've caught that particular one. And there's another. And another.'

Dr. Fetts shook her ash-blonde head. She could make out nothing but a series of zzt-zzt-zzt's.

Eddie glanced at the DF needle.

'Coming from NE by E. Should we try to locate?'

'Naturally,' she replied. 'But we'd better eat first. We don't know how far away it is, or what we'll find there. While I fix a hot meal, you get our field trip stuff ready.'

'O.K.,' he said with more enthusiasm than he had shown for a long time.

When he came back he ate everything in the large dish his mother had prepared on the unwrecked galley stove.

'You always did make the best stew,' he said.

'Thank you. I'm glad you're eating again, son. I am surprised. I thought you'd be sick about all this.'

He waved vaguely but energetically.

'The challenge of the unknown. I have a sort of feeling this is going to turn out much better than we thought. Much better.'

She came close and sniffed his breath. It was clean, innocent even of stew. That meant he'd taken Nodor, which probably meant he'd been sampling some hidden rye. Otherwise, how explain his reckless disregard of the possible dangers? It wasn't like him.

She said nothing, for she knew that if he tried to hide a bottle in his clothes or field sack while they were tracking down the radio signals, she would soon find it. And take it away. He wouldn't even protest, merely let her lift it from his limp hand while his lips swelled with resentment.

III

They set out. Both wore knapsacks and carried the panrads. He carried a gun over his shoulder, and she had snapped on to her sack her small black bag of medical and lab supplies.

High noon of late autumn was topped by a weak red sun that

barely managed to make itself seen through the eternal double layer of clouds. Its companion, an even smaller blob of lilac, was setting on the northwestern horizon. They walked in a sort of bright twilight, the best that Baudelaire ever achieved. Yet, despite the lack of light, the air was warm. It was a phenomenon common to certain planets behind the Horsehead Nebula, one being investigated but as yet unexplained.

The country was hilly, with many deep ravines. Here and there were prominences high enough and steep-sided enough to be called embryo mountains. Considering the roughness of the land, however, there was a surprising amount of vegetation. Pale green, red and yellow bushes, vines, and little trees clung to every bit of ground, horizontal or vertical. All had comparatively broad leaves that turned with the sun to catch the light.

From time to time, as the two Terrans strode noisily through the forest, small multicoloured insect-like and mammal-like creatures scuttled from hiding place to hiding place. Eddie decided to carry his gun in the crook of his arm. Then, after they were forced to scramble up and down ravines and hills and fight their way through thickets that became unexpectedly tangled, he put it back over his shoulder, where it hung from a strap.

Despite their exertions, they did not tire quickly. They weighed about twenty pounds less than they would have on Earth and, though the air was thinner, it was richer in oxygen.

Dr. Fetts kept up with Eddie. Thirty years the senior of the twenty-three-year-old, she passed even at close inspection for his older sister. Longevity pills took care of that. However, he treated her with all the courtesy and chivalry that one gave one's mother and helped her up the steep inclines, even though the climbs did not appreciably cause her deep chest to demand more air.

They paused once by a creek bank to get their bearings.

'The signals have stopped,' he said.

'Obviously,' she replied.

At that moment the radar-detector built into the panrad began to ping. Both of them automatically looked upwards.

'There's no ship in the air.'

'It can't be coming from either of those hills,' she pointed out. 'There's nothing but a boulder on top of each one. Tremendous rocks.'

'Nevertheless, it's coming from there, I think. Oh! Oh! Did

you see what I saw? Looked like a tall stalk of some kind being pulled down behind that big rock.'

She peered through the dim light. 'I think you were imagining things, son. I saw nothing.'

Then, even as the pinging kept up, the zzting started again. But after a burst of noise, both stopped.

'Let's go up and see what we shall see,' she said.

'Something screwy,' he commented. She did not answer.

They forded the creek and began the ascent. Half-way up, they stopped to sniff in puzzlement at a gust of some heavy odour coming downwind.

'Smells like a cageful of monkeys,' he said.

'In heat,' she added. If his was the keener ear, hers was the sharper nose.

They went on up. The RD began sounding its tiny hysterical gonging. Nonplussed, Eddie stopped. The DF indicated the radar pulses were not coming from the top of the hill they were climbing, as formerly, but from the other hill across the valley. Abruptly, the panrad fell silent.

'What do we do now?'

'Finish what we started. This hill. Then we go to the other one.'

He shrugged and then hastened after her tall slim body in its long-legged coveralls. She was hot on the scent, literally, and nothing could stop her. Just before she reached the bungalow-sized boulder topping the hill, he caught up with her. She had stopped to gaze intently at the DF needle, which swung wildly before it stopped at neutral. The monkey-cage odour was very strong.

'Do you suppose it could be some sort of radio-generating mineral?' she asked, disappointedly.

'No. Those groupings were semantic. And that smell. . . .'

'Then what—'

He didn't know whether to feel pleased or not that she had so obviously and suddenly thrust the burden of responsibility and action on him. Both pride and a curious shrinking affected him. But he did feel exhilarated. Almost, he thought, he felt as if he were on the verge of discovering what he had been looking for a long time. What the object of his search had been, he could not say. But he was excited and not very much afraid.

He unslung his weapon, a two-barrelled combination shot-gun and rifle. The panrad was still quiet.

'Maybe the boulder is camouflage for a spy outfit,' he said. He sounded silly, even to himself.

Behind him, his mother gasped and screamed. He whirled and raised his gun, but there was nothing to shoot. She was pointing at the hilltop across the valley, shaking, and saying something incoherent.

He could make out a long slim antenna seemingly projecting from the monstrous boulder crouched there. At the same time, two thoughts struggled for first place in his mind: one, that it was more than a coincidence that both hills had almost identical stone structures on their brows, and, two, that the antenna must have been recently stuck out, for he was sure he had not seen it the last time he looked.

He never got to tell her his conclusions, for something thin and flexible and irresistible seized him from behind. Lifted into the air, he was borne backwards. He dropped the gun and tried to grab the bands or tentacles around him and tear them off with his bare hands. No use.

He caught one last glimpse of his mother running off down the hillside. Then a curtain snapped down, and he was in total darkness.

IV

Eddie sensed himself, still suspended, twirled around. He could not know for sure, of course, but he thought he was facing in exactly the opposite direction. Simultaneously, the tentacles binding his legs and arms were released. Only his waist was still gripped. It was pressed so tightly that he cried out with pain.

Then, boot-toes bumping on some resilient substance, he was carried forward. Halted, facing he knew not what horrible monster, he was suddenly assailed – not by a sharp beak or tooth or knife or some other cutting or mangling instrument – but by a dense cloud of that same monkey perfume.

In other circumstances, he might have vomited. Now his stomach was not given the time to consider whether it should clean house or not. The tentacle lifted him higher and thrust him against something soft and yielding – something fleshlike and womanly – almost breastlike in texture and smoothness and warmth and in its hint of gentle curving.

He put his hands and feet out to brace himself, for he thought for a moment he was going to sink in and be covered up – enfolded – ingested. The idea of a gargantuan amoeba-thing hiding within a hollow rock – or a rocklike shell – made him writhe and yell and shove at the protoplasmic substance.

But nothing of the kind happened. He was not plunged into a smothering and slimy jelly that would strip him of his skin and then his flesh and then dissolve his bones. He was merely shoved repeatedly against the soft swelling. Each time, he pushed or kicked or struck at it. After a dozen of these seemingly purposeless acts, he was held away, as if whatever was doing it was puzzled by his behaviour.

He had quit screaming. The only sounds were his harsh breathing and the zzzts and pings from the panrad. Even as he became aware of them, the zzzts changed tempo and settled into a recognizable pattern of bursts – three units that crackled out again and again.

'Who are you? Who are you?'

Of course, it could just as easily have been, 'What are you?' or 'What the hell!' or 'Nor smoz ka pop?'

Or nothing – semantically speaking.

But he didn't think the latter. And when he was gently lowered to the floor, and the tentacle went off to only-God-knew-where in the dark, he was sure that the creature was communicating – or trying to – with him.

It was this thought that kept him from screaming and running around in the lightless and fetid chamber, brainlessly seeking an outlet. He mastered his panic and snapped open a little shutter in the panrad's side and thrust in his right-hand index finger. There he poised it above the key and in a moment, when the thing paused in transmitting, he sent back, as best he could, the pulses he had received. It was not necessary for him to turn on the light and spin the dial that would put him on the 1000 kc. band. The instrument would automatically key that frequency in with the one he had just received.

The oddest part of the whole procedure was that his whole body was trembling almost uncontrollably – one part excepted. That was his index finger, his one unit that seemed to him to have a definite function in this otherwise meaningless situation. It was the section of him that was helping him to survive – the only part that knew how – at that moment. Even his brain seemed to have no connexion with his finger. That digit was himself, and the rest just happened to be linked to it.

When he paused, the transmitter began again. This time the units were unrecognizable. There was a certain rhythm to them, but he could not know what they meant. Meanwhile, the RD was pinging. Something somewhere in the dark hole had a beam held tightly on him.

He pressed a button on the panrad's top, and the built-in flashlight illuminated the area just in front of him. He saw a wall of reddish-grey rubbery substance. On the wall was a roughly circular, light grey swelling about four feet in diameter. Around it, giving it a Medusa appearance, were coiled twelve very long, very thin tentacles.

Though he was afraid that if he turned his back to them the tentacles would seize him once more, his curiosity forced him to wheel about and examine his surroundings with the bright beam. He was in an egg-shaped chamber about thirty feet long, twelve wide, and eight to ten high in the middle. It was formed of a reddish-grey material, smooth except for irregular intervals of blue or red pipes. Veins and arteries?

A door-sized portion of the wall had a vertical slit running down it. Tentacles fringed it. He guessed it was a sort of iris and that it had opened to drag him inside. Starfish-shaped groupings of tentacles were scattered on the walls or hung from the ceiling. On the wall opposite the iris was a long and flexible stalk with a cartilaginous ruff around its free end. When Eddie moved, it moved, its blind point following him as a radar antenna tracks the thing it is locating. That was what it was. And unless he was wrong, the stalk was also a C.W. transmitter-receiver.

He shot the light around. When it reached the end farthest from him, he gasped. Ten creatures were huddled together facing him! About the size of half-grown pigs, they looked like nothing so much as unshelled snails; they were eyeless, and the stalk growing from the forehead of each was a tiny duplicate of that on the wall. They didn't look dangerous. Their open mouths were little and toothless, and their rate of locomotion must be slow, for they moved like snails, on a large pedestal of flesh – a foot-muscle.

Nevertheless, if he were to fall asleep they could overcome him by force of numbers, and those mouths might drip an acid to digest him, or they might carry a concealed poisonous sting.

His speculations were interrupted violently. He was seized, lifted, and passed on to another group of tentacles. He was carried beyond the antenna-stalk and towards the snail-beings. Just before he reached them, he was halted, facing the wall. An iris, hitherto invisible, opened. His light shone into it, but he could see nothing but convolutions of flesh.

His panrad gave off a new pattern of dit-dot-deet-dats. The iris widened until it was large enough to admit his body, if he were shoved in head first. Or feet first. It didn't matter. The convolutions straightened out and became a tunnel. Or a throat. From thousands of little pits emerged thousands of tiny, razor-sharp teeth. They flashed out and sank back in, and before they had disappeared thousands of other wicked little spears darted out and past the receding fangs.

Meat-grinder.

Beyond the murderous array, at the end of the throat, was a huge pouch of water. Steam came from it, and with it an odour like that of his mother's stew. Dark bits, presumably meat, and pieces of vegetables floated on the seething surface.

Then the iris closed, and he was turned around to face the slugs. Gently, but unmistakably, a tentacle spanked his buttocks. And the panrad zzzted a warning.

Eddie was not stupid. He knew now that the ten creatures were not dangerous unless he molested them. In which case he had just seen where he would go if he did not behave.

Again he was lifted and carried along the wall until he was shoved against the light grey spot. The monkey-cage odour, which had died out, became strong again. Eddie identified its source with a very small hole which appeared in the wall.

When he did not respond – he had no idea yet how he was supposed to act – the tentacles dropped him so unexpectedly that he fell on his back. Unhurt by the yielding flesh, he rose.

What was the next step? Exploration of his resources. Itemization: The panrad. A sleeping-bag, which he wouldn't need as long as the present too-warm temperature kept up. A bottle of Old Red Star capsules. A free-fall thermos with attached nipple. A box of A-2-Z rations. A Foldstove. Cartridges for his double-barrel, now lying outside the creature's boulderish shell. A roll of toilet paper. Toothbrush. Paste. Soap. Towel. Pills:

Nodor, hormone, vitamin, longevity, reflex, and sleeping. And a thread-thin wire, a hundred feet long when uncoiled, that held prisoner in its molecular structure a hundred symphonies, eighty operas, a thousand different types of musical pieces, and two thousand great books ranging from Sophocles and Dostoyevsky to the latest bestseller. It could be played inside the panrad.

He inserted it, pushed a button, and spoke. 'Eddie Fetts's recording of Puccini's *Che gelida manina,* please.'

And while he listened approvingly to his own magnificent voice, he zipped open a can he had found in the bottom of the sack. His mother had put into it the stew left over from their last meal in the ship.

Not knowing what was happening, yet for some reason sure he was for the present safe, he munched meat and vegetables with a contented jaw. Transition from abhorrence to appetite sometimes came easily for Eddie.

He cleaned out the can and finished with some crackers and a chocolate bar. Rationing was out. As long as the food lasted, he would eat well. Then, if nothing turned up, he would ... But then, he reassured himself as he licked his fingers, his mother, who was free, would find some way to get him out of his trouble.

She always had.

V

The panrad, silent for a while, began signalling. Eddie spot-lighted the antenna and saw it was pointing at the snailbeings, which he had, in accordance with his custom, dubbed familiarly. Sluggos he called them.

The Sluggos crept towards the wall and stopped close to it. Their mouths, placed on the tops of their heads, gaped like so many hungry young birds. The iris opened, and two lips formed into a spout. Out of it streamed steaming-hot water and chunks of meat and vegetables. Stew! Stew that fell exactly into each waiting mouth.

That was how Eddie learned the second phrase of Mother Polyphema's language. The first message had been. 'What are you?' This was, 'Come and get it!'

He experimented. He tapped out a repetition of what he'd last heard. As one, the Sluggos – except the one then being fed – turned to him and crept a few feet before halting, puzzled.

Inasmuch as Eddie was broadcasting, the Sluggos must have had some sort of built-in DF. Otherwise they wouldn't have been able to distinguish between his pulses and their Mother's.

Immediately after, a tentacle smote Eddie across the shoulders and knocked him down. The panrad zzzted its third intelligible message: 'Don't ever do that!'

And then a fourth, to which the ten young obeyed by wheeling and resuming their former positions.

'This way, children.'

Yes, they were the offspring, living, eating, sleeping, playing, and learning to communicate in the womb of their mother – the Mother. They were the mobile brood of this vast immobile entity that had scooped up Eddie as a frog scoops up a fly. This Mother. She who had once been just such a Sluggo until she had grown hog-size and had been pushed out of her Mother's womb. And who, rolled into a tight ball, had free-wheeled down her natal hill, straightened out at the bottom, inched her way up the next hill, rolled down, and so on. Until she found the empty shell of an adult who had died. Or, if she wanted to be a first class citizen in her society and not a prestigeless *occupée*, she found the bare top of a tall hill – any eminence that commanded a big sweep of territory – and there squatted.

And there she put out many thread-thin tendrils into the soil and into the cracks in the rocks, tendrils that drew sustenance from the fat of her body and grew and extended downwards and ramified into other tendrils. Deep underground the rootlets worked their instinctive chemistry; searched for and found the water, the calcium, the iron, the copper, the nitrogen, the carbons, fondled earthworms and grubs and larvae, teasing them for the secrets of their fats and proteins; broke down the wanted substance into shadowy colloidal particles; sucked them up the thready pipes of the tendrils and back to the pale and slimming body crouching on a flat space atop a ridge, a hill, a peak.

There, using the blueprints stored in the molecules of the cerebellum, her body took the building blocks of elements and fashioned them into a very thin shell of the most available material, a shield large enough so she could expand to fit it while her natural enemies – the keen and hungry predators that prowled twilighted Baudelaire – nosed and clawed it in vain.

Then, her evergrowing bulk cramped, she would resorb the hard covering. And if no sharp tooth found her during that process of a few days, she would cast another and a larger. And so on through a dozen or more.

Until she had become the monstrous and much reformed body of an adult and virgin female. Outside would be the stuff that so much resembled a boulder, that was, actually, rock: either granite, diorite, marble, basalt, or maybe just plain limestone. Or sometimes iron, glass, or cellulose.

Within was the centrally located brain, probably as large as a man's. Surrounding it, the tons of organs: the nervous system, the mighty heart, or hearts, the four stomachs, the microwave and longwave generators, the kidneys, bowels, tracheae, scent and taste organs, the perfume factory which made odours to attract animals and birds close enough to be seized, and the huge womb. And the antennae – the small one inside for teaching and scanning the young, and a long and powerful stalk on the outside, projecting from the shelltop, retractable if danger came.

The next step was from virgin to Mother, lower case to uppercase as designated in her pulse-language by a longer pause before a word. Not until she was deflowered could she take a high place in her society. Immodest, unblushing, she herself made the advances, the proposals, and the surrender.

After which, she ate her mate.

The clock in the panrad told Eddie he was in his thirtieth day of imprisonment when he found out that little bit of information. He was shocked, not because it offended his ethics, but because he himself had been intended to be the mate. And the dinner.

His finger tapped, 'Tell me, Mother, what you mean.'

He had not wondered before how a species that lacked males could reproduce. Now he found that, to the Mothers, all creatures except themselves were male. Mothers were immobile and female. Mobiles were male. Eddie had been mobile. He was, therefore, a male.

He had approached this particular Mother during the mating season, that is, midway through raising a litter of young. She had scanned him as he came along the creekbanks at the valley bottom. When he was at the foot of the hill, she had detected his odour. It was new to her. The closest she could come to it in her memorybanks was that of a beast similar to him. From her description, he guessed it to be an ape. So she had released from her repertoire its rut stench. When he seemingly fell into the trap, she had caught him.

He was supposed to attack the conception-spot, that light grey swelling on the wall. After he had ripped and torn it enough to begin the mysterious workings of pregnancy, he would have been popped into her stomach-iris.

Fortunately, he had lacked the sharp beak, the fang, the claw. And she had received her own signals back from the panrad.

Eddie did not understand why it was necessary to use a mobile for mating. A Mother was intelligent enough to pick up a sharp stone and mangle the spot herself.

He was given to understand that conception would not start unless it was accompanied by a certain titillation of the nerves – a frenzy and its satisfaction. Why this emotional state was needed, Mother did not know.

Eddie tried to explain about such things as genes and chromosomes and why they had to be present in highly-developed species.

Mother did not understand.

Eddie wondered if the number of slashes and rips in the spot corresponded to the number of young. Or if there were a large number of potentialities in the heredity-ribbons spread out under the conception-skin. And if the haphazard irritation and consequent stimulation of the genes paralleled the chance combining of genes in human male-female mating. Thus resulting in offspring with traits that were combinations of their parents.

Or did the inevitable devouring of the mobile after the act indicate more than an emotional and nutritional reflex? Did it hint that the mobile caught up scattered gene-nodes, like hard seeds, along with the torn skin, in its claws and tusks, that these genes survived the boiling in the stew-stomach, and were later passed out in the faeces? Where animals and birds picked them up in beak, tooth, or foot, and then, seized by other Mothers in this oblique rape, transmitted the heredity-carrying agents to the conception-spots while attacking them, the nodules being scraped off and implanted in the skin and blood of the swelling even as others were harvested? Later, the mobiles were eaten, digested, and ejected in the obscure but ingenious and never-ending cycle? Thus ensuring the continual, if haphazard, recombining of genes, chances for variations in offspring, opportunities for mutations, and so on?

Mother pulsed that she was nonplussed.

Eddie gave up. He'd never know. After all, did it matter?

He decided not, and rose from his prone position to request water. She pursed up her iris and spouted a tepid quartful into his thermos. He dropped in a pill, swished it around till it dissolved, and drank a reasonable facsimile of Old Red Star. He preferred the harsh and powerful rye, though he could have afforded the smoothest. Quick results were what he wanted. Taste didn't matter, as he disliked all liquor tastes. Thus he drank what the Skid Row bums drank and shuddered even as they did, renaming it Old Rotten Tar and cursing the fate that had brought them so low they had to gag such stuff down.

The rye glowed in his belly and spread quickly through his limbs and up to his head, chilled only by the increasing scarcity of the capsules. When he ran out – then what? It was at times like this that he most missed his mother.

Thinking about her brought a few large tears. He snuffled and drank some more and when the biggest of the Sluggos nudged him for a back-scratching, he gave it instead a shot of Old Red Star. A slug for Sluggo. Idly, he wondered what effect a taste for rye would have on the future of the race when these virgins became Mothers.

At that moment he was shaken by what seemed a life-saving idea. These creatures could suck up the required elements from the earth and with them duplicate quite complex molecular structures. Provided, of course, they had a sample of the desired substance to brood over in some cryptic organ.

Well, what easier to do than give her one of the cherished capsules? One could become any number. Those, plus the abundance of water pumped up through hollow underground tendrils from the nearby creek, would give enough to make a master-distiller green!

He smacked his lips and was about to key her his request when what she was transmitting penetrated his mind.

Rather cattily, she remarked that her neighbour across the valley was putting on airs because she, too, held prisoner a communicating mobile.

VI

The Mothers had a society as hierarchical as table-protocol in Washington or peck-order in a barnyard. Prestige was what counted, and prestige was determined by the broadcasting power, the height of the eminence on which the Mother sat, which governed the extent of her radar-territory, and the abundance and novelty and wittiness of her gossip. The creature that had snapped Eddie up was a queen. She had precedence over thirty-odd of her kind; they all had to let her broadcast first, and none dared start pulsing until she quit. Then, the next in order began, and so on down the line. Any of them could be interrupted at any time by Number One, and if any of the lower echelon had something interesting to transmit, she could break in on the one then speaking and get permission from the queen to tell her tale.

Eddie knew this, but he could not listen in directly to the hilltop-gabble. The thick pseudo-granite shell barred him from that and made him dependent upon her womb-stalk for relayed information.

Now and then Mother opened the door and allowed her young to crawl out. There they practiced beaming and broadcasting at the Sluggos of the Mother across the valley. Occasionally that Mother deigned herself to pulse the young, and Eddie's keeper reciprocated to her offspring.

Turnabout.

The first time the children had inched through the exit-iris, Eddie had tried, Ulysses-like, to pass himself off as one of them and crawl out in the midst of the flock. Eyeless, but no Polyphemus, Mother had picked him out with her tentacles and hauled him back in.

It was following that incident that he had named her Polyphema.

He knew she had increased her own already powerful prestige tremendously by possession of that unique thing – a transmitting mobile. So much had her importance grown that the Mothers on the fringes of her area passed on the news to others. Before he had learned her language, the entire continent was hooked-up. Polyphema had become a veritable gossip columnist; tens of thousands of hillcrouchers listened in eagerly to her accounts of her dealings with the walking paradox: a semantic male.

That had been fine. Then, very recently, the Mother across the valley had captured a similar creature. And in one bound she had become Number Two in the area and would, at the slightest weakness on Polyphema's part, wrest the top position away.

Eddie became wildly excited at the news. He had often daydreamed about his mother and wondered what she was doing. Curiously enough, he ended many of his fantasies with lip-mutterings, reproaching her almost audibly for having left him and for making no try to rescue him. When he became aware of his attitude, he was ashamed. Nevertheless, the sense of desertion coloured his thoughts.

Now that he knew she was alive and had been caught, probably while trying to get him out, he rose from the lethargy that had lately been making him doze the clock around. He asked Polyphema if she would open the entrance so he could talk directly with the other captive. She said yes. Eager to listen in on a conversation between two mobiles, she was very cooperative. There would be a mountain of gossip in what they would have to say. The only thing that dented her joy was that the other Mother would also have access.

Then, remembering she was still Number One and would broadcast the details first, she trembled so with pride and ecstasy that Eddie felt the floor shaking.

Iris open, he walked through it and looked across the valley. The hillsides were still green, red, and yellow, as the plants on Baudelaire did not lose their leaves during winter. But a few white patches showed that winter had begun. Eddie shivered from the bite of cold air on his naked skin. Long ago he had taken off his clothes. The womb-warmth had made garments too uncomfortable; moreover, Eddie, being human, had had to get rid of waste products. And Polyphema, being a Mother, had had periodically to flush out the dirt with warm water from one of her stomachs. Every time the tracheae-vents exploded streams that swept the undesirable elements out through her door-iris, Eddie had become soaked. When he abandoned dress, his clothes had gone floating out. Only by sitting on his pack did he keep it from a like fate.

Afterwards, he and the Sluggos had been dried off by warm air pumped through the same vents and originating from the mighty battery of lungs. Eddie was comfortable enough – he'd always liked showers – but the loss of his garments had been one more thing that kept him from escaping. He would soon freeze to death outside unless he found the yacht quickly. And he wasn't sure he remembered the path back.

So now, when he stepped outside, he retreated a pace or two

and let the warm air from Polyphema flow like a cloak from his shoulders.

Then he peered across the half-mile that separated him from his mother, but he could not see her. The twilight state and the dark of the unlit interior of her captor hid her.

He tapped in Morse, 'Switch to the talkie, same frequency.' Paula Fetts did so. She began asking him frantically if he were all right.

He replied he was fine.

'Have you missed me terribly, son?'

'Oh, very much.'

Even as he said this he wondered vaguely why his voice sounded so hollow. Despair at never again being able to see her, probably.

'I've almost gone crazy, Eddie. When you were caught I ran away as fast as I could. I had no idea what horrible monster it was that was attacking us. And then, half-way down the hill, I fell and broke my leg. . . .'

'Oh, no, mother!'

'Yes. But I managed to crawl back to the ship. And there, after I'd set it myself, I gave myself B.K. shots. Only, my system didn't react like it's supposed to. There are people that way, you know, and the healing took twice as long.

'But when I was able to walk, I got a gun and a box of dynamite. I was going to blow up what I thought was a kind of rock-fortress, an outpost for some kind of extee. I'd no idea of the true nature of these beasts. First, though, I decided to reconnoitre. I was going to spy on the boulder from across the valley. But I was trapped by this thing.

'Listen, son. Before I'm cut off, let me tell you not to give up hope. I'll be out of here before long and over to rescue you.'

'How?'

'If you remember, my lab kit holds a number of carcinogens for field work. Well, you know that sometimes a Mother's conception-spot when it is torn up during mating, instead of begetting young, goes into cancer – the opposite of pregnancy. I've injected a carcinogen into the spot and a beautiful carcinoma has developed. She'll be dead in a few days.'

'Mom! You'll be buried in that rotting mass!'

'No. This creature has told me that when one of her species dies, a reflex opens the labia. That's to permit their young – if any – to escape. Listen, I'll—'

A tentacle coiled about him and pulled him back through the iris, which shut.

When he switched back to C.W., he heard, 'Why didn't you communicate? What were you doing? Tell me! Tell me!'

Eddie told her. There was a silence that could only be interpreted as astonishment. After Mother had recovered her wits, she said, 'From now on, you will talk to the other male through me.'

Obviously, she envied and hated his ability to change wavebands, and, perhaps, had a struggle to accept the idea.

'Please,' he persisted, not knowing how dangerous were the waters he was wading in, 'please let me talk to my mother di—'

For the first time, he heard her stutter.

'Wha-wha-what? Your Mo-Mo-Mother?'

'Yes. Of course.'

The floor heaved violently beneath his feet. He cried out and braced himself to keep from falling and then flashed on the light. The walls were pulsating like shaken jelly, and the vascular columns had turned from red and blue to grey. The entrance-iris sagged open, like a lax mouth, and the air cooled. He could feel the drop in temperature in her flesh with the soles of his feet.

It was some time before he caught on.

Polyphema was in a state of shock.

What might have happened had she stayed in it, he never knew. She might have died and thus forced him out into the winter before his mother could escape. If so, and he couldn't find the ship, he would die. Huddled in the warmest corner of the egg-shaped chamber, Eddie contemplated that idea and shivered to a degree for which the outside air couldn't account.

VII

However, Polyphema had her own method of recovery. It consisted of spewing out the contents of her stew-stomach, which had doubtless become filled with the poisons draining out of her system from the blow. Her ejection of the stuff was the physical manifestation of the psychical catharsis. So furious was the flood that her foster son was almost swept out in the hot tide, but she, reacting instinctively, had coiled tentacles about him and the Sluggos. Then she followed the first upchucking by

28

emptying her other three waterpouches, the second hot and the third luke-warm and the fourth, just filled, cold.

Eddie yelped as the icy water doused him.

Polyphema's irises closed again. The floor and walls gradually quit quaking; the temperature rose; and her veins and arteries regained their red and blue. She was well again. Or so she seemed.

But when, after waiting twenty-four hours he cautiously approached the subject, he found she not only would not talk about it, she refused to acknowledge the existence of the other mobile.

Eddie, giving up hope of conversation, thought for quite a while. The only conclusion he could come to, and he was sure he'd grasped enough of her psychology to make it valid, was that the concept of a mobile female was utterly unacceptable.

Her world was split into two: mobile and her kind, the immobile. Mobile meant food and mating. Mobile meant – male. The Mothers were – female.

How the mobiles reproduced had probably never entered the hillcrouchers' minds. Their science and philosophy were on the instinctive body-level. Whether they had some notion of spontaneous generation or amoeba-like fission being responsible for the continued population of mobiles, or they'd just taken for granted they 'growed', like Topsy, Eddie never found out. To them, they were female and the rest of the protoplasmic cosmos was male.

That was that. Any other idea was more than foul and obscene and blasphemous. It was – unthinkable.

Polyphema had received a deep trauma from his words. And though she seemed to have recovered, somewhere in those tons of unimaginably complicated flesh a bruise was buried. Like a hidden flower, dark purple, it bloomed, and the shadow it cast was one that cut off a certain memory, a certain tract, from the light of consciousness. That bruise-stained shadow covered that time and event which the Mother, for reasons unfathomable to the human being, found necessary to mark KEEP OFF.

Thus, though Eddie did not word it, he understood in the cells of his body, he felt and knew, as if his bones were prophesying and his brain did not hear, what came to pass.

Sixty-six hours later by the panrad clock, Polyphema's entrance-lips opened. Her tentacles darted out. They came back in, carrying his helpless and struggling mother.

Eddie, roused out of a doze, horrified, paralysed, saw her toss her lab kit at him and heard an inarticulate cry from her. And saw her plunged, headforemost, into the stomach-iris.

Polyphema had taken the one sure way of burying the evidence.

Eddie lay face down, nose mashed against the warm and faintly throbbing flesh of the floor. Now and then his hands clutched spasmodically as if he were reaching for something that someone kept putting just within his reach and then moving away.

How long he was there he didn't know, for he never again looked at the clock.

Finally, in the darkness, he sat up and giggled inanely, 'Mother always did make good stew.'

That set him off. He leaned back on his hands and threw his head back and howled like a wolf under a full moon.

Polyphema, of course, was dead-deaf, but she could radar his posture, and her keen nostrils deduced from his body-scent that he was in terrible fear and anguish.

A tentacle glided out and gently enfolded him.

'What is the matter?' zzted the panrad.

He stuck his finger in the keyhole.

'I have lost my mother!'

'?'

'She's gone away, and she'll never come back.'

'I don't understand. *Here I am.*'

Eddie quit weeping and cocked his head as if he were listening to some inner voice. He snuffled a few times and wiped away the tears, slowly disengaged the tentacle, patted it, walked over to his pack in a corner, and took out the bottle of Old Red Star capsules. One he popped into the thermos; the other he gave to her with the request she duplicate it, if possible. Then he stretched out on his side, propped on one elbow like a Roman in his sensualities, sucked the rye through the nipple, and listened to a medley of Beethoven, Moussorgsky, Verdi, Strauss, Porter, Feinstein, and Waxworth.

So the time – if there were such a thing there – flowed around Eddie. When he was tired of music or plays or books, he listened in on the area hookup. Hungry, he rose and walked – or often just crawled – to the stew-iris. Cans of rations lay in his pack; he had planned to eat those until he was sure that – what was it he was forbidden to eat? Poison? Something had been devoured

by Polyphema and the Sluggos. But sometime during the music-
rye orgy, he had forgotten. He now ate quite hungrily and with
thought for nothing but the satisfaction of his wants.

Sometimes the door-iris opened, and Billy Greengrocer
hopped in. Billy looked like a cross between a cricket and a kan-
garoo. He was the size of a collie, and he bore in a marsupialian
pouch vegetables and fruit and nuts. These he extracted with
shiny green, chitinous claws and gave to Mother in return for
meals of stew. Happy symbiote, he chirruped merrily while his
many-faceted eyes, revolving independently of each other, looked
one at the Sluggos and the other at Eddie.

Eddie, on impulse, abandoned the 100 kc. band and roved the
frequencies until he found that both Polyphema and Billy were
emitting a 108 wave. That, apparently, was their natural signal.

When Billy had his groceries to deliver, he broadcast. Polyphema, in turn, when she needed them, sent back to him. There
was nothing intelligent on Billy's part; it was just his instinct
to transmit. And the Mother was, aside from the 'semantic' frequency, limited to that one band. But it worked out fine.

VIII

Everything was fine. What more could a man want? Free food,
unlimited liquor, soft bed, air-conditioning, showerbaths, music,
intellectual works (on the tape), interesting conversation (much
of it was about him), privacy, and security.

If he had not already named her, he would have called her
Mother Gratis.

Nor were creature comforts all. She had given him the
answers to all his questions, all. . . .

Except one.

That was never expressed vocally by him. Indeed, he would
have been incapable of doing so. He was probably unaware that
he had such a question.

But Polyphema voiced it one day when she asked him to do
her a favour.

Eddie reacted as if outraged.

'One does not—! One does not—!'

He choked, and then he thought, how ridiculous! She is not—
And looked puzzled, and said, 'But she is.'

He rose and opened the lab kit. While he was looking for a

scalpel, he came across the carcinogens. He threw them through the half-opened labia far out and down the hillside.

Then he turned and, scalpel in hand, leaped at the light grey swelling on the wall. And stopped, staring at it, while the instrument fell from his hand. And picked it up and stabbed feebly and did not even scratch the skin. And again let it drop.

'What is it? What is it?' crackled the panrad hanging from his wrist.

Suddenly, a heavy cloud of human odour – mansweat – was puffed in his face from a nearby vent.

'? ? ? ?'

And he stood, bent in a half-crouch, seemingly paralysed. Until tentacles seized him in fury and dragged him towards the stomach-iris, yawning man-sized.

Eddie screamed and writhed and plunged his finger in the panrad and tapped, 'All right! All right!'

And once back before the spot, he lunged with a sudden and wild joy; he slashed savagely; he yelled. 'Take that! And that, P . . .' and the rest was lost in a mindless shout.

He did not stop cutting, and he might have gone on and on until he had quite excised the spot had not Polyphema interferred by dragging him towards her stomach-iris again. For ten seconds he hung there, helpless and sobbing with a mixture of fear and glory.

Polyphema's reflexes had almost overcome her brain. Fortunately, a cold spark of reason lit up a corner of the vast, dark, and hot chapel of her frenzy.

The convolutions leading to the steaming, meat-laden pouch closed and the foldings of flesh rearranged themselves. Eddie was suddenly hosed with warm water from what he called the 'sanitation' stomach. The iris closed. He was put down. The scalpel was put back in the bag.

For a long time Mother seemed to be shaken by the thought of what she might have done to Eddie. She did not trust herself to transmit until her nerves were settled. When they were, she did not refer to his narrow escape. Nor did he.

He was happy. He felt as if a spring, tight-coiled against his bowels since he and his wife had parted, was now, for some reason, released. The dull vague pain of loss and discontent, the slight fever and cramp in his entrails, and the apathy that sometimes afflicted him, were gone. He felt fine.

Meanwhile, something akin to deep affection had been lighted, like a tiny candle under the draughty and overtowering roof of a cathedral. Mother's shell housed more than Eddie; it now curved over an emotion new to her kind. This was evident by the next event that filled him with terror.

For the wounds in the spot healed and the swelling increased into a large bag. Then the bag burst and ten mouse-sized Sluggos struck the floor. The impact had the same effect as a doctor spanking a newborn baby's bottom; they drew in their first breath with shock and pain; their uncontrolled and feeble pulses filled the ether with shapeless SOS's.

When Eddie was not talking with Polyphema or listening in or drinking or sleeping or eating or bathing or running off the tape, he played with the Sluggos. He was, in a sense, their father. Indeed, as they grew to hog-size, it was hard for their female parent to distinguish him from her young. As he seldom walked any more, and was often to be found on hands and knees in their midst, she could not scan him too well. Moreover, something in the heavywet air or in the diet had caused every hair on his body to drop off. He grew very fat. Generally speaking, he was one with the pale, soft, round, and bald offspring. A family likeness.

There was one difference. When the time came for the virgins to be expelled, Eddie crept to one end, whimpering, and stayed there until he was sure Mother was not going to thrust him out into the cold, hard, and hungry world.

That final crisis over, he came back to the centre of the floor. The panic in his breast had died out, but his nerves were still quivering. He filled his thermos and then listened for a while to his own tenor singing the 'Sea Things' aria from his favourite opera, Gianelli's *Ancient Mariner*. Suddenly, he burst out and accompanied himself, finding himself thrilled as never before by the concluding words.

> *And from my neck so free*
> *The Albatross fell off, and sank*
> *Like lead into the sea.*

Afterwards, voice silent but heart singing, he switched off the wire and cut in on Polyphema's broadcast.

Mother was having trouble. She could not precisely describe

to the continent-wide hook-up this new and almost inexpressible emotion she felt about the mobile. It was a concept her language was not prepared for. Nor was she helped any by the gallons of Old Red Star in her bloodstream.

Eddie sucked at the plastic nipple and nodded sympathetically and drowsily at her search for words. Presently, the thermos rolled out of his hand.

He slept on his side, curled in a ball, knees on his chest and arms crossed, neck bent forward. Like the pilot room chronometer whose hands reversed after the crash, the clock of his body was ticking backwards, ticking backwards . . .

In the darkness, in the moistness, safe and warm, well fed, much loved.

Cq! Cq!

This is Mother Hardhead pulsing.

Keep quiet all you virgins and Mothers, while I communicate. Listen, listen, all you who are hooked into this broadcast. Listen, and I will tell you how I left my Mother, how my two sisters and I grew our shells, how I dealt with the olfway, and why I have become the Mother with the most prestige, the strongest shell, the most powerful broadcaster and beamer, and the pulser of a new language.

First, before I tell my story, I will reveal to all you who do not know it that my father was a mobile.

Do not be nervequivered. This is a so-story. It is not a not-so-story.

Father was a mobile.

Mother pulsed, 'Get out!'

Then, to show she meant business, she opened her exit-iris.

That sobered us up and made us realize how serious she was. Before, when she snapped open her iris, she did it so we could practice pulsing at the other young crouched in the doorway to their Mothers' wombs, or else send a respectful message to the Mothers themselves, or even a quick one to Grandmother, far away on a mountainside. Not that she received, I think, because we young were too weak to transmit that far. Anyway, Grandmother never acknowledged receipt.

At times, when Mother was annoyed because we would all broadcast at once instead of asking her permission to speak one at a time or because we would crawl up the sides of her womb and then drop off the ceiling on to the floor with a thud, she would pulse at us to get out and build our own shells. She meant it, she said.

Then, according to our mood, we would either settle down or else get more boisterous. Mother would reach out with her tentacles and hold us down and spank us. If that did no good, she would threaten us with the olfway. That did the trick. That is, until she used him too many times. After a while, we got so we didn't believe there was an olfway. Mother, we thought, was creating a not-so-story. We should have known better, however, for Mother loathed not-so-stories.

Another thing that quivered her nerves was our conversation with Father in Orsemay. Although he had taught her his language, he refused to teach her Orsemay. When he wanted to send messages to us that he knew she wouldn't approve, he would pulse at us in our private language. That was another thing, I think, that finally made Mother so angry she cast us out despite Father's pleadings that we be allowed to remain four more seasons.

You must understand that we virgins had remained in the womb far longer than we should have. The cause for our overstay was Father.

He was the mobile.

Yes, I know what you're going to reply. All fathers, you will repeat, are mobiles.

But he was Father. He was the *pulsing* mobile.

Yes, he could too. He could pulse with the best of us. Or maybe he *himself* couldn't. Not directly. We pulse with organs in our body. But Father, if I understand him correctly, used a creature of some kind which was separate from his body. Or maybe it was an organ that wasn't attached to him.

Anyway, he had no internal organs or pulse-stalks growing from him to pulse with. He used this creature, this r-a-d-i-o, as he called it. And it worked just fine.

When he conversed with Mother, he did so in Motherpulse or in his own language, mobilepulse. With us he used Orsemay. That's like mobilepulse, only a little different. Mother never did figure out the difference.

When I finish my story, dearie, I'll teach you Orsemay. I've been beamed that you've enough prestige to join our Highest Hill sorority and thus learn our secret of communication.

Mother declared Father had two means of pulsing. Besides his radio, which he used to communicate with us, he could pulse in another and totally different manner. He didn't use dotdeet-ditdashes, either. His pulses needed air to carry them, and he sent them with the same organ he ate with. Boils one's stomach to think of it, doesn't it?

Father was caught while passing by my Mother. She didn't

know what mating-lust perfume to send downwind towards him so he would be lured within reach of her tentacles. She had never smelled a mobile like him before. But he did have an odour that was similar to that of another kind of mobile, so she wafted that towards him. It seemed to work, because he came close enough for her to seize him with her extra-uterine tentacles and pop him into her shell.

Later, after I was born, Father radioed me – in Orsemay, of course, so Mother wouldn't understand – that he had smelled the perfume and that it, among other things, had attracted him. But the odour had been that of a hairy tree-climbing mobile, and he had wondered what such creatures were doing on a bare hilltop. When he learned to converse with Mother, he was so surprised that she had identified him with that mobile.

Ah, well, he pulsed, it is not the first time a female has made a monkey of a man.

He also informed me that he had thought Mother was just an enormous boulder on top of the hill. Not until a section of the supposed rock opened out was he aware of anything out of the ordinary or that the boulder was her shell and held her body within. Mother, he radioed, is something like a dinosaur-sized snail, or jellyfish, equipped with organs that generate radar and radio waves and with an egg-shaped chamber big as the living room of a bungalow, a womb in which she bears and raises her young.

I didn't understand more than half of these terms, of course. Nor was Father able to explain them satisfactorily.

He did make me promise not to pulse Mother that he had thought she was just a big lump of mineral. Why, I don't know.

Father puzzled Mother. Though he fought her when she dragged him in, he had no claws or teeth sharp enough to tear her conception-spot. Mother tried to provoke him further, but he refused to react. When she realized that he was a pulse-sending mobile and released him to study him, he wandered around the womb. After a while he understood that Mother was beaming from her womb pulse-stalk. He learned how to talk with her by using his detachable organ, which he termed a panrad. Eventually, he taught her his language, mobile-pulse. When Mother learned that and informed other Mothers about it, her prestige became the highest in all the area. No Mother had ever thought of a new language. The idea stunned them.

Father said he was the only communicating mobile on this world. His s-p-a-c-e-s-h-i-p had crashed, and he would now remain forever with Mother.

Father learned the dinnerpulses when Mother summoned her young to eat. He radioed the proper message. Mother's nerves were quivered by the idea that he was semantic, but she opened her stew-iris and let him eat. Then Father held up fruit or other objects and let Mother beam at him with her wombstalk what the proper dotditdeetdashes were for each. Then he would repeat on his panrad the name of the object to verify it.

Mother's sense of smell helped her, of course. Sometimes it is hard to tell the difference between an apple and a peach just by pulsing it. Odours aid you.

She caught on fast. Father told her she was very intelligent — for a female. That quivered her nerves. She wouldn't pulse with him for several mealperiods after that.

One thing that Mother especially liked about Father was that when conception-time came, she could direct him what to do. She didn't have to depend on luring a non-semantic mobile into her shell with perfumes and then hold it to her conception-spot while it scratched and bit the spot to fight its way from the grip of her tentacles. Father had no claws, but he carried a detachable claw. He named it a s-c-a-l-p-e-l.

When I asked him why he had so many detachable organs, he replied that he was a man of parts.

Father was always talking nonsense.

But he had trouble understanding Mother, too.

Her reproductive processes amazed him.

'By G-o-d,' he beamed, 'who'd believe it? That a healing process in a wound would result in conception? Just the opposite of cancer.'

When we were adolescents and about ready to be shoved out of Mother's shell, we received Mother asking Father to mangle her spot again. Father replied no. He wanted to wait another four seasons. He had said farewell to two broods of his young, and he wanted to keep us around longer so he could give us a real education and enjoy us instead of starting to raise another group of virgins.

This refusal quivered Mother's nerves and upset her stew-stomach so that our food was sour for several meals. But she didn't act against him. He gave her too much prestige. All the Mothers were dropping Motherpulse and learning mobile from Mother as fast as she could teach it.

I asked, 'What's prestige?'

'When you send, the others have to receive. And they don't dare pulse back until you're through and you give your permission.'

'Oh, I'd like prestige!'

Father interrupted, 'Little Hardhead, if you want to get ahead, you tune in to me. I'll tell you a few things even your Mother can't. After all, I'm a mobile, and I've been around.'

And he would outline what I had to expect once I left him and Mother and how, if I used my brain, I could survive and eventually get more prestige than even Grandmother had.

Why he called me Hardhead, I don't know. I was still a virgin and had not, of course, grown a shell. I was as soft-bodied as any of my sisters. But he told me he was f-o-n-d of me because I was so hard-headed. I accepted the statement without trying to grasp it.

Anyway, we got eight extra seasons in Mother because Father wanted it that way. We might have got some more, but when winter came again, Mother insisted Father mangle her spot. He replied he wasn't ready. He was just beginning to get acquainted with his children – he called us Sluggos – and, after we left, he'd have nobody but Mother to talk to until the next brood grew up.

Moreover, she was starting to repeat herself, and he didn't think she appreciated him like she should. Her stew was too often soured or else so overboiled that the meat was shredded into a neargoo.

That was enough for Mother.

'Get out!' she pulsed.

'Fine! And don't think you're throwing me out in the cold, either!' zztd back Father. 'Yours is not the only shell in this world.'

That made Mother's nerves quiver until her whole body shook. She put up her big outside stalk and beamed her sisters and aunts. The Mother across the valley confessed that, during one of the times Father had basked in the warmth of the s-u-n while lying just outside Mother's opened iris, she had asked him to come live with her.

Mother changed her mind. She realized that, with him gone, her prestige would die and that of the hussy across the valley would grow.

'Seems as if I'm here for the duration,' radioed Father.

Then, 'Whoever would think your Mother'd be j-e-a-l-o-u-s?'

Life with Father was full of those incomprehensible semantic groups. Too often he would not, or could not, explain.

For a long time Father brooded in one spot. He wouldn't answer us or Mother.

Finally, she became overquivered. We had grown so big and boisterous and sassy that she was one continual shudder. And she must have thought that as long as we were around to communicate with him, she had no chance to get him to rip up her spot.

So, out we went.

Before we passed forever from her shell, she warned, 'Beware the olfway.'

My sisters ignored her, but I was impressed. Father had described the beast and its terrible ways. Indeed, he used to dwell so much on it that we had dropped the old term for it and used Father's. It began when he reprimanded her for threatening us too often with the beast when we misbehaved.

'Don't "cry wolf." '

He then beamed me the story of the origin of that puzzling phrase. He did it in Orsemay, of course, because Mother would lash him with her tentacles if she thought he was pulsing something that was not-so. The very idea of not-so strained her brain until she couldn't think straight.

I wasn't sure myself what not-so was, but I enjoyed his stories. And I, like the other virgins and Mother herself, began terming the killer 'the olfway.'

Anyway, after I'd beamed, 'Good sending, Mother,' I felt Father's strange stiff mobile-tentacles around me and something wet and warm falling from him on to me. He pulsed, 'Good l-u-c-k, Hardhead. Send me a message via hook-up sometimes. And be sure to remember what I told you about dealing with the olfway.'

I pulsed that I would. I left with the most indescribable feeling inside me. It was a nervequivering that was both good and bad, if you can imagine such a thing, dearie.

But I soon forgot it in the adventure of rolling down a hill, climbing slowly up the next one on my single foot, rolling down the other side, and so on. After about ten warm-periods, all my sisters but two had left me. They found hilltops on which to build their shells. But my two faithful sisters had listened to my ideas about how we should not be content with anything less than the highest hilltops.

'Once you've grown a shell, you stay where you are.'

So they agreed to follow me.

But I led them a long, long way, and they would complain that they were tired and sore and getting afraid of running into some meat-eating mobile. They even wanted to move into the empty shells of Mothers who had been eaten by the olfway or died when cancer, instead of young, developed in the conception-spots.

'Come on,' I urged. 'There's no prestige in moving into empties. Do you want to take bottom place in every community-pulsing just because you're too lazy to build your own covers?'

'But we'll resorb the empties and then grow our own later on.'

'Yes? How many Mothers have declared that? And how many have done it? Come on, Sluggos.'

We kept getting into higher country. Finally, I scanned the set-up I was searching for. It was a flat-topped mountain with many hills around it. I crept up it. When I was on top, I test-beamed. Its summit was higher than any of the eminences for as far as I could reach. And I guessed that when I became adult and had much more power, I would be able to cover a tremendous area. Meanwhile, other virgins would sooner or later be moving in and occupying the lesser hills.

As Father would have expressed it, I was on top of the world.

It happened that my little mountain was rich. The search-tendrils I grew and then sunk into the soil found many varieties of minerals. I could build from them a huge shell. The bigger the shell, the larger the Mother. The larger the Mother, the more powerful the pulse.

Moreover, I detected many large flying mobiles. Eagles, Father termed them. They would make good mates. They had sharp beaks and tearing talons.

Below, in a valley, was a stream. I grew a hollow tendril under the soil and down the mountainside until it entered the water. Then I began pumping it up to fill my stomachs.

The valley soil was good. I did what no other of our kind had ever done, what Father had taught me. My far-groping tendrils picked up seeds dropped by trees, flowers, and birds and planted them. I spread an underground net of tendrils around an apple tree. But I didn't plan on passing the tree's fallen fruit from tendril-frond to frond and so on up the slope and into my iris. I had a different destination in mind for them.

Meanwhile, my sisters had topped two hills much lower than mine. When I found out what they were doing, my nerves quivered. Both had built shells! One was glass; the other, cellulose!

'What do you think you're doing? Aren't you afraid of the olfway?'

'Pulse away, old grouch. Nothing's the matter with us. We're just ready for winter and mating-heat, that's all. We'll be Mothers, then, and you'll still be growing your big old shell. Where'll your prestige be? The others won't even pulse with you 'cause you'll still be a virgin and a half-shelled one at that!'

'Brittlehead! Woodenhead!'

'Yah! Yah! Hardhead!'

They were right – in a way. I was still soft and naked and helpless, an evergrowing mass of quivering flesh, a ready prey to any meat-eating mobile that found me. I was a fool and a gambler. Nevertheless, I took my leisure and sunk my tendrils and located ore and sucked up iron particles in suspension and built an inner shell larger, I think, than Grandmother's. Then I laid a thick sheath of copper over that so the iron wouldn't rust. Over that I grew a layer of bone made out of calcium I'd extracted from limestone rocks. Nor did I bother, as my sisters had done, to resorb my virgin's stalk and grow an adult one. That could come later.

Just as fall was dying, I finished my shells. Body-changing and growing began. I ate from my crops, and I had much meat, too, because I'd put up little cellulose latticework shells in the valley and raised many mobiles from the young that my far-groping tendrils had plucked from their nests.

I planned my structure with an end in mind. I grew my stomach much broader and deeper than usual. It was not that I was overly hungry. It was for a purpose, which I shall transmit to you later, dearie.

My stew-stomach was also much closer to the top of my shell than it is in most of us. In fact, I intentionally shifted my brain from the top to one side and raised the stomach in its place. Father had informed me I should take advantage of my ability to partially direct the location of my adult organs. It took me time, but I did it just before winter came.

Cold weather arrived.

And the olfway.

He came as he always does, his long nose with its retractable antennae sniffing out the minute encrustations of pure minerals that we virgins leave on our trails. The olfway follows his nose to wherever it will take him. This time it led him to my sister who had built her shell of glass. I had suspected she would be the first to be contacted by an olfway. In fact, that was one of the reasons I had chosen a hilltop further up the line. The olfway always takes the nearest shell.

When sister Glasshead detected the terrible mobile, she sent out wild pulse after pulse.

'What will I do? Do? *Do?*'

'Sit tight, sister, and hope.'

Such advice was like feeding on cold stew, but it was the best, and the only, that I could give. I did not remind her that she should have followed my example, built a triple shell, and not been so eager to have a good time by gossiping with others.

The olfway prowled about, tried to dig underneath her base, which was on solid rock, and failed. He did manage to knock off a chunk of glass as a sample. Ordinarily, he would then have swallowed the sample and gone off to pupate. That would have given my sister a season of rest before he returned to attack. In the meanwhile, she might have built another coating of some other material and frustrated the monster for another season.

It just so happened that that particular olfway had, unfortunately for sister, made his last meal on a Mother whose covering had also been of glass. He retained his special organs for dealing with such mixtures of silicates. One of them was a huge and hard ball of some material on the end of his very long tail. Another was an acid for weakening the glass. After he had dripped that over a certain area, he battered her shell with the ball. Not long before the first snowfall he broke through her shield and got to her flesh.

Her wildly alternating beams and broadcasts of panic and terror still bounce around in my nerves when I think of them. Yet I must admit my reaction was tinged with contempt. I do not think she had even taken the trouble to put boron oxide in her glass. If she had, she might. . . .

What's that? How dare you interrupt? . . . Oh, very well, I accept your humble apologies. Don't let it happen again, dearie. As for what you wanted to know, I'll describe later the substances that Father termed silicates and boron oxides and such. After my story is done.

To continue; the killer, after finishing Glasshead off, followed his nose along her trail back down the hill to the junction. There he had his choice of my other sister's trail or of mine. He decided on hers. Again he went through his pattern of trying to dig under her, crawling over her, biting off her pulse-stalks, and then chewing a sample of shell.

Snow fell. He crept off, sluggishly scooped a hole, and crawled in for the winter.

Sister Woodenhead grew another stalk. She exulted, 'He found my shell too thick! He'll never get me!'

Ah, sister, if only you had received from Father and not spent so much time playing with the other Sluggos. Then you would have remembered what he taught. You would have known that an olfway, like us, is different from most creatures. The majority of beings have functions that depend upon their structures. But the olfway, that nasty creature, has a structure that depends upon his functions.

I did not quiver her nerves by telling her that, now that he had secreted a sample of her cellulose-shell in his body, he was pupating around it. Father had informed me that some arthropods follow a life-stage that goes from egg to larva to pupa to adult. When a caterpillar pupates in its cocoon, for instance, practically its whole body dissolves, its tissues disintegrate. Then something reforms the pulpy whole into a structurally new creature with new functions, the butterfly.

The butterfly, however, never repupates. The olfway does. He parts company with his fellow arthropods in this peculiar ability. Thus, when he tackles a Mother, he chews off a tiny bit of the shell and goes to sleep with it. During a whole season, crouched in his den, he dreams around the sample – or his body does. His tissues melt and then coalesce. Only his nervous system remains intact, thus preserving the memory of his identity and what he has to do when he emerges from his hole.

So it happened. The olfway came out of his hole, nested on top of sister Woodenhead's dome, and inserted a modified ovipositor into the hole left by biting off her stalk. I could more or less follow his plan of attack, because the winds quite often blew my way, and I could sniff the chemicals he was dripping.

He pulped the cellulose with a solution of something or other, soaked it in some caustic stuff, and then poured on an evil-smelling fluid that boiled and bubbled. After that had ceased its violent action, he washed some more caustic on the enlarging depression and finished by blowing out the viscous solution through a tube. He repeated the process many times.

Though my sister, I suppose, desperately grew more cellulose, she was not fast enough. Relentlessly, the olfway widened the hole. When it was large enough, he slipped inside.

End of sister. . . .

The whole affair of the olfway was lengthy. I was busy, and I gained time by something I had made even before I erected my dome. This was the false trail of encrustations that I had laid, one of the very things my sisters had mocked. They did not understand what I was doing when I then back-tracked, a process which took me several days, and concealed with dirt my real track. But if they had lived, they would have comprehended. For the olfway turned off the genuine trail to my summit and followed the false.

Naturally, it led him to the edge of a cliff. Before he could check his swift pace, he fell off.

Somehow, he escaped serious injury and scrambled back up to the spurious path. Reversing, he found and dug up the cover over the actual tracks.

That counterfeit path was a good trick, one my Father taught me. Too bad it hadn't worked, for the monster came straight up the mountain, heading for me, his antennae ploughing up the loose dirt and branches which covered my encrustations.

However, I wasn't through. I had collected a number of large rocks and cemented them into one large boulder. The boulder itself was poised on the edge of the summit. Around its middle I had deposited a ring of iron, grooved to fit a rail of the same mineral. This rail led from the boulder to a point half-way down the slope. Thus, when the mobile reached that ridge of iron and followed it up the slope, I removed with my tentacles the little rocks that kept the boulder from toppling over the edge of the summit.

My weapon rolled down its track with terrific speed. I'm sure it would have crushed the olfway if he had not felt the rail vibrating with his nose. He sprawled aside. The boulder rushed by, just missing him.

Though disappointed, I did get another idea to deal with future olfways. If I deposited two rails half-way down the slope, one on each side of the main line, and sent three boulders down at the same time, the monster could leap aside from the centre, either way, and still get it on the nose!

He must have been frightened, for I didn't pip him for five warm-periods after that. Then he came back up the rail, not, as I had expected, up the opposite if much steeper side of the mountain. He was stupid, all right.

I want to pause here and explain that the boulder was my idea, not Father's. Yet I must add that it was Father, not Mother, who started me thinking original thoughts. I know it quivers all your nerves to think that a mere mobile, good for nothing but food and mating, could not only be semantic but could have a higher degree of semanticism.

I don't insist he had a higher quality. I think it was different, and that I got some of that difference from him.

To continue, there was nothing I could do while the olfway prowled about and sampled my shell. Nothing except hope. And hope, as I found out, isn't enough. The mobile bit off a piece of my shell's outer bone covering. I thought he'd be satisfied, and that, when he returned after pupating, he'd find the second sheath of copper. That would delay him until another season. Then he'd find the iron and have to retire again. By then it would be so frustrated he'd give up and go searching for easier prey.

I didn't know that an olfway never gives up and is very thorough. He spent days digging around my base and uncovered a place where I'd been careless in sheathing. All three elements of the shell could be detected. I knew the weak spot existed, but I hadn't thought he'd go that deep.

Away went the killer to pupate. When summer came, he crawled out of his hole. Before attacking me, however, he ate up my crops, upset my cage-shells and devoured the mobiles therein, dug up my tendrils and ate them, and broke off my waterpipe.

But when he picked up all the apples off my tree and consumed them, my nerves tingled. The summer before, I had transported, via my network of underground tendrils, an amount of a certain poisonous mineral to the tree. In so doing I killed the tendrils that did the work, but I succeeded in feeding to the roots minute amounts of the stuff – selenium, Father termed it. I grew more tendrils and carried more poison to the tree. Eventually, the plant was full of the potion, yet I had fed it so slowly that it had built up a kind of immunity. A kind of, I say, because it was actually a rather sickly tree.

I must admit I got the idea from one of Father's not-so stories, tapped out in Orsemay so Mother wouldn't be vexed. It was about a mobile – a female, Father claimed, though I find the concept of a female mobile too nervequivering to dwell on – a mobile who was put into a long sleep by a poisoned apple.

The olfway seemed not to have heard of the story. All he did was retch. After he had recovered, he crawled up and perched on top of my dome. He broke off my big pulse-stalk and inserted his ovipositor in the hole and began dripping acid.

I was frightened. There is nothing more panic-striking than being deprived of pulsing and not knowing at all what is going on in the world outside your shell. But, at the same time, his actions were what I had expected. So I tried to suppress my nerve-quiverings. After all, I knew the olfway would work on that spot. It was for that very reason that I had shifted my brain to one side and jacked up my oversize stomach closer to the top of my dome.

My sisters had scoffed because I'd taken so much trouble with my organs. They'd been satisfied with the normal procedure of growing into Mother-size. While I was still waiting for the water pumped up from the stream to fill my sac, my sisters had long before heated theirs and were eating nice warm stew. Meanwhile, I was consuming much fruit and uncooked meat, which sometimes made me sick. However, the rejected stuff was good for the crops, so I didn't suffer a complete loss.

As you know, once the stomach is full of water and well walled up, our body heat warms the fluid. As there is no leakage of heat except when we iris meat and vegetables in or out, the water comes to the boiling point.

Well, to pulse on with the story, when the mobile had scaled away the bone and copper and iron with his acids and made a hole large enough for his body, he dropped in for dinner.

I suppose he anticipated the usual helpless Mother or virgin, nerves numbed and waiting to be eaten.

If he did, his own nerves must have quivered. There was an iris on the upper part of my stomach, and it had been grown with the dimensions of a certain carnivorous mobile in mind.

But there was a period when I thought I hadn't fashioned the opening large enough. I had him half through, but I couldn't get his hindquarters past the lips. He was wedged in tight and clawing my flesh away in great gobbets. I was in such pain I shook my body back and forth and, I believe, actually rocked my shell on its base. Yet, despite my jerking nerves, I strained and struggled and gulped hard, oh, so hard. And finally, just when I was on the verge of vomiting him back up the hole through which he had come, which would have been the end of me, I gave a tremendous convulsive gulp and popped him in.

My iris closed. Nor, much as he bit and poured out searing acids, would I open it again. I was determined that I was going to keep this meat in my stew, the biggest piece any Mother had ever had.

Oh, he fought. But not for long. The boiling water pushed into his open mouth and drenched his breathing-sacs. He couldn't take a sample of that hot fluid and then crawl off to pupate around it.

He was through – and he was delicious.

Yes, I know that I am to be congratulated and that this information for dealing with the monster must be broadcast to every one of us everywhere. But don't forget to pulse that a mobile was partly responsible for the victory over our ancient enemy. It may quiver your nerves to admit it, but he was.

Where did I get the idea of putting me stew-sac just below the hole the olfway always makes in the top of our shells? Well, it was like so many I had. It came from one of Father's not-so stories, told in Orsemay. I'll pulse it sometime when I'm not so busy. After you, dearie, have learned our secret language.

I'll start your lessons now. First. . . .

What's that? You're quivering with curiosity? Oh, very well, I'll give you some idea of the not-so story, then I'll continue my lessons with this neophyte.

It's about eethay olfway and eethay eethray ittlelay igspay.

I

THE first mate of the *Gull* looked up from the naviga-tion desk and pointed to the magnified figures cast upon the in-formation screen by the spoolmike.

'If this is correct, sir, we're a hundred thousand kilometres from the second planet. There are ten planets in this system. Luckily, one is inhabitable. The second one.'

He paused. Captain Tu looked curiously at him, for the man was very pale and had ironically accented the *luckily*.

'Sir, the second planet must be Abatos.'

The captain's swarthy skin whitened to match the mate's. His mouth opened as if to form an oath, then clamped shut. At the same time his right hand made an abortive gesture towards his forehead, as if he had meant to touch it. His hand dropped.

'Very well, Mister Givens. We shall make an attempt to land. That is all we can do. Stand by for further orders.'

He turned away so none could see his face.

'Abatos, Abatos,' he murmured. He licked his dry lips and locked his hands behind his back.

Two short buzzes sounded. Midshipman Nkrumah passed his hand over an activating plate and said, 'Bridge,' to a plate that sprang into life and colour on the wall. A steward's face appeared.

'Sir, please inform the captain that Bishop André and Father Carmody are waiting for him in cabin 7.'

Captain Tu glanced at the bridge clock and tugged at the silver crucifix that hung from his right ear. Givens, Nkrumah, and Merkalov watched him intently, though they looked to one side when their eyes met his. He smiled grimly when he saw their expressions, unlocked his hands, and straightened his back. It was as if he knew his men were depending on him to preserve a calm that would radiate confidence in his ability to get them to safety. So, for a half minute, he posed monolithic in his sky-blue uniform that had not changed since the Twenty-First

Century. Though it was well known that he felt a little ridiculous when he wore it planetside, when he was on his ship he walked as a man clad in armour. If coats and trousers were archaic and seen only at costume balls or in historical stereos or on officers of interstellar vessels, they did give a sense of apartness and of glamour and helped enforce discipline. The captain must have felt as if he needed every bit of confidence and respect he could muster. Thus, the conscious striking of the pose; here was the thoughtful and unnervous skipper who was so sure of himself that he could take time to attend to social demands.

'Tell the bishop I'll be in to see him at once,' he ordered the midshipman.

He strode from the bridge, passed through several corridors, and entered the small lounge. There he paused in the doorway to look the passengers over. All except the two priests were there. None of them as yet was aware that the *Gull* was not merely going through one of the many transitions from normal space to perpendicular space. The two young lovers, Kate Lejeune and Pete Masters, were sitting in one corner on a sofa, holding hands and whispering softly and every now and then giving each other looks that ached with suppressed passion. At the other end of the room Mrs. Recka sat at a table playing double solitaire with the ship's doctor, Chandra Blake. She was a tall voluptuous blonde whose beauty was spoiled by an incipient double chin and dark halfmoons under her eyes. The half-empty bottle of bourbon on the table told of the origin of her dissipated appearance; those who knew something of her personal history also knew that it was responsible for her being on the *Gull*. Separated from her husband on Wildenwooly, she was going home to her parents on the faraway world of Diveboard on the Galaxy's rim. She'd been given the choice of him or the bottle and had preferred the simpler and more transportable item. As she was remarking to the doctor when the captain entered, bourbon never criticized you or called you a drunken slut.

Chandra Blake, a short dark man with prominent cheekbones and large brown eyes, sat with a fixed smile. He was very embarrassed at her loud conversation but was too polite to leave her.

Captain Tu touched his cap as he passed the four and smiled at their greetings, ignoring Mrs. Recka's invitation to sit at her table. Then he went down a long hall and pressed a button by the door of cabin 7.

It swung open and he strode in, a tall stiff gaunt man who looked as if he were made of some dark inflexible metal. He stopped abruptly and performed the seeming miracle of bending forward. He did so to kiss the bishop's extended hand, with a lack of grace and a reluctance that took all the meaning out of the act. When he straightened up, he almost gave the impression of sighing with relief. It was obvious that the captain liked to unbend to no man.

He opened his mouth as if to give them at once the unhappy news, but Father John Carmody pressed a drink into his hand.

'A toast, captain, to a quick trip to Ygdrasil,' said Father John in a low gravelly voice. 'We enjoy being aboard, but we've reason for haste in getting to our destination.'

'I will drink to your health and His Excellency's,' said Tu in a harsh clipped voice. 'As for the quick trip, I'm afraid we'll need a little prayer. Maybe more than a little.'

Father Carmody raised extraordinarily thick and tufted eyebrows but said nothing. This act of silence told much about his inner reactions, for he was a man who must forever be talking. He was short and fat, about forty, with heavy jowls, a thick shock of blue-black slightly wavy hair, bright blue and somewhat bulging eyes, a drooping left eyelid, a wide thick mouth, and a long sharp rocket-shaped nose. He quivered and shook and bounced with energy; he must always be on the move lest he explode; must be turning his hand to this and that, poking his nose here and there, must be laughing and chattering; must give the impression of vibrating inside like a great tuning fork.

Bishop André, standing beside him, was so tall and still and massive that he looked like an oak turned into a man, with Carmody the squirrel that raced around at his feet. His superb shoulders, arching chest, lean belly, and calves bursting with muscle told of great strength rigidly controlled and kept at a prizefighter's peak. His features did justice to the physique; he had a large high-cheekboned head topped by a mane of lion-yellow hair. His eyes were a glowing golden-green, his nose straight and classical in profile though too narrow and pinched when seen from the front; his mouth full and red and deeply indented at the corners. The bishop, like Father John, was the darling of the ladies of the diocese of Wildenwooly, but for a different reason. Father John was fun to be around. He made them giggle and laugh and made even their most serious problems seem not insurmountable. But Bishop André made them weak-kneed when he looked into their eyes. He was the kind of priest who caused them regret that he was not available for marrying. The worst part of that was that His Excellency knew the effect he had and hated it. At times he had been downright curt and was always just a little standoffish. But no woman could long remain offended at him. Indeed, as was well known, the bishop owed some of his meteoric rise to the efforts of the ladies behind the scenes. Not that he wasn't more than capable; it was just that he'd attained his rank faster than might have been expected.

Father John poured out a drink from a wine bottle, then filled two glasses with lemonade.

'I shall drink of the wine,' he said. 'You, Captain, will be forced to gag down this non-alcoholic beverage because you are on duty. His Excellency, however, refuses the cup that cheers, except as a sacrament, for reasons of principle. As for me, I take a little wine for my stomach's sake.'

He patted his large round paunch. 'Since my belly constitutes so much of me, anything I take for it I also take for my entire being. Thus, not only my entrails benefit, but my whole body glows with good health and joy and calls for more tonic. Unfortunately, the bishop sets me such an unendurably good example, I must restrain myself to this single cup. This, in spite of the fact that I am suffering from a toothache and could dull the pain with an extra glass or two.'

Smiling, he looked over the rim of his glass at Tu, who was grinning in spite of his tension, and at the bishop, whose set features and dignified bearing made him look like a lion deep in thought.

'Ah, forgive me, Your Excellency,' said the padre. 'I cannot help feeling that you are most immoderate in your temperance, but I should not have intimated as much. Actually, your asceticism is a model for all of us to admire, even if we haven't the strength of character to imitate it.'

'You are forgiven, John,' said the Bishop gravely. 'But I'd prefer that you confine your raillery – for I cannot help thinking that that is what it is – to times when no one else is around. It is not good for you to speak in such a manner before others, who might think you hold your bishop in some measure of contempt.'

'Now, God forgive me, I meant no such thing!' cried Carmody. 'As a matter of fact, my levity is directed at myself, because I enjoy too much the too-good things of this life, and instead of putting on wisdom and holiness, add another inch to my waistline.'

Captain Tu shifted uneasily, then suppressed his telltale movements. Obviously, this mention of God outside of church walls embarrassed him. Also, there just was no time to be chattering about trivial things.

'Let's drink to our good healths,' he said. He gulped his ade. Then, setting the glass on the table with an air of finality as if he would never get a chance to drink again, he said, 'The news I have is bad. Our translator engine cut out about an hour ago and left us stranded in normal space. The chief says he can't find a thing wrong with it, yet it won't work. He has no idea of how to start it again. He's a thoroughly competent man, and when he admits defeat, the problem is unsolvable.'

There was silence for a minute. Then Father John said, 'How close are we to an inhabitable planet?'

'About a hundred thousand kilometres,' replied Tu, tugging at the silver crucifix hanging from his ear. Abruptly realizing that he was betraying his anxiety, he let his hand fall to his side.

The padre shrugged his shoulders. 'We're not in free fall, so there's nothing wrong with our interplanetary drive. Why can't we set down on this planet?'

'We're going to try to. But I'm not confident of our success. The planet is Abatos.'

Carmody whistled and stroked the side of his long nose. André's bronzed face paled.

The little priest set down his glass and made a moue of concern.

'That is bad.' He looked at the bishop. 'May I tell the captain why we're so concerned about getting to Ygdrasil in a hurry?'

André nodded, his eyes downcast as if he were thinking of something that concerned the other two not at all.

'His Excellency,' said Carmody, 'left Wildenwooly for Ygdrasil because he thought he was suffering from hermit fever.'

The captain flinched but did not step back from his position close to the bishop. Carmody smiled and said, 'You needn't worry about catching it. He doesn't have it. Some of his symptoms matched those of hermit fever, but an examination failed to disclose any microbes. Not only that, His Excellency didn't develop a *typical* antisocial behaviour. But the doctors decided he should go to Ygdrasil, where they have better facilities than those on Wildenwooly, which is still rather primitive, you know. Also, there's a Doctor Ruedenbach there, a specialist in epileptoid diseases. It was thought best to see him, as His Excellency's condition was not improving.'

Tu held out his palms in a gesture of helplessness.

'Believe me, Your Excellency, this news saddens me and makes me regret even more this accident. But there is nothing . . .'

André came out of his reverie. For the first time he smiled, a slow, warm, and handsome smile. 'What are my troubles compared to yours? You have the responsibility of this vessel and its expensive cargo. And, far more important, the welfare of twenty-five souls.'

He began pacing back and forth, speaking in his vibrant voice.

'We've all heard of Abatos. We know what it may mean if the translator doesn't begin working again. Or if we meet the same fate as those other ships that tried to land on it. We're about eight light years from Ygdrasil and six from Wildenwooly, which means we can't get to either place in normal drive. We either get the translator started or else land. Or remain in space until we die.'

'And even if we are allowed to make planetfall,' said Tu, 'we may spend the rest of our lives on Abatos.'

A moment later, he left the cabin. He was halted by Carmody, who had slipped out after him.

'When are you going to tell the other passengers?'

Tu looked at his watch.

'In two hours. By then we'll know whether or not Abatos will let us pass. I can't put off telling them any longer, because they'll know something's up. We should have been falling to Ygdrasil by now.'

'The bishop is praying for us all now,' said Carmody. 'I shall concentrate my own request on an inspiration for the engineer. He's going to need it.'

'There's nothing wrong with that translator,' said Tu flatly, 'except that it won't work.'

Carmody looked shrewdly at him from under his thatched

eyebrows and stroked the side of his nose.

'You think it's not an accident that the engine cut out?'

'I've been in many tough spots before,' replied Tu, 'and I've been scared. Yes, scared. I wouldn't tell any man except you – or maybe some other priest – but I have been frightened. Oh, I know it's a weakness, maybe even a sin . . .'

Here Carmody raised his eyebrows in amazement and perhaps a little awe of such an attitude.

'. . . but I just couldn't seem to help it, though I swore that I'd never again feel that way, and I never allowed anyone to see it. My wife always said that if I'd allow myself now and then to show a little weakness, not much, just a little . . . Well, perhaps that may have been why she left me, I don't know, and it doesn't really matter any more, except . . .'

Suddenly realizing that he was wandering, the captain stopped, visibly braced himself, squared his shoulders, and said, 'Anyway, Father, this set-up scares me worse than I've ever been scared. Why, I couldn't exactly tell you. But I've a feeling that something caused that cut-out and for a purpose we won't like when we find out. All I have to base my reasoning on is what happened to those other three ships. You know, everybody's read about them, how the *Hoyle* landed and was never heard of again, how the *Priam* investigated its disappearance and couldn't get any closer than fifty kilometres because her normal space drive failed, and how the cruiser *Tokyo* tried to bull its way in with its drive dead and only escaped because it had enough velocity to take it past the fifty kilo limit. Even so, it almost burned up when it was going through the stratosphere.'

'What I can't understand,' said Carmody, 'is how such an agent could affect us while we're in translation. Theoretically, we don't even exist in normal space then.'

Tu tugged at the crucifix. 'Yes, I know. But we're *here*. Whatever did this has a power unknown to man. Otherwise It wouldn't be able to pinpoint us in translation so close to Its home planet.'

Carmody smiled cheerfully. 'What's there to worry about? If it can haul us in like fish in a net, it must want us to land. So we don't have to fret about planetfall.'

Suddenly he grimaced with pain. 'This rotten molar of mine,' he explained. 'I was going to have it pulled and a bud put in when I got to Ygdrasil. And I'd sworn to quit eating so much of that chocolate of which I'm perilously overfond and which has already cost me the loss of several teeth. And now I must pay for my sins, for I was in such a hurry I forgot to bring along any painkiller, except for the wine. Or was that a Freudian slip?'

'Doctor Blake will have pain pills.'

Carmody laughed. 'So he does! Another convenient oversight! I'd hoped to confine myself to the natural medicine of the grape, and ignore the tasteless and enervating laboratory-born nostrums. But I have too many people looking out for my welfare. Well, such is the price of popularity.'

He slapped Tu on the shoulder. 'There's adventure awaiting us, Bill. Let's get going.'

The captain did not seem to resent the familiarity. Evidently, he'd known Carmody for a long time.

'I wish I had your courage, Father.'

'Courage!' snorted the priest. 'I'm shaking in my hair shirt. But we must take what God sends us, and if we can like it, all the better.'

Tu allowed himself to smile. 'I like you because you can say something like that without sounding false or unctuous or – uh – priestly. I know you mean it.'

'You're blessed well right I do,' answered Carmody, then shifted from cheeriness to a more grave tone. 'Seriously, though, Bill, I do hope we can get going soon. The bishop is in a bad way. He looks healthy, but he's liable at any moment to have an attack. If he does, I'll be pretty busy with him for a while. I can't tell you much more about him because he wouldn't want me to. Like you, he hates to confess to any weakness; he'll probably reprimand me when I go back to the cabin for having mentioned the matter to you. That's one reason why he has said nothing to Doctor Blake. When he has one of his ... spells, he doesn't like anyone but me to take care of him. And he resents that little bit of dependency.'

'It's pretty bad, then? Hard to believe. He's such a healthy-looking man; you wouldn't want to tangle with him in a scrap. He's a *good* man, too. Righteous as they make them. I remember one sermon he gave us at St. Pius' on Lazy Fair. Gave us hell and scared me into living a clean life for all of three weeks. The saints themselves must have thought they'd have to move over for me, and then ...'

Seeing the look in Carmody's eyes, Tu stopped, glanced at

his watch, and said, 'Well, I've a few minutes to spare and I've not been doing as well as I might, though I suppose we all could say that, eh, Father? Could we step into your cabin? There's no telling what might happen in the next few hours and I'd like to be prepared.'

'Certainly. Follow me, my son.'

II

Two hours later, Captain Tu had told crew and passengers the truth over the bridge-viser. When his voice died and his grim gaunt face faded off the screen in the lounge, he left behind him silence and stricken looks. All except Carmody sat in their chairs as if the captain's voice had been an arrow pinning them to the cushions. Carmody stood in the centre of the lounge, a soberly clad little figure in the midst of their bright clothes. He wore no rings on his ears, his legs were painted a decent black, his puff-kilts were only moderately slashed, and his quilted dickie and suspenders were severe, innocent of golden spangles or jewels. Like all members of the Jairusite Order, he wore his Roman collar only when on planetside in memory of the founder and his peculiar but justified reason for doing so.

He shrewdly watched the passengers. Rocking back and forth on his heels, his forefinger tracing the length of his nose, he seemed to be interested in the announcement only from the view-point of how it was affecting them. There was no sign that he was concerned about himself.

Mrs. Recka was still sitting before her cards, her head bent to study them. But her hand went out more often to the bottle, and once she upset it with a noise that made Blake and the two young lovers jump. Without bothering to get up from her chair, she allowed the fifth to spill on the floor while she rang for the steward. Perhaps the significance of the captain's words had not penetrated the haze in her brain. Or perhaps she just did not care.

Pete Masters and Kate Lejeune had not moved or spoken a word. They huddled closer, if that were possible and squeezed hands even more tightly – pale-faced their heads nodded like two white balloons shaken by an internal wind, Kate's red painted mouth, vivid against her bloodless skin, hanging open like a gash in the sphere and by some miracle keeping the air inside her so her head did not collapse.

Carmody looked at them with pity for he knew their story far better than they realized. Kate was the daughter of a rich 'pelter-piper' on Wildenwooly. Pete was the son of a penniless 'tinwood-man' one of those armoured lumberjacks who venture deep into the planet's peculiarly dangerous forests in search of wishing-wood trees. After his father had been dragged into an under-water cavern by a snoligoster, Pete had gone to work for Old Man Lejeune. That he had courage was quickly proved for it took guts to pipe the luxuriously furred but savage-tempered agropelters out of their hollow trees and conduct them into the hands of the skinners. That he was also foolhardy was almost as swiftly demonstrated for he had fallen as passionately in love with Kate as she had with him.

When he had summoned up enough bravery to ask her father for her hand – Old Man Lejeune was as vicious and quickly angered as an agropelter itself and not to be charmed by any blowing on a pipe – he had been thrown out bodily with several bruises and contusions, a slight brain concussion, and a promise that if he got within speaking distance of her again he would lose both life and limb. Then had followed the old and inevitable story. After getting out of the hospital Pete had sent Kate messages through her widowed aunt. The aunt disliked her brother and was moreover such an intense devotee of the stereo romance-serials that she would have done almost anything to smooth the path of true love.

Thus it was that a copter had suddenly dropped on to the port outside Breakneck just before the *Gull* was to take off. After identifying themselves and purchasing tickets – which was all they had to do to get passage for there were no visas or pass-ports for human beings who wanted transportation between planets of the Commonwealth – they had entered cabin 9 next to the bishop's, and there stayed until just before the translator had broken down.

Kate's aunt had been too proud of her part as Cupid to keep her mouth shut. She'd told a half dozen friends in Breakneck after getting their solemn promises not to tell anyone. Result: Father Carmody had all the facts and some of the lies about the Masters-Lejeune affair. When the couple had slipped aboard he'd known at once what had happened and indeed was waiting for the outraged father to follow them with a band of tough skinners to take care of Pete. But the ship had flashed away, and now there was little chance they'd be met at Ygdrasil port with an order for the couple's detention. They'd be lucky if they ever arrived there.

Carmody walked to a spot before them and halted. 'Don't be frightened, kids,' he said. 'The captain's private opinion is that we won't have any trouble landing on Abatos.'

Pete Masters was a redhaired hawk-nosed youth with hollow cheeks and a too large chin. His frame was large but he'd not yet filled out with a man's muscles nor got over the slouch of the adolescent who grows too fast. He covered the delicate long-fingered hand of Kate with his big bony hand and said, glaring up at the priest, 'And I suppose he'll turn us over to the authorities as soon as we land?'

Carmody blinked at the brassiness of Pete's voice and leaned slightly forward as if he were walking against the wind of it.

'Hardly,' he said softly. 'If there's an authority on Abatos, we haven't met him yet. But we may, we may.'

He paused and looked at Kate. She was pretty and petite. Her long wheaten hair was caught up in back with a silver circlet; her large violet eyes turned up to meet his with a mixture of guilelessness and pleading.

'Actually,' said the padre, 'your father can't do a thing – legally – to stop you two unless you commit a crime. Let me see, you're nineteen, aren't you, Pete? And you, Kate, are only seventeen, right? If I remember the clauses in the Free Will Act, your being under age will not hamper your moving away from your father's house without his permission. You're of mobile age. On the other hand, according to law, you're not of nubile age. Biology, I know, contradicts that, but we also live in a social world, one of manmade laws. You may not get married without your father's consent. If you try to do so, he may legally restrain you. And will, no doubt.'

'He can't do a thing,' said Pete, fiercely. 'We're not going to get married until Kate is of age.'

He glared from under straw-coloured eyebrows. Kate's paleness disappeared under a flood of red, and she looked down at her slim legs, painted canary yellow with scarlet-tipped toenails. Her free hand plucked at her Kelly-green puffkilt.

Carmody's smile remained.

'Forgive a nosy priest who is interested because he doesn't

want to see you hurt. Or to have you hurt anybody. But I know your father, Kate. I know he's quite capable of carrying out his threat against Pete. Would you want to see him kidnapped, brutally beaten up, perhaps killed?'

She raised her large eyes to him, her cheeks still flaming. She was very beautiful, very young, very intense.

'Daddy wouldn't dare!' she said in a low but passionate voice. 'He knows that if anything happens to Pete, I'll kill myself. I said so in the note I left him, and he knows I'm just as stubborn as he. Daddy won't hurt Pete because he loves me too much.'

'Just don't bother talking to him, honey,' said Pete. 'I'll handle this. Carmody, we don't want any interference, well meant or not. We just want to be left alone.'

Father John sighed. 'To be left alone is little enough to desire. Unfortunately, or perhaps fortunately, it's one of the rarest things in this universe, almost as rare as peace of mind or genuine love for mankind.'

'Spare me your clichés,' said Pete. 'Save them for church.'

'Ah, yes, I did see you once at St. Mary's, didn't I?' replied Father John, stroking the side of his nose. 'Two years ago during that outbreak of hermit fever. Hmm.'

Kate put her hand on the young man's wrist. 'Please, darling. He means well, and what he says is true, anyway.'

'Thank you, Kate.'

Carmody hesitated, then, looking thoughtful and sad, he reached into the puffkilt's pocket and pulled out a slip of yellow paper. He held it out to Kate, who took it with a trembling hand.

'This was given to the steward just before our ship took off,' he said. 'It was too late then for anything to be done; unless it's a matter of supreme importance, the ship's schedule is adhered to.'

Kate read the message and paled again. Pete, reading over her shoulder, became red, and his nostrils flared. Tearing the paper from her, he jumped up.

'If Old Man Lejeune thinks he can jail me by accusing me of stealing his money, he's crazy!' he snarled. 'He can't prove it because I didn't do it! I'm innocent, and I'll prove it by volunteering for chalarocheil! Or any truth drug they want to give me! That'll show him up for the liar he is!'

Father John's eyes widened. 'Meanwhile, you two will be

held, and Kate's father will take steps to get her back or at least remove her to the other end of the Galaxy. Now, I'd like to suggest . . .'

'Never mind your needlenosing suggestions,' barked Pete.

He crumpled the paper and dropped it on the floor. 'Come on, Kate, let's go to our cabin.'

Submissively, she rose, though she shot a look at Pete as if she'd like to express her opinion. He ignored it.

'Do you know,' he continued, 'I'm glad we're being forced to land on Abatos. From what I've read, the *Tokyo* determined that it's a habitable planet, perhaps another Eden. So Kate and I ought to be able to live fairly easy on it. I've got my Power-kit in my cabin; with it we can build a cabin and till the soil and hunt and fish and raise our children as we wish. And there'll be no interference from anyone – no one at all.'

Father John cocked his head to one side and let his left eyelid droop. 'Adam and Eve, heh? Won't you two become rather lonely? Besides, how do you know what dangers Abatos holds?'

'Pete and I need nobody else,' replied Kate quietly. 'And we're not afraid of anything at all.'

'Except your father.'

But the two were walking away hand in hand; they might not have heard him.

He leaned over to pick up the paper, grunting as he did so. Straightening up with a sigh, he smoothed it out and read it.

Doctor Blake rose from the table and approached him. He smiled with a mixture of affability and reproach.

'Aren't you being a little bit too officious?'

Carmody smiled. 'You've known me for a long time, Chandra. You know that this long sharp nose of mine is an excellent sign of my character, and that I would not put my hand in the flame to deny that I am a needlenosing busybody. However, my excuse is that I am a priest and that that is a professional attribute. No escaping it. Moreover, I happen to be interested in those kids; I want them to get out of this mess without being hurt.'

'You're likely to get the shape of your nose changed. That Pete looks wild enough to swing on you.'

Father John rubbed the end of his nose. 'Won't be the first time it's been busted. But I doubt if Pete'd hit me. One good thing about popping off if you're a priest. Even the roughest hesitate about hitting you. Almost like striking a woman. Or

God's representative. Or both. We cowards sometimes take advantage of that.'

Blake snorted. 'Coward?' Then, 'Kate's not even of your religion, Father, and Pete might as well not be.'

Carmody shrugged and spread his palms out as if to show that his hands were for anybody who needed them. A few minutes later, he was pressing the buzzer by the bishop's door. When he heard no answering voice, he turned as if to go, then stopped, frowning. Abruptly, as if obeying an inner warning, he pushed in on the door. Unlocked, it swung open. He gasped and ran into the room.

The bishop was lying face up on the middle of the floor, his arms and legs extended crucifix-wise, his back arched to form a bow, his eyes open and fixed in a state at a point on the ceiling. His face was flushed and glistening with sweat; his breath hissed; bubbles of foam escaped from his lax mouth. Yet there was nothing of the classic seizure about him, for the upper part of his body seemed to be immobile, almost as if it were formed of wax just on the verge of melting from some internal heat. The lower part, on the contrary, was in violent movement. His legs thrashed and his pelvis stabbed upwards. He looked as if a sword had cut an invisible path through the region of his abdomen and severed the nerves and muscles that connected the two halves. The trunk had cast off the hips and legs and said, 'What you do is no concern of mine.'

Carmody closed the door and hastened to do that which needed doing for the bishop.

III

The *Gull* chose to settle upon a spot in the centre of the only continent of Abatos, a globe-encircling mass large as Africa and Asia put together, all of it in the northern hemisphere.

'Best landing I ever made,' said Tu to his first mate. 'Almost as if I were a machine, I set her down so easy.' Aside, he muttered, 'Perhaps I've saved the best for the last.'

Carmody did not come from the bishop's cabin until twenty-four hours later. After telling the doctor and the captain that André was resting quietly and did not wish to be disturbed, Carmody asked what they'd found out so far. Obviously, he'd been eaten up with curiosity while locked in the cabin, for he had a hundred questions ready and could not fire them out fast enough.

They could tell him little, though their explorations had covered much territory. The climate seemed to be about what you'd find in midwest America in May. The vegetation and animal life paralleled those of Earth, but of course there were many unfamiliar species.

'Here's something strange,' said Doctor Blake. He picked up several thin disks, cross-sections of trees, and handed them to the priest. 'Pete Masters cut these with his Powerkit. Apparently he's been looking for the best kind of wood with which to build a cabin – or maybe I should say a mansion; he has some rather grandiose ideas about what he's going to do here. Notice the grain and the distance between the rings. Perfect grain. And the rings are separated by exactly the same length. Also, no knots or worm-holes of any kind.

'Pete pointed out these interesting facts, so we cut down about forty trees of different types with the ship's Survival Kit saw. And all specimens showed the same perfection. Not only that, but the number of rings, plus the Mead method of photostatic dating, proved that every tree was exactly the same age. All had been planted ten thousand years ago!'

'The only comment I could make would be an understatement,' said Carmody. 'Hmmm. The even spacing of the growth rings would indicate that the seasons, if any, follow a regular pattern, that there have been no irregular stretches of wetness and dryness but a static allotment of rain and sunshine. But these woods are wild and untended. How account for the lack of damage from parasites? Perhaps there are none.'

'Don't know. Not only that, the fruit of these trees is very large and tasty and abundant – all looking as if they'd come from stock carefully bred and protected. Yet we've seen no signs of intelligent life.'

Blake's black eyes sparkled, and his hands seesawed with excitement.

'We took the liberty of shooting several animals so we could examine them. I did a fast dissection on a small zebra-like creature, a wolf with a long copper-coloured snout, a yellow red-crested corvine, and a kangarooish non-marsupial. Even my hasty study turned up several astonishing facts, though one of them could have been determined by any layman.'

He paused, then burst out, 'All were females! And the dating of their bones indicated that they, like the trees, were ten thousand years old!'

Father John's tufted eyebrows could rise no higher; they looked like untidy wings flapping heavily with a freight of amazement.

'Yes, we've detected no males at all among any of the millions of beasts that we've seen. Not a one. All, all females!'

He took Carmody's elbow and escorted him towards the woods. 'Ten thousand years old the skeletons were. But that wasn't all that was marvellous about them. Their bones were completely innocent of evolutionary vestiges, were perfectly functional. Carmody, you're an amateur paleontologist, you should know how unique that is. On every planet where we've studied fossil and contemporary skeletons, we've found that they display tag-ends of bones that have degenerated in structure because of loss of function. Consider the toes of a dog, the hoofs of a horse. The dog, you might say, walks on his fingers and has lost his big toe and reduced his thumb to a small size. The horse's splint bones were once two toes, the hoof representing the main toe that hardened and on which the fossil horse put his main weight. But this zebra had no splint bones, and the wolf showed no vestiges of toes that had lost their function. The same with the other creatures I studied. Functionally perfect.'

'But, but,' said Father John, 'you know that evolution on other planets doesn't follow exactly the same pattern laid down on Earth. Moreover, the similarity between a terrestrial and a non-terrestrial type may be misleading. As a matter of fact, likenesses between Earth types may be deceiving. Look how the isolated Australian marsupials developed parallels to placentals. Though not at all related to the higher mammals of the other continents, they evolved dog-like, mouse-like, mole-like, and bear-like creatures.'

'I'm quite aware of that,' replied Blake, a little stiffly. 'I'm no ignoramus, you know. There are other factors determining my opinion, but you talk so much you've given me no chance to tell you.'

Carmody had to laugh. 'I? Talk? I've hardly got in a word. Never mind. I apologize for my gabbiness. What else is there?'

'Well, I had some of the crewmen do some looking around. They brought in hundreds of specimens of insects, and of course I'd no time for anything except a hasty glance. But there were none with any correspondence to larval forms as we know them on Earth. All adult forms. When I thought of that, I realized something else we'd all seen but hadn't been impressed by, mostly, I suppose, because the deductions were too overwhelming or because we just weren't looking for such a thing. We saw no young among the animals.'

'Puzzling, if not frightening,' said Carmody. 'You may release my elbow, if you wish. I'll go with you willingly. Which reminds me, where are you taking me?'

'Here!'

Blake stopped before a redwoodish tree towering perhaps two hundred feet. He indicated a very large hole in the trunk, about two feet from the ground. 'This cavity is not the result of disease or damage by some animal. It obviously is part of the tree's structure.'

He directed the beam of a flashlight into the dark interior. Carmody stuck his head into the hole and after a moment withdrew it, looking thoughtful.

'There must be about ten tons of that jelly-like substance inside,' he said. 'And there are bones embedded deep within it.'

'Wherever you go, you find these jelly trees, as we now call them,' said Blake. 'About half of them hold animal skeletons.'

'What are they? A sort of Venusian fly-trap?' asked the priest, involuntarily taking a backward step. 'No, they couldn't be that, or you'd not have allowed me to stick my head in. Or does it, like many men, find theological subjects distasteful?'

Blake laughed, then sobered quickly.

'I've no idea *why* these bones are there nor what purpose the jelly serves,' he said. 'But I can tell you *how* they got there. You see, while we were flying around, mapping and observing, we witnessed several killings by the local carnivora. There are two types we were glad we didn't run into on the ground, though we've means to repel them if we see them soon enough. One's a cat about the size of a Bengal tiger, leopard-like except for big round ears and tufts of grey fur on the backs of its legs. The other's a ten-foot-high black-furred mammal built like a tyrannosaurus with a bear's head. Both prey on the zebras and the numerous deer and antelope. You'd think that their fleet-footed prey would keep the killers swift and trim, but they don't. The big cats and the struthiursines are the fattest and laziest meat-eaters you ever saw. When they attack, they don't sneak up through the grass and then make a swift but short run. They walk boldly into view, roar a few times, wait until the majority of the herd have dashed off, then select one from the several submissive animals that have refused to flee, and kill it. Those that have been spared then drift off. They're not frightened by the sight of the killer devouring one of their sisters. No, they just appear uneasy.

'As if that weren't extraordinary enough, the sequel positively astounds you. After the big killer has gorged himself and leaves, the small carrion-eaters then descend, yellowish crows and brown-and-white foxes. The bones are well cleaned. But they aren't left to bleach in the sun. Along comes a black ape with a long lugubrious face – the undertaker ape, we call him – and he picks the bones up and deposits them in the jelly inside the nearest jelly tree. Now, what do you think of that?'

'I think that, though it's a warm day, I have a sudden chill. I . . . oh, there's His Excellency. Excuse me.'

The priest hurried across the daisy-starred meadow, a long black case in his hand. The bishop did not wait for him but stepped from the shadow of the ship into the light. Though the yellow sun had risen only an hour ago above the purplish mountains to the east, it was very bright. When it struck the bishop's figure, it seemed to burst into flame around him and magnify him, almost as if its touch were that of a golden god imparting some of his own magnificence to him. The illusion was made all the stronger by the fact that André showed no signs of his recent illness. His face glowed, and he strode swiftly towards the crowd at the forest's edge, his shoulders squared and his deep chest rising and falling as if he were trying to crowd all the planet's air into his lungs.

Carmody, who met him half-way, said, 'You may well breathe this superb air, Your Excellency. It has a tang and freshness that is quite virginal. Air that had never been breathed by man before.'

André looked about him with the slowness and sure majesty of a lion staking out a new hunting territory. Carmody smiled slightly. Though the bishop made a noble figure of a man, he gave at that moment just the hint of a poseur, so subtle that only one with Carmody's vast experience could have detected it. André, catching the fleeting indentations at the corners of the little priest's lips, frowned and raised his hands in protest.

'I know what you are thinking.'

66

Carmody bent his neck to gaze at the bright green grass at their feet. Whether he did so to acknowledge that the reprimand was just or to hide another emotion, he managed to veil his eyes. Then, as if realizing it was not good to conceal his thoughts, he raised his head to look his bishop in the eyes. His gesture was similar to André's and had dignity but none of the other man's beauty, for Carmody could never look beautiful, except with the more subtle beauty that springs from honesty.

'I hope you can forgive me, Your Excellency. But old habits die hard. Mockery was so long a part of me before I was converted – indeed, was a necessity if one was to survive on the planet where I lived, which was Dante's Joy, you know – that it dug deep into my nervous system. I believe that I am making a sincere effort to overcome the habit; but, being human, I am sometimes lax.'

'We must strive to be more than human,' replied André, making a gesture with his hand which the priest, who knew him well, interpreted as a sign to drop the subject. It was not peremptory, for he was almost always courteous and patient. His time was not his; the lowliest were his masters. Had Carmody persisted in dwelling on that line of thought, he would have allowed it. The priest, however, accepted his superior's decision.

He held out a slender black case six feet long.

'I thought that perhaps Your Excellency would like to try the fishing here. It may be true that Wildenwooly has a Galaxy-wide reputation for the best fishing anywhere, but there's something about the very looks of Abatos that tells me we'll find fish here to put a glow in our hearts – not to mention a whale of an appetite in our mouths. Would you care to try a few casts? It might benefit Your Excellency.'

André's smile was slow and gentle, ending in a huge grin of delight. 'I'd like that very much, John. You could have suggested nothing better.'

He turned to Tu. 'Captain?'

'I think it'll be safe. We've sent out survey copters. They reported some large carnivores but none close. However, some of the herbivores may be dangerous. Remember, even a domestic bull may be a killer. The copter crews did try to get some of the larger beasts to charge and failed. The animals either ignored them or ambled away. Yes, you may go fishing, though I wish the lake weren't so far off. What about a copter dropping you off there and picking you up later?'

André said, 'No thank you. We can't get the feel of this planet by flying over it. We'll walk.'

The first mate held out two pistols of some sort.

'Here you are, Reverends. Something new. Sonos. Shoots a subsonic beam that panics man or beast, makes 'em want to get to hell and away as fast as they can, if you'll pardon the expression.'

'Of course. But we can't accept them. Our order is never permitted to carry arms, for any reason.'

'I wish you'd break the rule this time,' said Tu. 'Rules aren't made to be broken; no captain would subscribe to that proverb. But there are times when you have to consider their context.'

'Absolutely not,' replied the bishop, looking keenly at Carmody, who'd stretched out his hand as if to take a sono.

At the glance, the priest dropped his hand. 'I merely wished to examine the weapon,' said Carmody. 'But I must admit I've never thought much of that rule. It's true that Jairus had his peculiar power over beasts of prey. However, that fact didn't necessarily endow his disciples with a similar gift. Think of what happened on Jimdandy because St. Victor refused a gun. Had he used one, he'd have saved a thousand lives.'

The bishop closed his eyes and murmured so that only Carmody could hear. '*Even though I walk in the dark valley . . .*'

Carmody murmured back, 'But the dark is sometimes cold, and the hairs on the back of the neck rise with fear, though I become hot with shame.'

'Hmm. Speaking of shame, John, you always manage, somehow, while deprecating yourself, to leave me discomfited and belittled. It's a talent which, perhaps, should be possessed by the man who is most often with me, for it cuts down my inclination to grow proud. On the other hand . . .'

Carmody waved the long case in his hand. 'On the other hand, the fish may not wait for us.'

André nodded and began walking towards the woods. Tu said something to a crewman, who ran after the two priests and gave the little one a ship-finder, a compass that would always point in the *Gull*'s direction. Carmody flashed a grin of thanks and, shoulders set jauntily, bounced after the swiftly striding bishop, the case whipping behind him like a saucy antenna. He whistled an old old tune – 'My Buddy.' Though seemingly carefree, his eyes looked everywhere. He did not fail to see Pete Masters and Kate Lejeune slipping hand in hand into the woods in another direction. He stopped in time to keep from bumping into the bishop, who had turned and was frowning back towards the ship. At first Carmody thought he, too, had noticed the young couple, then saw he was gazing at Mrs. Recka and First Mate Givens. They were standing to one side and talking very intensely. Then they began walking slowly across the meadow towards the towering hemisphere of the *Gull*. André stood motionless until the couple went into the ship and, a moment later, came out. This time Mrs. Recka had her pocketbook, a rather large one whose size was not enough to conceal the outlines of a bottle within. Still talking, the two went around the curve of the vessel and presently came into sight of the priests again, though they could not be seen by Tu or the crew members.

Carmody murmured, 'Must be something in the air of this planet . . .'

'What do you mean by that?' said the bishop, his features set very grim, his green eyes narrowed but blazing.

'If this is another Eden, where the lion lies down with the lamb, it is also a place where a man and woman . . .'

'If Abatos is fresh and clean and innocent,' growled the bishop, 'it will not remain so very long. Not while we have people like those, who would foul any nest.'

'Well, you and I will have to content ourselves with fishing.'

'Carmody, don't grin when you say that! You sound almost as if you were blessing them instead of condemning!'

The little priest lost his half-smile. 'Hardly. I was neither condemning nor blessing. Nor judging them beforehand, for I don't actually know what they have in mind. But it is true that I have too wide a streak of the earth earthy, a dabble of Rabelais, perhaps. It's not that I commend. It's just that I understand too well, and . . .'

Without replying, the bishop turned away violently and resumed his longlegged pace. Carmody, somewhat subdued, followed at his heels, though there was often room enough for the two to walk side by side. Sensitive to André's moods, he knew that it was best to keep out of his sight for a while. Meanwhile, he'd interest himself in his surroundings.

The copter survey crews had reported that between the mountains to the east and the ocean to the west the country was much alike: a rolling, sometimes hilly land with large prairies interspersed with forests. The latter seemed more like parks than untamed woods. The grass was a succulent kind kept cropped by the herbivores; many of the trees had their counterparts among the temperate latitudes of Earth; only here and there were thick tangled stretches that might properly be called wild. The lake towards which the two were headed lay in the centre of just such a 'jungle'. The widely spaced oaks, pines, cypresses, beeches, sycamores, and cedars here gave way to an island of the jelly-containing redwoods. Actually, they did not grow close together but gave that impression because of the many vines and lianas that connected them and the tiny parasitic trees, like evergreens, that grew horizontally out of cracks in their trunks.

It was darker under these great vegetation-burdened limbs, though here and there shafts of sunlight slanted, seeming like solid and leaning trunks of gold themselves. The forest was alive with the colour and calls of bright birds and the dark bodies and chitterings of arboreal animals. Some of these looked like monkeys; when they leapt through the branches and came quite close, the resemblance was even more amazing. But they were evidently not sprung from a protosimian base; they must have been descended from a cat that had decided to grow fingers instead of claws and to assume a semi-upright posture. Dark brown on the back, they had grey-furred bellies and chests and long prehensile tails tufted at the end with auburn. Their faces had lost the pointed beastish look and become flat as an ape's. Three long thick feline whiskers bristled from each side of their thin lips. Their teeth were sharp and long, but they picked and ate a large pear-shaped berry that grew on the vines. Their slitted pupils expanded in the shade and contracted in the sunlit spaces. They chattered among themselves and behaved in general like monkeys, except that they seemed to be cleaner.

'Perhaps they've cousins who evolved into humanoid beings,' said Carmody aloud, partly because he'd the habit of talking to himself, partly to see if the bishop were out of his mood.

'Heh?' said André, stopping and also looking at the creatures, who returned his gaze just as curiously. 'Oh, yes, Sokoloff's Theory of the Necessary Chance. Every branch of the animal kingdom as we know it on Earth seems to have had its opportunity to develop into a sentient being some place in the Galaxy.

The vulpoids of Kubeia, the avians of Albireo IV, the cetaceoids of Oceanos, the molluscs of Baudelaire, the Houyhnhnms of Somewhere Else, the so-called lying bugs of Münchausen, the ... well, I could go on and on. But on almost every Earth-type planet we find that this or that line of life seized the evolutionary chance given by God and developed intelligence. All, with some exceptions, going through an arboreal simian stage and then flowering into an upright creature resembling man.'

'And all thinking of themselves as being in God's image, even the porpoise-men of Oceanos and the land-oysters of Baudelaire,' added Carmody. 'Well, enough of philosophy. At least, fish are fish, on any planet.'

They had come out of the forest on to the lake shore. It was a body of water about a mile wide and two long, fed by a clear brook to the north. Grass grew to the very edge, where little frogs leaped into the water at their approach. Carmody uncased their two rods but disengaged the little jet mechanisms that would have propelled their bait-tipped lines far out over the lake.

'Really not sporting,' he said. 'We ought to give these foreign piscines a chance, eh?'

'Right,' replied the bishop, smiling. 'If I can't do anything with my own right arm, I'll go home with an empty basket.'

'I forgot to bring along a basket, but we can use some of those broad leaves of the vines to wrap our catch in.'

An hour later they were forced to stop because of the pile of finny life behind them, and these were only the biggest ones. The rest had been thrown back. André had hooked the largest, a magnificent trout of about thirty pounds, a fighter who took twenty minutes to land. After that, sweating and breathing hard but shining-eyed, he said, 'I'm hot. What do you say to a swim, John?'

Carmody smiled at the use of his familiar name again and shouted, 'Last one in is a Sirian!'

In a minute two naked bodies plunged into the cold clear waters at exactly the same time. When they came up, Carmody sputtered, 'Guess we're both Sirians, but you win, for I'm the ugliest. Or does that mean that I win?'

André laughed for sheer joy, then sped across the lake in a fast crawl. The other did not even try to follow him but floated on his back, eyes closed. Once he raised his head to determine how the bishop was getting along but lay back when he saw that he was in no trouble. André had reached the other shore and was returning at a slower but easy pace. When he did come back and had rested for a while on the beach, he said, 'John, would you mind climbing out and timing me in a dive? I'd like to see if I'm still in good form. It's about seven feet here, not too deep.'

Carmody climbed on to the grassy shore, where he set his watch and gave the signal. André plunged under. When he emerged he swam back at once. 'How'd I do?' he called as he waded out of the water, his magnificent body shining wet and golden brown in the late afternoon sun.

'Four minutes, three seconds,' said Carmody. About forty seconds off your record. But still better, I'll bet, than any other man in the Galaxy. You're still the champ, Your Excellency.'

André nodded, smiling slightly. 'Twenty years ago I set the record. I believe that if I went into rigorous training again, I could equal it again or even beat it. I've learned much since then about control of my body and mind. Even then I was not entirely at ease in the pressure and gloom of the underwater. I loved it, but my love was tinged just a little with terror. An attitude that is almost, you might say, one's attitude towards God. Perhaps too much so, as one of my parishioners was kind enough to point out to me. I think he meant that I was paying too much attention to what should have been only a diversion for my idle moments.

'He was correct, of course, though I rather resented his remarks at the time. He couldn't have known that it was an irresistible challenge to me to float beneath the bright surface, all alone, feel myself buoyed as if in the arms of a great mother, yet also feel her arms squeezing just a little too tight. I had to fight down the need to shoot to the surface and suck in life-giving air, yet I was proud because I could battle that panic, could defeat it. I felt always as if I was in danger but because of that very danger was on the verge of some vital discovery about myself – what, I never found out. But I always thought that if I stayed down long enough, could keep out the blackness and the threat of loss of consciousness, I would find the secret.

'Strange thought, wasn't it? It led me to study the neo-Yoga disciplines which were supposed to enable one to go into suspended animation, death-in-life. There was a man on Gandhi who could stay buried alive for three weeks, but I could never determine if he was faking or not. He was some help to me, however. He taught me that if I would, as he put it, go dead here, first of all,' and André touched his left breast, 'then here,' and he touched his loins, 'the rest would follow. I could become as an embryo floating in the amniotic sac, living but requiring no breath, no oxygen except that which soaked through the cells, as he put it. An absurd theory, scientifically speaking, yet it worked to some extent. Would you believe it, I now have to force myself to rise because it seems so safe and nice and warm under there, even when the water is very cold, as in this lake?'

While he talked, he'd been wiping the water from his skin with his quilted dickie, his back turned to Carmody. The priest knew his bishop was embarrassed to expose himself. He himself, though he knew his body looked ugly and grotesque beside the other's perfect physique, was not at all ill-at-ease. In common with most of the people of his time, he'd been raised in a world where nudity on the beach and in the private home was socially accepted, almost demanded. André, born in the Church, had had a very strict upbringing by devout parents who had insisted that he follow the old pattern even in the midst of a world that mocked.

It was of that he spoke now, as if he'd guessed what Carmody was thinking.

'I disobeyed my father but once,' he said. 'That was when I was ten. We lived in a neighbourhood composed mainly of agnostics or members of the Temple of Universal Light. But I had some very good pals among the local gang of boys and tomboys, and just once they talked me into going swimming in the river, skin-style. Of course my father caught me; he seemed to have an instinct for detecting when sin was threatening any of his family. He gave me the beating of my life – may his soul rest in peace,' he added without conscious irony.

' "Spare the rod and spoil the child" was ever his favourite maxim, yet he had to whip me just that one time in my life. Or rather, I should say twice, because I tore loose from him while he was strapping me in front of the gang, plunged into the river, and dived deep, where I stayed a long time in an effort to frighten my father into thinking I'd drowned myself. Eventually, of course, I had to come up. My father resumed the punishment. He was no more severe the second time, though. He couldn't have been without killing me. As a matter of fact, he almost did. If it weren't for modern science's ability to do away with scars, I'd still bear them on my back and legs. As it is, they're still here,' and he pointed to indicate his heart.

He finished drying himself and picked up his puffkilt. 'Well, that was thirty-five years ago and thousands of light-years away, and I dare say the beating did me a tremendous amount of good.'

He looked at the clear sky and at the woods, arched his deep chest in a great breath, and said, 'This is a wonderful and unspoiled planet, a testimony to God's love for the beauty of His creatures and His generosity in scattering them across the universe, almost as if He had had to do so! Here I feel as if God is in His heaven and all's right with the world. The symmetry and fruitfulness of those trees, the clean air and waters, the manifold songs of those birds and their bright colours . . .'

He stopped, for he suddenly realized what Carmody had just previously noticed. There was none of the noisy but melodious twitterings and chirpings and warblings nor the chattering of the monkeys. All was hush. Like a thick blanket of moss, a silence hung over the forest.

'Something's scared those animals,' whispered Carmody. He shivered, though the westering sun was yet hot, and he looked around. Near them, on a long branch that extended over the lake's edge, sat a row of catmonkeys that had appeared as if from nowhere. They were grey-furred except for a broad white mark on their chests, roughly in the form of a cross. Their head-hair grew thick and forward and fell over their foreheads like a monk's cowl. Their hands were placed over their eyes in a monkey-see-no-evil attitude. But their eyes shone bright between their fingers, and Carmody, despite his sense of uneasiness, felt a prickling of laughter and murmred, 'No fair peeking.'

A deep cough sounded in the forest; the monk-monks, as he'd tagged them, cowered and crowded even closer together.

'What could that be?' said the bishop.

'Must be a big beast. I've heard lions cough; they sounded just like that.'

Abruptly, the bishop reached out a large square hand and closed Carmody's little pudgy hand in it.

Alarmed at the look on André's face, Carmody said, 'Is another seizure coming on?'

The bishop shook his head. His eyes were glazed. 'No. Funny, I felt for a moment almost as I did when my father caught me.'

74

He released the other's hand and took a deep breath. 'I'll be all right.'

He lifted his kilt to step into it. Carmody gasped. André jerked his head upright and gave a little cry. Something white was looming in the shadow of the trees, moving slowly but surely, the focus and cause of the silence that spread everywhere. Then it grew darker as it stepped into the sunshine and stopped for a moment, not to adjust its eyes to the dazzle but to allow the beholders to adjust their eyes to him. He was eight feet tall and looked much like a human being and moved with such dignity and such beauty that the earth seemed to give way respectfully at each footstep. He was long-bearded and naked and massively male, and the eyes were like those of a granite statue of a god that had become flesh, too terrible to look straight into.

He spoke. They knew then the origin of that cough that had come from the depth of lungs deep as an oracle's well. His voice was a lion's roar; it made the two pygmies clasp each other's hands again and unloosed their muscles so that they thought they'd come apart. Yet they did not think of how amazing it was that he should speak in their tongue.

'Hello, my sons!' he thundered.

They bowed their heads.

'Father.'

IV

An hour before sunset, André and Carmody ran out of the woods. They were in a hurry because of the tremendous uproar that had aroused the forest for miles around. Men were yelling, and a woman was screaming, and something was growling loudly. They arrived just in time to see the end. Two enormous beasts, bipedal heavily tailed creatures with bearish heads, were racing after Kate Lejeune and Pete Masters. Kate and Pete were running hand in hand, he pulling her so fast that she seemed to fly through the air with every step. In his other hand he carried his powersaw. Neither had a sono-gun with which to defend themselves, although Captain Tu had ordered that no one be without the weapon. A moment later it was seen that the gun would have made no difference, for several crewmen who had been standing by the ship had turned their sonos against the beasts. Undeterred by the panicking effects of the beams, the monsters sprang after the couple and caught them half-way across the meadow.

Though unarmed, André and Carmody ran at the things, their fists clenched. Pete turned in his captor's grasp and struck it across the muzzle with the sharp edge of his saw. Kate screamed loudly, then fainted. Suddenly, the two were lying in the grass, for the animals had dropped them and were walking almost leisurely towards the woods. That neither the sonos nor the priests had scared them off was evident. They brushed by the latter without noticing them, and if the former had affected their nervous systems at all, they gave no signs.

Carmody looked once at the young woman and yelled, 'Doctor Blake! Get Blake at once!'

Like a genie summoned by the mention of his name, Blake was there with his little black kit. He at once called for a stretcher; Kate, moaning and rolling her head from side to side, was carried into the ship's hospital. Pete raged until Blake ordered him out of the room.

'I'll get a gun and kill those beasts. I'll track them down if it takes me a week. Or a year! I'll trap them and . . .'

Carmody pushed him out of the room and into the lounge, where he made the youth sit down. With a shaking hand, he lit two cigarettes.

'It would do you no good to kill them,' he said. 'They'd be up and around in a few days. Besides, they're just animals who were obeying their master's commands.'

He puffed on his cigarette while with one hand he snapped his glow-wire lighter shut and put it back in his pocket.

'I'm just as shaken up as you. Recent events have been too fast and too inexplicable for my nervous system to take them in stride. But I wouldn't worry about Kate being hurt, if I were you. I know she looked pretty bad, but I'm sure she'll be all right and in a very short time, too.'

'You blind optimistic ass!' shouted Pete. 'You *saw* what happened to her!'

'She's suffering from hysterics, not from any physical effects of her miscarriage,' replied Carmody calmly. 'I'll bet that in a few minutes, when Blake has her calmed down with a sedative, she'll walk out of the hospital in as good a condition as she was in this morning. I know she will. You see, son, I've had a talk with a being who is not God but who convinces you that *he* is

76

the nearest equivalent.'

Pete became slack-jawed. 'What? What're you talking about?'

'I know I sound as if I were talking nonsense. But I've met the owner of Abatos. Or rather *he* has talked to me, and what *he* has shown the bishop and me is, to understate, staggering. There are a hundred things we'll have to let you and everybody else know in due time. Meanwhile, I can give you an idea of *his* powers. They range in terrible spectrum from such petty, but amazing deeds as curing my toothache with a mere laying on of hands to bringing dead bones back to life and reclothing them with flesh. I have seen the dead arise and go forth. Though, I must admit, probably to be eaten again.'

Frowning, he added, 'The bishop and I were permitted to perform – or should I say commit? – a resurrection ourselves. The sensation is not indescribable, but I prefer not to say anything about it at present.'

Pete rose with clenched fists, his cigarette shredding under the pressure.

'You must be crazy.'

'That would be nice if I were, for I'd be relieved of an awful responsibility. And if the choice were mine, I'd take incurable insanity. But I'm not to get off so easily.'

Suddenly, Father John lost his calmness; he looked as if he were going to break into many pieces. He buried his face in his hands, while Pete stared stunned. Then the priest as abruptly lowered his hands and presented once again the sharp-nosed, round and smiling features the world knew so well.

'Fortunately, the ultimate decision will not be mine but His Excellency's. And though it is cowardly to be glad because I may pass the buck on to him, I must confess that I will be glad. His is the power in this case, and though power has its glory, it also has its burdens and griefs. I wouldn't want to be in the bishop's shoes at this moment.'

Pete didn't hear the priest's last words. He was gazing at the hospital door, just opening. Kate stepped out, a little pale but walking steadily. Pete ran to her; they folded each other in their arms; then she was crying.

'Are you all right, honey?' Pete kept saying over and over.

'Oh, I feel fine,' she replied, still weeping. 'I don't understand why, but I do. I'm suddenly healed. There's nothing wrong down there. It was as if a hand passed over me, and strength flowed out of it, and all was well with my body.'

Blake, who had appeared behind her, nodded in agreement.

'Oh, Pete,' sobbed Kate, 'I'm all right, but I lost our baby! And I know it was because we stole that money from Daddy. It was our punishment. It was bad enough running away, though we had to do that because we loved each other. But we should never have taken that money!'

'Hush, honey, you're talking too much. Let's go to our cabin where you can rest.'

Gently he directed her out of the lounge while he glared defiantly at Carmody.

'Oh, Pete,' she wailed, 'all that money, and now we're on a planet where it's absolutely no good at all. Only a burden.'

'You talk too much, baby,' said Pete, a roughness replacing the gentleness in his voice. They disappeared down the corridor. Carmody said nothing. Eyes downcast, he, too, walked to his cabin and shut the door behind him.

A half hour later, he came out and asked for Captain Tu. Told that Tu was outside, he left the *Gull* and found an attentive group at the edge of the meadow on the other side of the ship. Mrs. Recka and the first mate were the centre of attraction.

'We were sitting under one of those big jelly trees and passing the bottle back and forth and talking of this and that,' said Givens. 'Mostly about what we'd do if we found out we were stranded here for the rest of our lives.'

Somebody snickered. Givens flushed but continued evenly.

'Suddenly, Mrs. Recka and I became very sick. We vomited violently and broke out into a cold sweat. By the time we'd emptied our stomachs, we were sure the whisky had been poisoned. We thought we'd die in the woods, perhaps never to be found, for we were quite a distance from the ship and in a rather secluded spot.

'But as suddenly as it had come, the illness went away. We felt completely happy and healthy. The only difference was, we both were absolutely certain that we'd never again want to touch a drop of whisky.'

'Or any other alcoholic drink,' added Mrs. Recka, shuddering.

Those who knew of her weakness gazed curiously and somewhat doubtfully at her. Carmody tapped the captain's elbow and drew him off to one side.

'Is the radio and other electronic equipment working by now?' he asked.

'They resumed operation about the time you two showed up. But the translator still refuses to budge. I was worried when you failed to report through your wrist radios. For all I knew, some beast of prey had killed you, or you'd fallen into the lake and drowned. I organized a search party, but we'd not gone half a mile before we noticed the needles on our ship-finders whirling like mad. So we returned. I didn't want to be lost in the woods, for my primary duty is to the ship, of course. And I couldn't send out a copter crew, for the copters simply refused to run. They're working all right now, though. What do you think of all this?'

'Oh, I know *who* is doing this. And *why*.'

'For God's sake, man, *who*?'

'I don't know if it is for God's sake or not. ...' Carmody glanced at his watch. 'Come with me. There is someone you must meet.'

'Where are we going?'

'Just follow me. *He* wants a few words with you because you are the captain, and your decision will have to be given also. Moreover, I want you to know just what we are up against.'

'Who is *he*? A native of Abatos?'

'Not exactly, though *he* has lived here longer than any native creature of this planet.'

Tu adjusted the angle of his cap and brushed dust flakes from his uniform. He strode through the corridors of the noisy jungle as if the trees were on parade and he were inspecting them.

'If *he* has been here longer than ten thousand years,' said the captain unconsciously stressing the personal pronoun as Carmody did, 'then *he* must have arrived long before English and its descendant tongue, Lingo, were spoken, when the Aryan speech was still only the property of a savage tribe in Europe. How can we talk with him? Telepathy?'

'No. *He* learned Lingo from the survivor of the crash of the *Hoyle*, the only ship *he* ever permitted to get through.'

'And where is this man?' asked Tu, annoyedly glancing at a choir of howling monkeys on an overhead branch.

'No man. A woman, a medical officer. After a year here, she committed suicide. Built a funeral pyre and burned herself to death. There was nothing left of her but ashes.'

'Why?'

'I imagine because total cremation was the only way she could put herself beyond *his* reach. Because otherwise *he* might have placed her bones in a jelly tree and brought her back to life.'

Tu halted. 'My mind understands you, but my sense of belief is numb. Why did she kill herself when, if you are not mistaken, she had eternal life before her or at least a reasonable facsimile thereof?'

'*He – Father* – says that she could not endure the thought of living forever on Abatos with him as her only human, or human-oid, companion. I know how she felt. It would be like sharing the world with only God to talk to. Her sense of inferiority and her loneliness must have been overwhelming.'

Carmody stopped suddenly and became lost in thought, his head cocked to one side, his left eyelid drooping.

'Hmm. That's strange. *He* said that we, too, could have *his* powers, become like *him*. Why didn't *he* teach her? Was it because *he* didn't want to share? Come to think of it, *he's* made no offer of dividing *his* dominions. Only wants substitution. Hmm. All or none. Either *he* or . . . or what?'

'What the hell are you talking about?' barked Captain Tu irritatedly.

'You may be right at that,' said Carmody absently. 'Look, there's a jelly tree. What do you say we do a little poking and prying, heh? It's true that *he* forbade any needlenosing on the part of us extra-Abatosians; it's true that this may be another garden of Eden and that I, a too true son of Adam, alas, may be re-enacting another fall from grace, may be driven out with flaming swords – though I wouldn't mind being expelled back to some familiar planet – may even be blasted with lightning for blaspheming against the local deity. Nevertheless, I think a little delving into the contents of that cavity may be as profitable as any dentist's work. What do you say, Captain? The conse-quences could be rather disastrous.'

'If you mean am I afraid, all I can say is that you know better than that,' growled Tu. 'I'll let no priest get ahead of me in guts. Go ahead. I'll back you up all the way.'

'Ah,' said Carmody, walking briskly up to the foot of the enormous redwood, 'ah, but you've not seen and talked to the Father of Abatos. It's not a matter of backing me up, for there's little you could do if we should be discovered. It's a matter of giving me moral courage, of shaming me with your presence so that I won't run like a rabbit if *he* should catch me red-handed.'

With one hand he took a small vial out of his pocket and with the other a flashlight, whose beam he pointed into the dark O. Tu looked over his shoulder.

'It quivers, almost as if it were alive,' said the captain in a low voice.

'It emits a faint humming, too. If you put your hand lightly on its surface, you can feel the vibration.'

'What are those whitish things embedded in it? Bones?'

'Yes, the hollow goes rather deep, doesn't it? Must be below the surface of the ground. See that dark mass in one corner? An antelope of some sort, I'd say. Looks to me as if the flesh were being built up in layers from the inside out; the outer muscles and skin aren't re-created yet.'

The priest scooped out a sample of the jelly, capped the vial, and put it back in his pocket. He did not rise but kept playing his beam over the hollow.

'This stuff really makes a Geiger counter dance. Not only that, it radiates electromagnetic waves. I think that radio waves from this jelly damped out our wrist speakers and sonos and played havoc with our ship-finders. Hey, wait a minute! Notice those very minute white threads that run through the whole mass. Nerve-like, aren't they?'

Before Carmody could protest, Tu stooped and dipped out a handful of the quivering gelatinous mass. 'Do you know where I've seen something like this before? This stuff reminds me of the protein transistors we use in the translator.'

Carmody frowned. 'Aren't they the only living parts of the machine? Seems to me I read that the translator won't rotate the ship through perpendicular space unless these transistors are used.'

'Mechanical transistors could be used,' corrected Tu. 'But they would occupy a space as large as the spaceship itself. Protein transistors take up very little area; you could carry the *Gull*'s on your back. Actually, that part of the translator is not only a series of transistors but a memory bank. Its function is to "remember" normal space. It has to retain a simulacrum of real or "horizontal" space as distinguished from perpendicular. While one end of the translator is "flopping us over", as the phrase goes, the protein end is reconstruction an image of what the space at our destination looks like, down to the last electron. Sounds very much like sympathetic magic, doesn't it? Build an effigy, and shortly you establish an affinity between reality and counterfeit.'

'What happened to the protein banks?'

'Nothing that we could tell. They functioned normally.'

'Perhaps the currents aren't getting through. Did the engineer check the synapses or just take a reading on the biostatic charge of the whole? The charge could be normal, you know, yet any transmission could be blocked.'

'That's the engineer's province. I wouldn't dream of questioning his work, any more than he would mine.'

Carmody rose. 'I'd like to talk to the engineer. I've a layman's theory, but like most amateurs, I may be overly enthusiastic because of my ignorance. If you don't care, I'd rather not discuss it now. Especially here, where the forest may have ears, and . . .'

Though the captain had not even opened his mouth, the priest had raised his finger for silence in a characteristic gesture. Suddenly, it was aparent that he *did* have his silence, for there was not a sound in the weeds except the faint soughing of the wind through the leaves.

'*He* is around,' whispered Carmody. 'Throw that jelly back in, and we'll get away from this tree.'

Tu raised his hand to do so. At that moment a rifle shot cracked nearby. Both men jumped. 'My God, what fool's doing that?' cried Tu. He said something else, but his voice was lost in the bedlam that broke out through the woods, the shrieks of birds, the howling of monkeys, the trumpetings, neighings, and roaring of thousands of other animals. Then, as abruptly as it had begun, it stopped, almost as if by signal. Silence fell. Then, a single cry. A man's.

'It's Masters,' groaned Carmody.

There was a rumble, as of some large beast growling deep in its chest. One of the leopard-like creatures with the round ears and the grey tufts on its legs padded out from the brush. It held Pete Masters' dangling body between its jaws as easily as a cat holds a mouse. Paying no attention to the two men, it ran past them to the foot of an oak, where it stopped and laid the youth down before another intruder.

Father stood motionless as stone, one nailless hand resting upon his long red-gold beard, his deeply sunken eyes downcast, intent on the figure on the grass. He did not move until Pete, released from his paralysis, writhed in a passion of abjectness and called out for mercy. Then he stooped and touched the youth briefly on the back of his head. Pete leaped to his feet and, holding his head and screaming as if in pain, ran away through the trees. The leopardess remained couchant, blinking slowly like a fat and lazy housecat.

Father spoke to her. While he stalked off into the woods, she turned her green eyes upon the two men. Neither felt like testing her competence as a guard.

Father stopped under a tree overgrown with vines from which hung fat heavy pods like white hairless coconuts. Though the lowest was twelve feet high, he had no difficulty in reaching up and squeezing it in his hand. It cracked open with a loud report, and water shot from the crushed shell. Tu and Carmody paled; the captain muttered, 'I'd rather tackle that big cat than him.'

The giant wheeled, and, washing his hands with the water, strode towards them. 'Would you like to crush coconuts in one hand too, Captain?' he thundered. 'That is nothing. I can show you how you may also do that. I can tear that young beech tree out of the ground by the roots, I can speak a word to Zeda here, and she will heel like a dog. That is nothing. I can teach you the power. I can hear your whisper even at a distance of a hundred yards, as you realize by now. And I could catch you within ten seconds, even if you had a head start and I were sitting down. That is nothing. I can tell instantly where any of my daughters are on the face of Abatos, what state of health they are in, and when they've died. That is nothing. You can do the same, provided you become like that priest there. You could even raise my dead, if you had the will to be like Father John. I may take your hand and show you how you could bring life again to the dead body, though I do not care to touch you.'

'For God's sake, say no,' breathed Carmody. 'It's enough that the bishop and I should have been exposed to that temptation.'

Father laughed. Tu grabbed hold of Carmody's hand. He could not have answered the giant if he had wished, for his mouth opened and closed like a fish's out of water, and his eyeballs popped.

'There's something about his voice that turns the bowels to

water and loosens the knees,' said the priest, then fell silent. Father stood above them, wiping his hands on his beard. Aside from that magnificent growth and a towering roach on his head, he was absolutely bald. His pale red skin was unblemished, glowing with perfect blood beneath the thin surface. His high-bridged nose was septumless, but the one nostril was a flaring Gothic one. Red teeth glistened in his mouth; a blue-veined tongue shot out for a moment like a flame; then the black-red lips writhed and closed. All this was strange but not enough to make these star-travelled men uncomfortable. The voice and the eyes stunned them, the thunder that seemed to shake their bones so they rattled, and the black eyes starred with silver splinters. Stone come to flesh.

'Don't worry, Carmody. I will not show Tu how to raise the dead. Unlike you and André, he'd not be able to do it, anyhow. Neither would any of the others, for I've studied them, and I know. But I have need of you, Tu. I will tell you why, and when I have told you, you will see there is nothing else for you to do. I will convince you by reason, not by force, for I hate violence, and indeed am required by the nature of my being not to use it. Unless an emergency demands it.'

Father talked. An hour later, he stopped. Without waiting for either of them to say a word, even if they'd been capable, he turned and strode away, the leopardess a respectable distance behind his heels. Presently, the normal calls of the wood animals began. The two men shook themselves and silently walked back to the ship. At the meadow's edge, Carmody said, 'There's only one thing to do. Call a Council of the Question of Jairus. Fortunately, you fill the bill for the kind of layman required as moderator. I'll ask the bishop's permission, but I'm sure he'll agree it's the only thing to do. We can't contact our superiors and refer a decision to their judgement. The responsibility rests on us.'

'It's a terrible burden,' said the captain.

At the ship they asked about the bishop, to be told he had walked away into the forest only a short time before. The wrist radios were working, but no answer came from André. Alarmed, the two decided to go back into the forest to search for him. They followed the path to the lake, while Tu checked every now and then through his radio with a copter circling overhead. They'd reported the bishop was not by the lakeshore, but Carmody thought he might be on his way to it or perhaps was just sitting some place and meditating.

About a mile from the *Gull* they found him lying at the foot of an exceptionally tall jelly tree. Tu halted suddenly.

'He's having an attack, Father.'

Carmody turned away and sat down on the grass, his back to the bishop. He lit a cigarette but dropped it and crushed it beneath his heel.

'I forgot *he* doesn't want us to smoke in the woods. Not for fear of fire. *He* doesn't like the odour of tobacco.'

Tu stood by the priest, his gaze clinging to the writhing figure beneath the tree. 'Aren't you going to help him? He'll chew off his tongue or dislocate a bone.'

Carmody hunched his shoulders and shook his head. 'You forget that *he* cured our ills to demonstrate *his* powers. My rotten tooth, Mrs. Recka's alcoholism. His Excellency's seizures.'

'But, but . . .'

'His Excellency has entered into this so-called attack voluntarily and is in no danger of breaking bones or lacerating his tongue. I wish that were all there were to it. Then I'd know what to do. Meanwhile, I suggest you do the decent thing and turn your back, too. I didn't care for this the first time I witnessed it; I still don't.'

'Maybe you won't help, but I sure as hell am going to,' said Tu. He took a step, halted, sucking in his breath.

Carmody turned to look, then rose. 'It's all right. Don't be alarmed.'

The bishop had given a final violent spasm, a thrusting of the pelvis that raised his arched body completely off the ground. At the same time he gave a loud racking sob. When he fell back, he crumpled into silence and motionlessness.

But it was not towards him but towards the hollow in the tree that Tu stared. Out of it was crawling a great white snake with black triangular markings on its back. Its head was large as a watermelon; its eyes glittered glassy green; its scales dripped with white-threaded jelly.

'My God,' said Tu, 'isn't there any end to it? It keeps coming and coming. Must be forty or fifty feet long.'

His hand went to the sono-gun in his pocket. Carmody restrained him with another shake of his head.

'That snake intends no harm. On the contrary, if I understand these animals, it knows dimly that it has been given life again and feels a sense of gratitude. Perhaps *he* has made them aware that *he* resurrects them so that *he* may warm himself in their automatic worship. But, of course, *he* would never stand for what that beast is doing. *He*, if you've not noticed, can't endure to touch *his* secondhand progeny. Did you perceive that after *he* had touched Masters, *he* washed *his* hands with coconut water? Flowers and trees are the only things *he* handles.'

The snake had thrust its head above the bishop's and was touching his face with its flickering tongue. André groaned and opened his eyes. Seeing the reptile, he shuddered with fear, then grew still and allowed it to caress him. After determining that it meant him no harm, he stroked its back.

'Well, if the bishop should take over from Father, he at least will give these animals what they have always wanted and have not got from *him*, a tenderness and affection. His Excellency does not hate these females. Not yet.'

In a louder voice, he added, 'I hope to God that such a thing does not come to pass.'

Hissing with alarm, the snake slid off into the grass. André sat up, shook his head as if to clear it, rose to greet them. His face had lost the softness it had held while he was caressing the serpent. It was stern, and his voice was challenging.

'Do you think it is right to come spying upon me?'

'Your pardon, Your Excellency, we were not spying. We were looking for you because we have decided that the situation demands a Council of the Question of Jairus.'

Tu added, 'We were concerned because Your Excellency seemed to be having another attack.'

'Was I? Was I? But I thought that *he* had done away ... I mean ...'

Sadly, Carmody nodded, '*He* has. I wonder if Your Excellency would forgive me if I gave an opinion. I think that you were not having an epileptoid seizure coincidentally with sparking the snake with its new life. Your seeming attack was only a mock-up of your former illness.

'I see you don't understand. Let me put it this way. The doctor on Wildenwooly had thought that your sickness was psychosomatic in origin and had ordered you to Ygdrasil where a more competent man could treat it. Before you left, you told me that he thought that your symptoms were symbolic behaviour and pointed the way to the seat of your malady, a suppressed ...'

'I think you should stop there,' said the bishop coldly.

'I had intended to go no further.'

They began walking back to the ship. The two priests dropped behind the captain, who strode along with his eyes fixed straight ahead of him.

The bishop said, hesitantly, 'You too experienced the glory – perhaps perilous, but nevertheless a glory – of bringing the dead back to life. I watched you, as you did me. You were not unmoved. True, you did not fall to the ground and become semiconscious. But you trembled and moaned in the grip of ecstasy.'

He cast his eyes to the ground, then, as if ashamed of his hesitancy, raised them to glare unflinchingly.

'Before your conversion, you were very much a man of this world. Tell me, John, is not this fathering something like being with a woman?'

Carmody looked to one side.

'I want neither your pity nor you revulsion,' said André. 'Just the truth.'

Carmody sighed deeply.

'Yes, the two experiences are very similar. But the fathering is even more intimate because, once entered upon, there is no control at all, absolutely no withdrawal from the intimacy; your whole being, mind and body, are fused and focused upon the event. The feeling of oneness – so much desired in the other and so often lacking – is inescapable here. You feel as if you were the recreator and the recreated. Afterwards, you have a part of the animal in you – as you well know – because there is a little spark in your brain that is a piece of its life, and when the spark moves you know that the animal you raised is moving. And when it dims you know it is sleeping, and when it flares you know it is in panic or some other intense emotion. And when the spark dies, you know the beast has died too.

'Father's brain is a constellation of such sparks, of billions of stars that image brightly their owner's vitality. *He* knows where every individual unit of life is on this planet, *he* knows when it is gone, and when *he* does, *he* waits until the bones have been refleshed, and then *he* fathers forth ...'

'*He fathers-forth whose beauty is past change:*
Praise him!' André burst out.

87

Startled, Carmody raised his eyes. 'Hopkins, I think, would be distressed to hear you quoting his lines in this context. I think perhaps he might retort with a passage from another of his poems.

'Man's spirit will be fleshbound when found at best,
But uncumbered: meadow-down is not distressed
For a rainbow footing it nor he for his bones risen.'

'Your quote supports mine. *His bones risen.* What more do you need?'

'*But uncumbered.* What is the penalty for this ecstasy? This world is beautiful, yes, but is it not sterile, dead-ended? Well, never mind that now. I wished to remind Your Excellency that this power and glory come from a sense of union and control over brutes. The world is *his* bed, but who would lie forever in it? And why does *he* now wish to leave it, if it is so desirable? For good? Or for evil?'

V

An hour later, the three entered the bishop's cabin and sat down at the bare round table in its centre. Carmody was carrying a little black bag, which he put under his chair without commenting on it. All were dressed in black robes, and as soon as André had given the opening ritual prayer, they put on the masks of the founder of the order. For a moment there was silence as they looked at each other from behind the assumed anonymous safety of identical features; brown skin, kinky hair, flat nose, thick lips. And with the intense West Africanness of the face, the maker of the masks had managed to impart to them the legendary gentleness and nobility of soul that had belonged to Jairus Cbwaka.

Captain Tu spoke through rigid lips.

'We are gathered here in the name of His love and of His love to formulate the temptation, if any, that confronts us, and take action, if any, against it. Let us speak as brothers, remembering each time we look across the table and see the face of the founder that he never lost his temper except upon one occasion nor forgot his love except upon one occasion. Let us remember his agonies caused by that forgetfulness and what he has directed us, priest and layman, to do. Let us be worthy of his spirit in the presence of the seeming of his flesh.'

'I would like it better if you didn't rattle through the words so fast,' said the bishop. 'Such a pace destroys the spirit of the thing.'

'It doesn't remedy anything for you to criticize my conducting.'

'Rebuke well taken. I ask you to forgive me.'

'Of course,' Tu said, somewhat uncomfortably. 'Of course. Well to business.'

'I speak for Father,' said the bishop.

'I speak against Father,' said Carmody.

'Speak for Father,' said Tu.

'Thesis: Father represents the forces of good. *He* has offered the Church the monopoly of the secret of resurrection.'

'Antithesis.'

'Father represents the forces of evil, for *he* will unloose upon the Galaxy a force which will destroy the Church if she tries to monopolize it. Morever, even if she should refuse to have anything to do with it, it will destroy mankind everywhere and consequently our Church.'

'Development of thesis.'

'All *his* actions have been for good. Point. *He* has cured our illnesses major and minor. Point. *He* stopped Masters and Lejeune from carnal intercourse and perhaps did the same to Recka and Givens. Point. *He* made the former confess they had stolen money from Lejeune's father, and since then Lejeune has come to me for spiritual advice. She seemed to consider very seriously my suggestion that she have nothing to do with Masters and to return to her father, if the chance came, in an attempt to solve their problems with his consent. Point. She is studying a manual I gave her and may be led to the Church. That will be Father's doing and not Masters', who has neglected the Church though he is nominally a member of our body. Point. Father is forgiving, for *he* didn't allow the leopardess to harm Masters, even after the youth's attempt at killing *him*. And *he* has said that the captain may as well release Masters from the brig, for *he* fears nothing, and our criminal code is beneath his comprehension. *He* is sure that Masters won't try again. Therefore, why not forget about his stealing a gun from the ship's storeroom and let him loose? We are using force to get our goal of punishment, and that is not necessary, for according to the laws of psycho-dynamics which *he* has worked out during ten thousand years of solitude, a person who uses violence as a means to an end is self-punished, is robbed of a portion of his powers. Even *his* original act of getting the ship down here has hurt *him* so much that it will be some time before he recovers the full use of *his* psychic energies.

'I enter a plea that we accept *his* offer. There can be no harm because *he* wishes to go as a passenger. Though I, of course, possess no personal funds, I will write out an authorization on the Order for *his* ticket. And I will take *his* place upon Abatos while *he* is gone.

'Remember, too, that the decision of this particular Council will not commit the Church to accept *his* offer. We will merely put *him* under our patronage for a time.'

'Antithesis.'

'I have a blanket statement that will answer most of thesis's points. That is, that the worst evil is that which adopts the lineaments of good, so that one has to look hard to distinguish the true face beneath the mask. Father undoubtedly learned from the *Hoyle* survivor our code of ethics. He has avoided close contact with us so we may not get a chance to study his behaviour in detail.

'However, these are mostly speculations. What can't be denied is that this act of resurrection is a drug, the most powerful and insidious that mankind has ever been exposed to. Once one has known the ecstasies attendant upon it, one wishes for more. And as the number of such acts is limited to the number of dead available, one wishes to enlarge the ranks of the dead so that one may enjoy more acts. And Father's set-up here is one that "combines the maximum of temptation with the maximum of opportunity". Once a man has tasted the act, he will seriously consider turning his world into one like Abatos.

'Do we want that? I say no. I predict that if Father leaves here, *he* will open the way to such a possibility. Won't each man who has the power begin thinking of himself as a sort of god? Won't he become as Father, dissatisfied with the original unruly rude chaotic planet as he found it? Won't he find progress and imperfection unbearable and remodel the bones of his creatures to remove all evolutionary vestiges and form perfect skeletons? Won't he suppress mating among the animals – and perhaps among his fellow human beings – while allowing the males to die unresurrected until none but the more pliable and amenable females are left and there is no chance of young being born? Won't he make a garden out of his planet, a beautiful but sterile and unprogressive paradise? Look, for example, at the method of hunting that the fat and lazy beasts of prey use. Consider its disastrous results, evolutionarily speaking. In the beginning they picked out the slowest and stupidest herbivores to kill. Did this result in the survivors breeding swifter and more intelligent young? Not at all. For the dead were raised, and caught and killed again. And again. So that now when a leopardess or bitch wolf goes out to eat, the unconditioned run away and the conditioned stand trembling and paralysed and meekly submit to slaughter like tame animals in a stockyard. And the uneaten return to graze unconcernedly within leaping distance of the killer while she is devouring their sister. This is a polished planet, where the same event slides daily through the same smooth groove.

'Yet even the lover of perfection, Father, has become bored and wishes to find a pioneer world where *he* may labour until *he* has brought it to the same state as Abatos. Will this go on forever until the Galaxy will no longer exhibit a multitude of worlds, each breathtakingly different from the other, but will show you everywhere a duplicate of Abatos, not one whit different? I warn you that this is one of the very real perils.

'Minor points. *He* is a murderer because *he* caused Kate Lejeune to miscarry, and . . .'

'Counterpoint. *He* maintains that it was an accident that Kate lost her foetus, that *he* had his two beasts chase her and Masters out of the woods because they were having carnal intercourse. And *he* could not tolerate that. Point. Such an attitude is in *his* favour and shows that *he* is good and on the side of the Church and of God.'

'Point. It would not have mattered to *him* if Pete and Kate had been bound in holy matrimony. Carnal intercourse *per se* is objectionable to *him*. Why, I don't know. Perhaps the act offends his sense of property because *he* is the sole giver of life on this world. But I say *his* interference was evil because it resulted in the loss of a human life, and that *he* knew it would . . .'

'Point,' said the bishop, somewhat heatedly. 'This is, as far as we know, a planet without true death and true sin. We have brought those two monsters with us, and *he* cannot endure either one.'

'Point. We did not ask to come but were forced.'

'Order,' said the moderator. 'The Question first, then the formulation of the temptation, as laid down in the rules. If we say yes, and Father goes with us, one of us must remain to take *his* place. Otherwise, so *he* insists, this world will go to wrack and ruin in *his* absence.'

The moderator paused, then said, 'For some reason, *he* has limited the choice of *his* substitutes to you two.'

'Point,' said the bishop. 'We are the only candidates because we have sworn total abstinence from carnal intercourse. Father seems to think that women are even greater vessels of evil than men. *He* says that bodily copulation involves a draining off of the psychic energy needed for the act of resurrection and implies also that there is something dirty – or perhaps I should say, just too physical and animal – about the act. I do not, of course, think *his* attitude entirely justified, nor do I agree at all that women are on the same plane with animals. But you must remember that *he* has not seen a woman for ten thousand years, that perhaps the female of his own species might justify *his* reaction. I gathered from *his* conversation that there is a wide gap between the sexes of *his* kind on *his* home planet. Even so, *he* is kind to our women passengers. *He* will not touch them, true, but *he* says that any physical contact with us is painful to *him*, because it robs *him* of *his*, what shall I say, sanctity? On the other hand, with flowers and trees . . .'

'Point. What you have told us indicates *his* aberrated nature.'

'Point, point. You have confessed you dare not say such a thing to *his* face, that you are awed by the sense of the power that emanates from *him*. Point. *He* acts as one who has taken a vow of chastity; perhaps *his* nature is such that too close a contact does besmirch him, figuratively speaking. I take this religious attitude to be one more sign in *his* favour.'

'Point. The devil himself may be chaste. But for what reason? Because he loves God or because he fears dirt?'

'Time,' said Tu, 'time for the chance of reversal. Has thesis or antithesis altered his mind on any or all points? Do not be backward in admitting it. Pride must fall before love of truth.'

The bishop's voice was firm. 'No change. And let me reaffirm that I do not think Father is God. But *he* has Godlike powers. And the Church should use them.'

Carmody rose and gripped the table's edge. His head was

thrust aggressively forward, his stance was strange in contrast to the tender melancholy of the mask.

'Antithesis reports no change, too. Very well. Thesis has stated that Father has Godlike powers. I say, so has man, within limits. Those limits are what he may do to material things through material means. I say that Father is limited to those means, that there is nothing at all supernatural about *his* so-called miracles. As a matter of fact, man can do what Father is doing, even if on a primitive scale.

'I have been arguing on a spiritual level, hoping to sway thesis with spiritual points before I revealed to you my discoveries. But I have failed. Very well. I will tell you what I have found out. Perhaps then thesis will change his mind.'

He stooped and picked up the little black bag and laid it on the table before him. While he spoke, he kept one hand upon it, as if to enforce attention towards it.

'Father's powers, I thought, might be only extensions of what we humans may do. *His* were more subtle because *he* had the backing of a much older science than ours. After all, we are able to rejuvenate the old so that our life span is about a hundred and fifty. We build organs of artificial flesh. Within a limited period we may revive the dead, provided we can freeze them quickly enough and then work on them. We've even built a simple brain of flesh – one on the level of a toad's. And the sense of the numinous and of panic is nothing new. We have our own sonobeams for creating a like effect. Why could he not be using similar methods?

'Just because we saw *him* naked and without a machine in *his* hand didn't mean that *his* effects were produced by mental broadcast. We couldn't conceive of science without metal mechanisms. But what if *he* had other means? What about the jelly trees, which display electromagnetic phenomena? What about the faint humming we heard?

'So I borrowed a microphone and oscilloscope from the engineer, rigged up a sound detector, put it in the bag, and set out to nose around. And I observed that His Excellency was also making use of his time before the Question, that he was talking again to *him*. And while doing so, the jelly trees nearby were emiting subsonics at four and thirteen cycles. You know what those do. The first massages the bowels and causes peristalsis. The second stimulates a feeling of vague overpowering oppression. There were other sonics, too, some sub, some super.

'I left Father's neighbourhood to investigate elsewhere. Also, to do some thinking. It's significant, I believe, that we have had little chance or inclination to do any meditating since we've been here. Father has been pushing us, has kept us off balance. Obviously, *he* wants to keep our minds blurry with too rapid a pace of events.

'I did some fast thinking, and I concluded that the resurrection act itself was not touched off by *his* spark of genesis. Far from it. It is completely automatic, and it comes when the newly formed body is ready for a shock of bio-electricity from the protoplasm-jelly.

'But he knows when it is ready and taps the wave-lengths of life blooming anew, feeds upon them. How? There must be a two-way linkage between *his* brainwaves and the jelly's. We know that we think in symbols, that a mental symbol is basically a complex combination of brainwaves issuing as series of single images. *He* triggers off certain pre-set mechanisms in the jelly with *his* thoughts, that is, with a mental projection of a symbol.

'Yet not anyone may do it, for we two priests, dedicated to abstention from carnal intercourse, were the only ones able to tap in on the waves. Evidently, a man has to have a peculiar psychosomatic disposition. Why? I don't know. Maybe there is something spiritual to the process. But don't forget that the devil is spiritual. However, the mind-body's actions are still a dark continent. I can't solve them, only speculate.

'As for *his* ability to cure illnesses at a distance, *he* must diagnose and prescribe through the medium of the tree-jelly. It receives and transmits, takes in the abnormal or unhealthy waves our sick cells broadcast and sends out the healthy waves to suppress or cancel the unhealthy. There's no miracle about the process. It works in accordance with materialistic science.

'I surmise that when Father first came here, *he* was fully aware that the trees originated the ecstasy, that *he* was merely tuning in. But after millennia of solitude and an almost continuous state of drugging ecstasy, *he* deluded *himself* into thinking that it was *he* who sparked the new life.

'There are a few other puzzling points. How did *he* catch our ship? I don't know. But *he* knew about the translator motor from the *Hoyle* survivor and was thus able to set up the required wavelengths to neutralize the workings of the protein "normal space" memory banks. *He* could have had half the jelly trees of Abatos broadcasting all the time, a trap that would inevitably catch a passing ship.'

Tu said, 'What happened to his original spaceship?'

'If we left the *Gull* to sit out in the rain and sun for ten thousand years, what would happen to it?'

'It'd be a heap of rust. Not even that.'

'Right. Now I suspect strongly that Father, when *he* first came here, had a well-equipped laboratory on his ship. His science was able to mutate genes at will, and he used his tools on the native trees to mutate them into these jelly trees. That also explains why he was able to change the animals' genetic pattern so that their bodies lost their evolutionary vestiges, became perfectly functional organisms.'

The little man in the mask sat down. The bishop rose. His voice was choked.

'Admitting that your researches and surmises have indicated that Father's powers are unspiritual gimmickry – and in all fairness it must be admitted that you seem to be right – admitting this, then, I still speak for Father.'

Carmody's mask cocked to the left. 'What?'

'Yes. We owe it to the Church that she get this wonderful tool in her hands, this tool which, like anything in this universe, may be used for evil or for good. Indeed, it is mandatory that she gets control of it, so that she may prevent those who would misuse it from doing so, so that she may become stronger and attract more to her fold. Do you think that eternal life is no attraction?

'Now – you say that Father has lied to us. I say *he* has not. *He* never once told us that *his* powers were purely spiritual. Perhaps, being of an alien species, *he* misunderstands our strength of comprehension and took it for granted that we would see how *he* operates.

'However, that is not the essence of my thesis. The essence is that we must take Father along and give the Church a chance to decide whether or not to accept *him*. There is no danger in doing that, for *he* will be alone among billions. And if we should leave *him* here, then we will be open to rebuke, perhaps even a much stronger action from the Church, for having been cowards enough to turn down *his* gift.

'I will remain here, even though my motives are questioned

by those who have no right to judge me. I am a tool of God as much as Father is; it is right that we both be used to the best of our abilities; Father is doing no good for Church or man while isolated here; I will endure my loneliness while waiting for your return with the thought that I am doing this as a servant who takes joy in his duty.'

'What a joy!' Carmody shouted. 'No! I say that we reject Father once and for all. I doubt very much that *he* will allow us to go, for *he* will think that, faced with spending the rest of our lives here and then dying – for I don't think *he*'ll resurrect us unless we say yes – we will agree. And *he*'ll see to it that we are cooped up inside the ship, too. We won't dare step outside, for we'll be bombarded with panic-waves or attacked by *his* beasts. However, that remains to be seen. What I'd like to ask thesis is this: Why can't we just refuse *him* and leave the problem of getting *him* off Abatos to some other ship? He can easily trap another. Or perhaps, if we get to go home, we may send a government craft to investigate.'

'Father has explained to me that we represent *his* only sure chance. He may have to wait another ten millennia before another ship is trapped. Or forever. It works this way. You know that translation of a vessel from one point in normal space to the other occurs simultaneously, as far as outside observers are affected. Theoretically, the ship rotates the two co-ordinates of its special axis, ignoring time, disappears from its launching point, reappearing at the same time at its destination. However, there is a discharging effect, a simulacrum of the ship, built of electromagnetic fields, which radiates at six points from the starting place, and speeds at an ever-accelerating rate at six right-angles from there. These are called "ghosts". They've never been seen, and we've no instruments that can detect them. Their existence is based on Guizot's equations, which have managed to explain how electromagnetic waves may exceed the speed of light, though we know from Auschweig that Einstein was wrong when he said that the velocity of light was the absolute.

'Now, if you were to draw a straight line from Wildenwooly to Ygdrasil, you would find that Abatos does not lie between, that it is off to one side of the latter. But it is at right-angles to it, so that one of the "ghosts" passes here. The electromagnetic net that the trees sent up stopped it cold. The result was that the *Gull* was literally sucked along the line of power, following this particular ghost to Abatos instead of to Ygdrasil. I imagine that we appeared for a flickering millisecond at our original destination, then were yanked back to here. Of course, we were unaware of that, just as the people on Ygdrasil never saw us.

'Now – the voyages between Ygdrasil and Wildenwooly are infrequent, and the field has to mesh perfectly with the ghost, otherwise the ghost passes between the pulses. So that *his* chances of catching another are very few.'

'Yes, and that is why *he* will never allow us to leave. If we go without him and send a warship back to investigate, it may be able to have defences built in to combat his trees' radiations. So we represent *his* sole ticket. And I say *no* even if we must remain marooned!'

So the talk raged for two hours until Tu asked for the final formulations.

'Very well. We have heard. Antithesis has stated the peril of the temptation as being one that will make man a sterile anarchistic pseudo-god.

'Thesis has stated that the peril is that we may reject a gift which would make our Church once again the universal, in numbers as well as in claim, because she would literally and physically hold the keys to life and death.

'Thesis, please vote.'

'I say we accept Father's offer.'

'Antithesis.'

'No. Refuse.'

Tu placed his large and bony hands on the table.

'As moderator and judge, I agree with antithesis.'

He removed his mask. The others, as if reluctant to acknowledge both identity and responsibility, slowly took off their disguises. They sat glaring at each other, and ignored the captain when he cleared his throat loudly. Like the false faces they had discarded, they had dropped any pretence of brotherly love.

Tu said, 'In all fairness, I must point out one thing. That is, that as a layman of the Church, I may concur in the agreement to reject Father as a passenger. But as a captain of the Saxwell Company's vessel, it is my duty when landing upon an unscheduled stop to take on any stranded non-active who wishes to leave, provided he has passage money and there is room for him. That is Commonwealth law.'

'I don't think we need worry about anybody paying for *his*

passage,' said the padre. 'Not now. However, if *he* should have the money, *he*'d present you with a nice little dilemma.'

'Yes, wouldn't *he*? I'd have to report my refusal, of course. And I'd face trial and might lose my captaincy and would probably be earthbound the rest of my life. Such a thought is – well, unendurable.'

André rose. 'This has been rather trying. I think I'll go for a walk in the woods. If I meet Father, I will tell *him* our decision.'

Tu also stood up. 'The sooner the better. Ask *him* to reactivate our translator at once. We won't even bother leaving in orthodox style. We'll translate and get our fixings later. Just so we get away.'

Carmody fumbled in his robe for a cigarette. 'I think I'll talk to Pete Masters. Might be able to drive some sense into his head. Afterwards, I'll take a walk in the woods, too. There's much hereabouts to learn yet.'

He watched the bishop walk out and grimly shook his head.

'It went hard to go against my superior,' he said to Tu. 'But His Excellency, though a great man, is lacking in the understanding that comes from having sinned much yourself.'

He patted his round paunch and smiled as if all were right, though not very convincingly.

'It's not fat alone that is stuffed beneath my belt. There are years of experience of living in the depths packed solidly there. Remember that I survived Dante's Joy. I've had my belly full of evil. At its slightest taste, I regurgitate it. I tell you, captain, Father is rotten meat, ten thousand years old.'

'You sound as if you're not quite certain.'

'In this world of shifting appearances and lack of true self-knowledge, who is?'

VI

Masters had been released after he had promised Tu that he would make no more trouble. Carmody, not finding the youth inside, walked out and called him over the wrist radio. No reply.

Still carrying his black bag, the padre hurried into the woods as fast as his short legs would go. He hummed as he passed beneath the mighty branches, called out to the birds overhead, stopped once to bow gravely to a tall heron-like bird with dark purple mask-markings over its eyes, then staggered off laughing and holding his sides when it replied with a call exactly like a plunger withdrawing from a stopped drain, finally sat down beneath a beech to wipe his streaming face with a handkerchief.

'Lord, Lord, there are more things in this universe ... surely You must have a sense of humour,' he said out loud. 'But then, I mustn't identify a purely human viewpoint with You and make the anthropomorphic fallacy.'

He paused, said in a lower tone as if not wanting Anyone to hear, 'Well, why not? Aren't we, in one sense, the focus of creation, the Creator's image? Surely He too likes to feel a need for relief and finds it in laughter. Perhaps His laughter does not come out as mere meaningless noise but is manifested on a highly economical and informative level. Perhaps He tosses off a new galaxy, instead of having a belly-laugh. Or substitutes a chuckle with a prodding of a species up the Jacob's ladder of evolution towards a more human state.

'Or, old-fashioned as it sounds, indulges in the sheer joy of a miracle to show His children that his is *not* an absolutely orderly clockwork universe. Miracles are the laughter of God. Hmm, not bad. Now, where did I leave my notebook? I knew it. Back in my cabin. That would have made such a splendid line for an article. Well, no matter. I shall probably recall it, and posterity won't die if I don't. But they'll be the poorer, and ...'

He fell silent as he heard Masters and Lejeune nearby. Rising he walked towards them, calling out so they wouldn't think he was eavesdropping.

They were facing each other across a tremendous fringe-topped toadstool. Kate had quit talking, but Pete, his face red as his hair, continued angrily as if the priest did not exist. He gestured wildly with one fist, while the other hung by his side, clenching a powersaw handle.

'That's final! We're not going back to Wildenwooly. And don't think I'm afraid of your father, 'cause I'm afraid of no-body. Sure, he won't press charges against us. He can afford to be noble-hearted. The Commonwealth will prosecute us for him. Are you so stupid you don't remember that it's the law that the Board of Health must take into custody anyone who's been put on notice as guilty of unhealthy practices? Your father must have sent word on to Ygdrasil by now. We'll be detained as soon as we put foot on it. And you and I will be sent to an institution. We won't even get to go together to the same place. They never send partners-in-misdoing to the same resort. And how do I know that I won't have lost you then? Those rehabilitation homes do things to people, change their outlooks. You might lose your love for me. Probably that would be fine with them. They'd say you were gaining a healthy attitude in getting rid of me.'

Kate raised her large violet eyes to his. 'Oh, Pete, that would never ever happen. Don't talk such stuff. Besides, Daddy wouldn't report us. He knows I'd be taken away for a long time, and he couldn't stand that. He won't inform the government; he'll send his own men after us.'

'Yeah? What about that telegram to the *Gull* just before we left?'

'Daddy didn't mention the money. We'd have been held for a juvenile misdemeanour only.'

'Sure, and then his thugs would have beaten me up and dropped me off in the Twogee Woods. I suppose you'd like that?'

Tears filled Kate's eyes. 'Please, Pete, don't. You know I love you more than anybody else in the world.'

'Well, maybe you do, maybe you don't. Anyway, you forget that this priest knows about the money, and his duty is to report us.'

'Perhaps I am a priest,' said Carmody, 'but that doesn't automatically classify me as nonhuman. I wouldn't dream of reporting you. Needlenose though I am, I am not a malicious trouble-maker. I'd like to help you out of your predicament, though just now I must confess to a slight inclination to punch you in the nose for the way you are talking to Kate. However, that is neither here nor there. What is important is that I'm under no compulsion to tell the authorities, even though your act was not told to me in confession.

'But I do believe you should follow Kate's advice and go back to her father and confess all and try to come to an agreement. Perhaps he would consent to your marriage if you were to promise him to wait until you had proved yourself capable of supporting Kate happily. And proved that your love for her is based on more than sexual passion. Consider his feelings. He's as much concerned in this as you. More, for he's known her far longer, loved her a greater time.'

'Ah, to hell with him and the whole situation!' shouted Pete.

He walked off and seated himself under a tree about twenty yards away. Kate wept softly. Carmody offered her a handkerchief, saying, 'A trifle sweaty, perhaps, but sanitary with sanctity.' He smiled at his own wit with such self-evident enjoyment, mingled with self-mockery, that she could not help smiling back at him. While she dried her tears, she gave him her free hand to hold.

'You are sweet and patient, Kate, and very much in love with a man who is, I'm afraid, afflicted with a hasty and violent temper. Now, tell me true, is not your father much the same? Wasn't that part of the reason you ran away with Pete, to get away from a too-demanding, jealous, hot-headed father? And haven't you found out since that Pete is so much like your father that you have traded one image for its duplicate?'

'You're very perceptive. But I love Pete.'

'Nevertheless, you should go home. Pete, if he really loves you, will follow you and try to come to an honest and open contract with your father. After all, you must admit that your taking the money was not right.'

'No,' she said, beginning to weep again, 'it wasn't. I don't want to be a weakling and put the blame on Pete, for I did agree to take the money, even if it was his suggestion. I did so in a weak moment. And ever since, it's been bothering me. Even when I was in the cabin with him and should have been deliriously happy, that money bothered me.'

Masters jumped up and strode towards them, the powersaw swinging in his hand. It was a wicked-looking tool, with a wide thin adjustable blade spreading out like a fan from a narrow motorbox. He held the saw like a pistol, his hand around the butt and one finger on the trigger.

'Take your paws off her,' he said.

Kate withdrew her hand from Carmody's grip, but she faced the youth defiantly. 'He isn't hurting me. He's giving me real warmth and understanding, trying to help.'

'I know these old priests. He's taking advantage of you so he can hug and pinch you and . . .'

'Old?' exploded the padre. 'Listen, Masters, I'm only forty . . .'

He laughed. 'Almost got me going, didn't you?' He turned to Kate. 'If we do get off of Abatos, go home to your father. I'll be stationed at Breakneck for a while; you may see me as often as you wish, and I'll do my best to help you. And though I foresee some years of martyrdom for you, placed between two fires like Pete and your father, I think you're made of strong stuff.'

His eyes twinkling, he added, 'Even if you do look fragile and exceedingly beautiful and very huggable and pinchable.'

At the moment a deer trotted into the little glade. Rusty red, flecked with tiny white spots edged in black, her large liquid black eyes unafraid, she danced up to them and held out her nose inquiringly towards Kate. She seemed to know that Kate was the only female there.

'Evidently one of those unconditioned to being killed by the beasts of prey,' said Carmody. 'Come here, my beauty. I do believe that I brought along some sugar for just such an occasion. What shall I call you? Alice? Everybody is mad at this party, but we've no tea.'

The girl gave a soft cry of delight and touched the doe's wet black nose. It licked her hand. Pete snorted with disgust.

'You'll be kissing it next.'

'Why not?' She put her mouth on its snout.

His face became even redder. Grimacing, he thrust the blade-edge of the saw against the animal's neck, and pressed the trigger. The doe dropped, taking Kate with it, for she had no warning to remove her arms from around its neck. Blood spurted over the saw and Pete's chest and over her arm. The fan-edge of the tool, emitting supersonic waves capable of eating through granite, had sliced a thin plane through the beast's cells.

Masters stared, white-faced now. 'I only touched it. I didn't really mean to pull the trigger. I must have nicked its jugular vein. The blood, the blood . . .'

Carmody's face was also pale, and his voice shook.

'Luckily, the doe won't remain dead. But I hope you keep the sight of this blood in your mind the next time you feel anger. It could just as easily be human, you know.'

He quit talking to listen. The forest sounds had ceased, overcome by a rush of silence, like the shadow of a cloud. Then, the striding legs and stone eyes of Father.

His voice roared around them as if they were standing beneath a waterfall.

'Anger and death in the air! I feel them when the beasts of prey are hungry. I came quickly, for I knew that these killers were not mine. And I also came for another reason, Carmody, for I have heard from the bishop of your investigations and of your mistaken conclusions and the decision which you forced upon the captain and the bishop. I came to show you how you have deceived yourself about my powers, to teach you humility towards your superiors.'

Masters gave a choked cry, grabbed Kate's hand with his bloodied hand, and began half-running, half-stumbling, dragging her after him. Carmody, though trembling, stood his ground.

'Shut off your sonics. I know how you create awe and panic in my breast.'

'You have your device in that bag. Check it. See if there are any radiations from the trees.'

Obediently, the man fumbled at the lock of his case, managed after two tries to get it open. He twisted a dial. His eyes grew wide when it had completed its circuit.

'Convinced? There are no sonics at that level, are there? Now – keep one eye on the oscilloscope but the other on me.'

Father scooped from the hole of the nearest tree a great handful of the jelly and plastered it over the bloodied area of the doe's neck. 'This liquid meat will close up the wound, which is small to begin with, and will rebuild the devastated cells. The jelly sends out probing waves to the surrounding parts of the wound, identifies their structure and hence the structure of the missing or ruptured cells, and begins to fill in. But not unless I direct the procedure. And I can, if necessary, do without the jelly. I do not need it, for my power is good because it comes from God. You should spend ten thousand years with no one to talk to but God. Then you would see that it is impossible for me to do anything but good, that I see to the mystical heart of things, feel its pulse as nearer than that of my body.'

He had placed his hand over the glazed eyes. When he withdrew it, the eyes were a liquid shining black again, and the doe's flanks rose and fell. Presently it got on its hoofs, thrust a nose towards Father, was repelled by a raised hand, wheeled, and bounded off.

'Perhaps you would like to call for another Question,' roared Father. 'I understand that new evidence permits it. Had I known that you were filled with such a monkey-like curiosity – and had reasoning powers on a monkey's level – I should have shown you exactly what I am capable of.'

The giant strode away. Carmody stared after him. Shaken, he

said to himself, 'Wrong? Wrong? Have I been lacking in humility, too contemptuous of His Excellency's perceptiveness because he lacked my experience ... I thought. Have I read too much into his illness, mistaken its foundations?'

He took a deep breath. 'Well, if I'm wrong, I will confess it. Publicly, too. But how small this makes me. A pygmy scurrying around the feet of giants, tripping them up in an effort to prove myself larger than they.'

He began walking. Absently, he reached up to a branch from which hung large apple-like fruit.

'Hmm. Delicious. This world is an easy one to live in. One need not starve nor fear death. One may grow fat and lazy, be at ease in Zion, enjoy the ecstasy of re-creation. That is what you have wanted with one part of your soul, haven't you? God knows you are fat enough, and if you give others the impression of bursting with energy, you often do so with a great effort. You have to ignore your tiredness, appear bristling with eagerness for work. And your parishioners, yes, and your superiors, too, who should know better, take your labour for granted and never pause to wonder if you, too, are tired or discouraged or doubtful. Here there would be no such thing.'

Half-eaten, the apple was discarded for red-brown berries from a brush. Frowning, muttering, he ate them, his eyes always on the retreating shoulders and golden-red roach of Father.

'Yet. . . .?'

After a while, he laughed softly. 'It is indeed a paradox, John I. Carmody, that you should be considering again the temptation after having talked Tu and André out of it. And it would be an everlasting lesson – one that you are not, I hope, too unintelligent to profit from – if you talked yourself into changing your mind. Perhaps you have needed this because you have not considered how strong was the bishop's temptation, because you felt a measure – oh, only a tinge, but nevertheless a tinge – of contempt for him because he fell so easily and you resisted so easily.

'Hah, you thought you were so strong, you had so many years of experience packed beneath your belt! It was grease and wind that swelled you out, Carmody. You were pregnant with ignorance and pride. And now you must give birth to humiliation. No, humility, for there is a difference between the two, depending on one's attitude. God give you insight for the latter.

'And admit it, Carmody, admit it. Even in the midst of the shock at seeing the deer killed, you felt a joy because you had an excuse to resurrect the animal and to feel again that ecstasy which you know should be forbidden because it *is* a drug and *does* take your mind from the pressing business of your calling. And though you told yourself you weren't going to do it, your voice was feeble, lacking the authority of conviction.

'On the other hand, doesn't God feel ecstasy when He creates, being The Artist? Isn't that part of creating? Shouldn't we feel it, too? But if we do, doesn't that make us think of ourselves as godlike? Still, Father says that *he* knows from whence he derives *his* powers. And if *he* acts aloof, *noli me tangere, he* could be excused by reason of ten thousand years of solitude. God knows, some of the saints were eccentric enough to have been martyred by the very Church that later canonized them.

'But it's a drug, this resurrection business. If it is, you are correct, the bishop is wrong. Still, alcohol, food, the reading of books, and many other things may become drugs. The craving for them can be controlled, they may be used temperately. Why not the resurrection, once one has got over the first flush of intoxication? Why not, indeed?'

He threw away the berries and tore off a fruit that looked like a banana with a light brown shell instead of soft peelings.

'Hmm. *He* keeps an excellent cuisine. Tastes like roast beef with gravy and a soupçon of onions. Loaded with protein, I'll bet. No wonder Father may be so massively, even shockingly, male, so virile-looking, yet a strict vegetarian.

'Ah, you talk too much to yourself. A bad habit you picked up on Dante's Joy and never got rid of, even after *that* night when you were converted. That was a terrible time, Carmody, and only by the grace ... Well, why don't you shut up, Carmody?'

Suddenly, he dropped behind a bush. Father had come to a large hill which rose from the forest and was bare of trees except for a single giant crowning it. The huge O at the base of its trunk showed its nature, but where the others of its kind were brown-trunked and light-green-leaved, this had a shiny white bark and foliage of so dark a green that it looked black. Around its monstrous white roots, which swelled above the ground, was a crowd of animals. Lionesses, leopardesses, bitch wolves, struthi-ursines, a huge black cow, a rhino, a scarlet-faced gorilla, a cow-elephant, a moa-like bird capable of gutting an elephant with its beak, a man-sized crested green lizard, and many others. All massed together, moving restlessly but ignoring each other, silent.

When they saw Father, they gave a concerted, muted roar, a belly-deep rumble. Moving aside for him, they formed an aisle through which he walked.

Carmody gasped. What he had mistaken for the exposed white roots of the tree were piles of bones, a tumulus of skeletons.

Father halted before them, turned, addressed the beasts in a chanting rhythm in an unknown tongue, gestured, describing large and small wheels that interwove. Then he stooped and began picking up the skulls one by one, kissing them on their grinning teeth, replacing them tenderly. All this while the beasts crouched silently and motionless, as if they understood what he was saying and doing. Perhaps, in a way, they did, for through them, like wind rippling fur, ran a current of anticipation.

The padre, straining his eyes, muttered, 'Humanoid skulls. *His* size, too. Did *he* come here with them, and they died? Or did *he* murder them? If so, why the ceremony of loving, the caresses?'

Father put down the last grisly article, lifted his hands upwards and out in a sign that took in the skies, then brought them in so they touched his shoulders.

'*He*'s come from the heavens? Or *he* means *he* identifies *himself* with the sky, the whole universe, perhaps? Pantheism? Or what?'

Father shouted so loudly that Carmody almost jumped up from behind the bush and revealed himself. The beasts growled an antiphony. The priest balled his fists and raised his head, glaring fiercely. He seemed to be gripped with anger. He looked like a beast of prey, so much did his snarling face resemble the assembled animals'. They, too, had been seized with fury. The big cats yowled. The pachyderms trumpeted. The cow and bears bellowed. The gorilla beat her chest. The lizard hissed like a steam engine.

Again Father shouted. The spell that held them in restraint was shattered. *En masse*, the pack hurled itself upon the giant. Without resistance, he went down beneath the heaving sea of hairy backs. Once, a hand was thrust above the screaming *mêlée*, making a circular motion as if it were still carrying out the prescribed movements of a ritual. Then it was engulfed in a lioness' mouth, and the spurting stump fell back.

Carmody had been grovelling in the dirt, his fingers hooked into the grass, obviously restraining himself from leaping up to join the slaughter. At the moment he saw Father's hand torn off, he did rise, but his facial expression was different. Fright showed on it, and horror. He ran off into the woods, doubled over so the bush would conceal him from the chance gaze of the animals. Once, he stopped behind a tree, vomited, then raced off again.

Behind him rose the thunder of the blood-crazed killers.

VII

The enormous melon-striped moon rose shortly after nightfall. Its bright rays glimmered on the hemisphere of the *Gull* and on the white faces gathered at the meadow's edge. Father John walked out of the forest's darkness. He stopped and called out, 'What is the matter?'

Tu disengaged himself from the huddled group. He pointed at the open main port of the ship, from which light streamed.

Father John gasped, '*Him*? Already?'

The majestic figure stood motionless at the foot of the portable steps, waiting as if he could stand there patiently for another ten thousand years.

Tu's voice, though angry, was edged with doubt.

'The bishop has betrayed us! He's told *him* of the law that we must accept *him* and has given *him* passage money!'

'And what are you going to do about it?' said Carmody, his gravelly voice even rougher than usual.

'Do? What else can I do but take *him* on? Regulations require it. If I refuse – why, why, I'd lose my captaincy. You know that. The most I can do is put off leaving until dawn. The bishop may have changed his mind by then.'

'Where is His Excellency?'

'Don't Excellency that traitor. He's gone off into the woods and become another Father.'

'We must find him and save him from himself!' cried Carmody.

'I'll go with you,' said Tue. 'I'd let him go his own way to hell, except that the enemies of our Church would mock us. My

God, a bishop, too!'

Within a few minutes, the two men, armed with flashlights, ship-finders and sonobeams, walked into the forest. Tu also wore a pistol. They went alone because the padre did not want to expose his bishop to the embarrassment that would be his if confronted by a crowd of angry men. Moreover, he thought they'd have a better chance of talking him back into his senses if just his old friends were there.

'Where in hell could we find him?' groaned the captain. 'God, it's dark in here. And look at those eyes. There must be thousands.'

'The beasts know something extraordinary is up. Listen, the whole forest's awake.'

'Celebrating a change of reign. The King is dead; long live the King. Where could he be?'

'Probably the lake. That's the place he loved best.'

'Why didn't you say so? We could have been there in two minutes in a copter.'

'There'll be no using the copter tonight.'

Father John flashed his light on the ship-finder. 'Look how the needle's whirling. I'll bet our wrist radios are dead.'

'Hello, *Gull, Gull*, come in, come in . . . You're right. It's out. Christ, those eyes glowing, the trees are crawling with them. Our sonos are kaput too. Why don't our flashes go out?'

'I imagine because *he* knows that they enable *his* beasts to locate us more quickly. Try your automatic. Its mechanism is electrically powered, isn't it?'

Tu groaned again. 'Doesn't work. Oh, for the old type!'

'It's not too late for you to turn back,' said Carmody. 'We may not get out of the woods alive if we do locate the bishop.'

'What's the matter with you? Do you think I'm a coward? I allow no man, priest or not, to call me that.'

'Not at all. But your primary duty is to the ship, you know.'

'And to my passengers. Let's go.'

'I thought I was wrong. I almost changed my mind about Father,' said the priest. 'Perhaps *he* was using *his* powers, which didn't depend entirely on material sources, for good. But I wasn't sure. So I followed *him*, and then, when I witnessed *his* death, I knew I'd been right, that evil would come from any attempted use of *him*.'

'*His* death? But *he* was at the *Gull* a moment ago.'

Carmody hurriedly told Tu what he'd seen.

'But, but ... I don't understand. Father can't stand the touch of *his* own creatures, and *he* exercises perfect control over them. Why the mutiny? How could *he* have come back to life so quickly, especially if *he* were torn to pieces? Say, maybe there's more than one Father, twins, and he's playing tricks on us. Maybe *he* just has control over a few animals. *He*'s a glorified lion-tamer, and *he* uses his trained beasts when *he*'s around us. And *he* ran into a group he couldn't handle.'

'You are half-right. First, it was a mutiny, but one that *he* drove them into, a ritual mutiny. I felt *his* mental command; it almost made me jump in and tear *him* apart, too. Second, I imagine *he* came back to life so quickly because the white tree is an especially powerful and swiftly acting one. Third, *he* is playing tricks on us, but not the kind you suggest.'

Carmody, slowing his pace, puffed and panted. 'I'm paying for my sins now. God help me, I'm going on a diet. I'll exercise, too, when this affair is over. I loathe my fat carcass. But what about when I'm seated hungry at a table piled high with the too-good things of life, created in the beginning to be enjoyed? What then?'

'I could tell you what then, but we've no time for talk like that. Stick to the point,' Tu growled. His contempt for self-indulgers was famous.

'Very well. As I said, it was obviously a ritual of self-sacrifice. It was that knowledge which sent me scurrying off in an unsuccessful search for the bishop. I meant to tell him that Father was only half-lying when *he* said *he* derived *his* powers from God and that *he* worshipped God.

'*He* does. But the god is *himself*! In his vast egoism *he* resembles the old pagan deities of Earth, who were supposed to have slain themselves and then, having made the supreme sacrifice, resurrected themselves. Odin, for instance, who hung himself from a tree.'

'But *he* wouldn't have heard of them. Why would *he* imitate them?'

'*He* doesn't have to have heard of our Earth myths. After all, there are certain religious rites and symbols that are universal, that sprang up spontaneously on a hundred different planets. Sacrifice to a god, communion by eating the god, sowing and reaping ceremonies, the concept of being a chosen people, the symbols of the circle and the cross. So Father may have brought the idea from *his* home world. Or *he* may have thought it up as the highest possible act *he* was capable of. Man must have a religion, even if it consists of worshipping himself.

'Also, don't forget that *his* ritual, like most, combined religion with practicality. *He*'s ten millennia old and has preserved *his* longevity by going from time to time into the jelly tree. *He* thought *he*'d be going with us, that it'd be some time before *he* could grow a tree on an alien world. A rejuvenation treatment is part of the re-creation, you know. The calcium deposit in your vascular system, the fatty deposits in your brain cells, the other degenerations that make you old, are left out of the process. You emerge fresh and young from the tree.'

'The skulls?'

'The entire skeleton isn't necessary for the re-creation, though it's the custom to put it in. A sliver of bone is enough, for a single cell contains the genetic pattern. You see, I'd overlooked something. That was the problem of how certain animals may be conditioned into being killed by the carnivores. If their flesh is rebuilt around the bones according to the genetic record alone, then the animal should be without memory of its previous life. Hence, its nervous system would contain no conditioned reflexes. But it does. Therefore, the jelly must also reproduce the contents of the neural system. How? I surmise that at the very moment of dying the nearest jelly-deposit records the total wave output of the cells, including the complex of waves radiated by the "knotted" molecules of the memory. Then it reproduces it.

'So, Father's skulls are left outside, and when *he* rises, *he* is greeted with their sight, a most refreshing vision to *him*. Remember, *he* kissed them during the sacrifice. *He* showed his love for *himself*. Life kissing death, knowing *he* had conquered death.'

'Ugh!'

'Yes and that is what will happen to the Galaxy if Father leaves here. Anarchy, a bloody battle until only one person is left to each planet, stagnation, the end of sentient life as we know it, no goal . . . Look, there's the lake ahead!'

Carmody halted behind a tree. André was standing by the shore, his back turned to them. His head was bent forward as if in prayer or meditation. Or perhaps grief.

'Your Excellency,' said the padre softly, stepping out from

behind the tree.

André started. His hands, which must have been placed together on his chest, flew out to either side. But he did not turn.
He sucked in a deep breath, bent his knees, and dived into the
lake.

Carmody yelled, 'No!' and launched himself in a long flat
dive. Tu was not long behind him but stopped short of the
edge. He crouched there while the little waves caused by the disappearance of the two spread, then subsided into little rings,
moonlight haloed on a dark flat mirror. He removed his coat
and shoes but still did not leap in. At that moment a head broke
the surface and a loud whoosh sounded as the man took in a
deep breath.

Tu called, 'Carmody? Bishop?'

The other sank again. Tu jumped in, disappeared. A minute
passed. Then three heads emerged simultaneously. Presently,
the captain and the little priest stood gasping above the limp
form of André.

'Fought me,' said Carmody hoarsely, his chest rising and
falling quickly. 'Tried push me off. So . . . put my thumbs behind
his ears . . . where jaw meets . . . squeezed . . . went limp but
don't know if he'd breathed water . . . or I'd made him unconscious . . . or both . . . no time talk now . . .'

The priest turned the bishop over so he was face downward,
turned the head to one side, and straddled the back on his knees.
Palms placed outwards on the other's shoulders, he began the
rhythmic pumping he hoped would push the water out and the
breath in.

'How could he do it?' said Tu. 'How could he, born and
raised in the faith, a consecrated and respected bishop, betray
us? Who'd have thought it? Look what he did for the Church
on Lazy Fair; he was a great man. And how could he, knowing
all it meant, try to kill himself?'

'Shut your damn mouth,' replied Carmody, harshly. 'Were
you exposed to *his* temptations? What do you know of his
agonies? Quit judging him. Make yourself useful. Give me a
count by your watch so I can adjust my pumpings. Here we go.
One . . . two . . . three . . .'

Fifteen minutes later, the bishop was able to sit up and hold
his head between his hands. Tu had walked off a little distance
and stood there, back turned to them. Carmody knelt down and

said, 'Do you think you can walk now, Your Excellency? We ought to get out of this forest as quickly as possible. I feel danger in the air.'

'There's more than just danger. There's damnation,' said André feebly.

He rose, almost fell, was caught by the other's strong hand.

'Thank you. Let's go. Ah, old friend, why didn't you let me sink to the bottom and die where *he* would not have found my bones and no man would have known of my disgrace?'

'It's never too late, Your Excellency. The fact that you regretted your bargain and were driven by remorse . . .'

'Let's hurry back before it does become too late. Ah, I feel the spark of another life being born. You know how it is, John. It glows and grows and flares until it fills your whole body and you're about to burst with fire and light. This one is powerful. It must be in a nearby tree. Hold me, John. If I go into another seizure, drag me away, no matter how I fight.

'You have felt what I did, you seem to be strong enough to fight against it, but I have fought against something like it all my life and never revealed it to anyone, even denied it in my prayers – the worst thing I could do – until the too-long-punished body took over and expressed itself in my illness. Now I fear that . . . Hurry, hurry!'

Tu grabbed André's elbow and helped Carmody propel him onwards through the darkness, lit only by the priest's beam. Overhead was a solid roof of interlacing branches.

Something coughed. They stopped, frozen.

'Father?' whispered Tu.

'No. His representative, I fear.'

Twenty yards away, barring their path, crouched a leopardess, spotted and tufted, five hundred pounds ready to spring. Its green eyes blinked, narrowing in the beam; its round ears were cocked forward. Abruptly, it rose and stalked slowly towards them. It moved with a comic mixture of feline grace and over-stuffed waddle. At another time they might have chuckled at this creature, its fat sheathing its spring-steel muscles and its sagging swollen belly. Not now, for it could – and probably would – tear them to bits.

Abruptly, the tail, which had been moving gently back and forth, stiffened out. It roared once, then sprang at Father John, who had stepped out in front of Tu and André.

Father John yelled. His flashlight sailed through the air and into the brush. The big cat yowled and bounded off. There were two sounds: a large body crashing through the bushes and Father John cursing heartily, not with intended blasphemy but for the sake of an intense relief.

'What happened?' said Tu. 'And what are you doing down on your knees?'

'I'm not praying. I'll save that for later. This perilous flashlight went out, and I can't find it. Get down here and help me and be useful. Get your hands dirty for once; we're not on your perilous vessel, you know.'

'What happened?'

'Like a cornered rat,' groaned Carmody, 'I fought. Out of sheer desperation I struck with my fist and accidentally hit it on its nose. I couldn't have done better if I'd planned it. These beasts of prey are fat and lazy and cowardly after ten thousand years of easy living on conditioned victims. They have no real guts. Resistance scares them. This one would not have attacked if it hadn't been urged by Father, I'm sure. Isn't that so, Your Excellency?'

'Yes. *He* showed me how to control any animal on Abatos anywhere. I'm not advanced enough as yet to recognize the individual when she's out of sight and transmit mental commands, but I can do so at close range.'

'Ah, I've found this doubly perilous flashlight.'

Carmody turned the beam on and rose. 'Then I was wrong in thinking my puny fist had driven off that monster? You instilled panic in it?'

'No. I cancelled out Father's wavelengths and left the cat on its own. Too late, of course – once it had begun an attack, its instinct would urge it on. We owe its flight to your courage.'

'If my heart would stop hammering so hard, I'd believe more in my courage. Well, let's go. Does Your Excellency feel stronger?'

'I'll keep up with any pace you set. And don't use the title. My action in defying the Question Council's decision constituted an automatic resignation. You know that.'

'I know only what Tu has told me Father told him.'

They walked on. Occasionally, Carmody flashed his light behind him. While doing this he became aware that the leopardess or one of its sisters was following them by some forty yards.

'We are not alone,' he said. André said nothing, and Tu, mis-understanding him, began to pray in a very low voice. Carmody did not elucidate but urged them to walk faster.

Suddenly, the shadow of the forest fell away before the bright-ness of the moon. There was still a crowd on the meadow, but it was away from the edge, gathered beneath the curve of the ship. Father was not in sight.

'Where is *he*?' called Father John. An echo answered from the meadow's other side, followed at once by the giant's appear-ance in the main port. Stooping, Father walked through it and down the steps to the ground, there to resume his motionless vigilance.

André muttered, 'Give me strength.'

Carmody spoke to the captain. 'You must make a choice. Do what your faith and intelligence tell you is best. Or obey the regulations of Saxwell and the Commonwealth. Which is it to be?'

Tu was rigid and silent, cast into thought like bronze. With-out waiting for a reply, Carmody started to walk towards the ship. Half-way across the meadow, he stopped and raised clenched fists and cried, 'No use trying that panic trick on us, Father! Knowing what *you* are doing, and how, we may fight against it, for we are men!'

His words were lost to the people around the ship. They were yelling at each other and scrambling for a place on the steps so they could get inside. Father must have evoked a battery of waves from the surrounding trees, more powerful than anything used before. It struck like a tidal wave, carrying all before it. All except Carmody and André. Even Tu broke and ran for the *Gull*.

'John,' moaned the bishop. 'I'm sorry. But I can't stand it. Not the subsonics. No. The betrayal. The recognition of what I've been fighting against since manhood. It's not true that when you first see the face of your unknown enemy you have the battle half-won. I can't stand it. The need I have for this damnable communion . . . I'm sorry, believe me. But I must . . .'

He whirled and ran back into the forest. Carmody chased after him, shouting, but his short legs were quickly outdistanced. Ahead of him, out of the darkness, came a coughing roar. A scream. Silence.

Unhesitatingly, the priest plunged on, his light stabbing before him. When he saw the cat crouching over the crumpled form, one grey-furred paw tearing at its victim's groin, he shouted again and charged. Snarling, the leopardess arched its back, seemed ready to rear on its hind legs and bat at the man with its bloodied claws, then roared, turned, and bounded away.

It was too late. There'd be no bringing back the bishop this time. Not unless . . .

Carmody shuddered and lifted the sagging weight in his arms and staggered back across the meadow. He was met by Father.

'Give me the body,' thundered the voice.

'No! You'll not put him in your tree. I'm taking him back to the ship. After we get home we'll give him a decent burial. And you might as well quit broadcasting your panic. I'm angry, not scared. And we're leaving in spite of you, and we're not taking you. So do your damnedest!'

Father's voice became softer. It sounded sad and puzzled.

'You do not understand, man. I went aboard your vessel and into the bishop's cabin and tried to sit down in a chair that was too small for me. I had to sit on the cold and hard floor, and while I waited I thought of going out into vast and empty space again and to all the many strange and uncomfortable and sickeningly undeveloped worlds. It seemed to me that the walls were getting too close and were collapsing in upon me. They would crush me. Suddenly, I knew I could not endure their nearness for any time at all, and that, though our trip would be short, I'd soon be in other too-small rooms. And there would be many of the pygmies swarming about me, crushing each other and possibly me in an effort to gape at me, to touch me. There would be millions of them, each trying to get his dirty little hairy paws on me. And I thought of the planets crawling with unclean females ready to drop their litters at a moment's notice and all the attendant uncleanliness. And the males mad with lust to get them with child. And the ugly cities stinking with refuse. And the deserts that scab those neglected worlds, the disorder, the chaos, the uncertainty. I had to step out for a moment to breathe again the clean and certain air of Abatos. It was then that the bishop appeared.'

'You were terrified by the thought of change. I would pity you, except for what you have done to him,' said Carmody, nodding down at the form in his arms.

'I do not want your pity. After all, I am Father. You are a

man who will crumble into dust forever. But do not blame me. He is dead because of what he was, not because of me. Ask his real father why he did not give him love along with his blows and why he shamed him without justifying why he should be shamed and why he taught him to forgive others but not himself.

'Enough of this. Give me him. I liked him, could almost stand his touch. I will raise him to be my companion. Even I want someone to talk to who can understand me.'

'Out of the way,' demanded Carmody, 'André made his choice. He trusted me to take care of him, I know. I loved the man, though I did not always approve of what he did or was. He was a great man, even with his weakness. None of us can say anything against him. Out of the way, before I commit the violence which you say you so dread but which does not keep you from sending wild beasts to bring about your will. Out of the way!'

'You do not understand,' murmured the giant, one hand pulling hard upon his beard. The black, silver-splintered eyes stared hard, but he did not lift his hand against Carmody. Within a minute, the priest had carried his burden into the *Gull*. The port shut softly, but decisively, behind him.

Some time later, Captain Tu, having disposed of his major duties in translating the ship, entered the bishop's cabin. Carmody was there, kneeling by the side of the bed that held the corpse.

'I was late because I had to take Mrs. Recka's bottle away from her and lock her up for a while,' he explained. He paused, then, 'Please don't think I'm hateful. But right is right. The bishop killed himself and doesn't deserve burial in consecrated ground.'

'How do you know?' replied Carmody, his head still bent, his lips scarcely moving.

'No disrespect to the dead, but the bishop had power to control the beasts, so he must have ordered the cat to kill him. It was suicide.'

'You forget that the panic waves which Father caused in order to get you and me quickly into the ship also affected any animals in the area. The leopardess may have killed the bishop just because he got in the way of her flight. How are we to know any different?

'Also, Tu, don't forget this. The bishop may be a martyr. He knew that the one thing that would force Father to stay on Abatos would be for himself to die. Father would not be able to ensure the idea of leaving *his* planet fatherless. André was the only one among us that could take over the position Father had vacated. He was ignorant at that time, of course, that Father had changed his mind because of his sudden claustrophobia.

'All the bishop could know was that his death would chain Father to Abatos and free us. And if he deliberately slew himself by means of the leopardess, does that make him any less a martyr? Women have chosen death rather than dishonour and been canonized.

'We shall never know the bishop's true motive. We'll leave knowledge of that to Another.

'As for the owner of Abatos, my feeling against *him* was right. Nothing *he* said was true, and *he* was as much a coward as any of *his* fat and lazy beasts. *He* was no god. *He* was the Father ... of Lies.'

THE luxury liner blew up, and with it went Jones.

He had been leaning on the railing, his eyes on the moon's image dancing on the waves and his thoughts on his wife. He had left her in Hawaii; he would, he hoped, never see her again. He had also been thinking of his mother in California and wondering how it would be to live again with her. He wasn't unhappy or happy about either prospect. He had just been meditating.

Then the enemy, in one of the first moves of the undeclared war, had torpedoed the ship from beneath. And Jones, utterly unwarned, was thrown high into the air as if he had bounced off a tremendous springy diving board.

He plunged deep. The blackness crushed him. He became panicky, and lost that delicate sense of poise that he was able to maintain when he was swimming in the sunlight open waters. He wanted to scream and then to ascend on the scream, like a circus acrobat on a rope, to the uncloseted air and the bright moon.

Before the cry for help came, before the waters poured their heavy blackness down his lungs, his head broke the surface, and he gulped in light and breath. Then he looked around and saw that the ship was gone and that he was alone. There was nothing for him to do but seize a floating piece of debris and hang on with the hope that the day would bring airplanes or another ship.

An hour later, the sea suddenly heaved and split, and a long dark back emerged. It looked like a whale, for it had the rounded head and the sloping-away body. Yet it did not move the tail up and down to propel itself forward, nor roll to one side, nor do anything but lie there. Jones knew that it must be a new type of submarine, but he was not sure because it looked so alive. There was about it that indefinable air that distinguishes the animate from the inanimate.

His doubts were settled a moment later when the smooth, curved back was suddenly broken by a long rod pushing up from the centre. The shaft grew until it was twenty feet high, halted, and then flowered at its end into grids of various sizes and shapes. Retractable radar antennae.

So this was the enemy. It had come up from the depths where it had been hiding after its deadly blow. It wished to survey the destruction and, perhaps, pick up any surivors for questioning. Or to make sure that none lived.

Even with that thought he did not try to swim away. What could he do? Better to take a chance that they would treat him decently. He did not want to sink into the abyss below, into the darkness and the pressure.

He trod water while the sub turned its blind snout towards him. No men appeared from the hatches suddenly popping open upon the sleek deck. There was no sign of life except that men must be presumed to be below and turning the faceless, eyeless grids of the radar towards him.

Not until it was almost upon him did he see how it planned to take him prisoner. A large, round port in the whale-shaped head swung in. The sea rushed into it and carried Jones with it. He struggled, for he could not endure the idea of being scooped up in this monstrous parody of a cow catcher, gulped like a sardine chased by a mobile can. Moreover, the very thought of a door swinging open and showing him nothing but blackness beyond was enough to make him want to scream.

In the next moment, the port slid shut behind him, and he found himself hemmed in by water and walls and darkness. He struggled frantically against an enemy that he could not hold in his hands. He cried out from the bottom of his being for a breath of air and a spark of light and a door that would lead him out of this chamber of panic and death. Where was the door, the door, the door? Where . . .?

There were moments when he almost awoke, when he was suspended in that twilight world between dark sleep and bright wakefulness. It was then that he heard a voice that was new to him. It sounded like a woman's, soft, caressing and sympathetic. Sometimes it was urgent with the hint that he'd better not try to hold anything back.

Hold back? Hold back what? What?

Once he felt rather than heard a series of tremendous impacts – thunder from somewhere, and a sense of being squeezed in a giant fist. That, too, passed.

The voice returned for a while. Then it faded off and sleep came.

He did not awaken swiftly. He had to struggle up through blanket after blanket of semiconsciousness, throwing each one off with desperation tempered with a frantic hope that the next would be the last. And just as he was about to give up, to sink again beneath the choking and heavy layers, to quit breathing and fighting, he awoke.

He was crying out loud and trying to wave his arms and he thought, just for a moment, that the closet door had opened and light and his mother had entered.

But it was not so. He was not back in the locked closet. He was not six years old, and it was not his mother who had rescued him. Certainly that was not her voice, nor was it the voice of his father, the man who had locked him in the closet.

It came from a speaker set into the wall. It did not talk in the tongue of the enemy, as he had expected, but in English. It droned on and on, oddly half-metallic, half-maternal, and it told him what had been taking place in the last twelve hours.

He was shocked to know he had been unconscious that long. While he assimilated that knowledge, he ran his eyes over his cell, taking stock. It was seven feet long, four wide, and six high. It was bare except for the cot on which he lay and certain indispensable plumbing. A bulb burned directly above him, hot and naked.

The discovery that he was hemmed within such a place, narrow as a tomb and with no exit that he could see, made him leap from the cot. Or try to, for he found that his arms and legs were bound inside broad plastic bands.

The voice filled the cell.

'Do not be alarmed, Jones. And do not try to make those hysterical and hopeless struggles that you made before I was forced to give you a sedative. If you suffer from severe claustrophobia, you must endure it.'

Jones did not struggle. He was too numbed by the disclosure that he was the only human being upon the submarine. It was a robot speaking to him – perhaps the sub itself, directed electronically from a mother ship.

He took some time, turning the matter over in his mind .. but he could bring himself to feel no lessening of the terror. It would have been bad enough to be imprisoned with the living enemy, but an enemy that was steel skin and plastic bones and electronic veins and radar eyes and germanium brains was an enemy that filled him with an overpowering dread. How could you fight against anybody – anything – like that?

He checked his fear with the thought that, after all, he was in no way worse off. How would this machine differ from the enemy itself, the creature from the creator? It was the enemy who had built this automatic fish, and he would model it exactly after his own thought processes, his own ideology. Whichever way the living enemy would have acted, just so would this monster.

Now that he was conscious, he remembered what the robot had said to him and what he had answered. He had awakened from his near-drowning and seen a long, plastic arm withdrawing into a hole in the wall. The hole had been covered with a small port, but not before he had caught a glimpse of the needles at the end of the arm. Later, he was to understand that the arm needles had shot adrenalin into him to stimulate his heart, and another chemical – unknown to the American – to cause his internal muscles to reject the water he had swallowed.

The sub wanted him alive. The question was, for what?

It was not long until he knew. The machine or mechanical 'brain' or whatever you wanted to call it had also injected a drug that would put him in a light hypnotic state. And it had given him a key word which, uttered after the effect of the drug died off, would enable him to remember what had happened. Now that the voice had uttered that magical key to his unconscious – it was from the enemy's language, so he did not understand it – everything came back in a rush.

He understood everything that the sub had thought fit to tell him. In the first place, she was one of the new experimental craft the enemy had built shortly before the war began. She was wholly automatic, not because the enemy had no men to spare, for God knew they had millions to throw away on the battlefield, but because a submarine that did not have to carry a great amount of supplies and air-making equipment for a crew and that did not have to consider living space, could be much smaller and efficient and stay at sea longer. The machinery required to run her occupied much less space than sailors.

The entire craft was designed for sleekness and speed and deadliness. She carried forty torpedoes, and when these were expended she would return to her mother ship somewhere in the Pacific. If need be, she did not have to rise to the surface at any time during her entire cruise. But her makers had put in orders to the effect that she should, if it was safe, take some prisoners and pry loose from them valuable information.

'Then,' said the voice with its hint of metal. 'I would have shot you back into the sea from which I picked you. But when, during the questioning, I found that you were an electronics specialist, I decided to keep you and take you back to the base. I am required to bring back any valuable prisoners. It is lucky for you that you turned out to be a man we can use. Otherwise. . . .'

The cold echoes hung in the room. Jones shivered. He could see in his mind's eye the port swinging inward, the sea rushing in, his own struggles, and then the irresistible plastic arms shoving him out into the black and silent depths.

He wondered briefly how much *Keet VI* had found out about him. No sooner thought than answered. Memory flooded in, and he knew all the rest that had happened.

To begin with, the sub was as human as it was possible for a machine to be. It 'thought' of itself as *Keet VI* – which meant *Whale VI* – and spoke in terms that might have fooled a non-expert into thinking it was conscious of itself. Jones knew better. No mechanical 'brain' had been built yet that was self-conscious. But it was set up so that it gave that impression. And Jones, after a while, adopted the natural fallacy of thinking of it as a living being. Or as a woman. For *Keet's* makers had fallen into their own trap and, believing that ships are female, had unconsciously built and endowed *Keet* with a feminine psychology.

Otherwise, how could you explain that *Keet* seemed almost tenderly solicitous of him? Knowing that he was a valuable male, that the men back upon the mother ship wanted a man like Jones who had information and talents they could use, *Keet* was prepared to do all she could to keep his body alive. That was why she had fed him intravenously and why she had stopped questioning him when she had stumbled upon a particularly tender and painful area of his brain.

What was that sensitive part? Why, nothing other than that night long ago in time, but so near in effect, when his father had locked him in that dark closet because he, Jones, would not confess that he had stolen a quarter from his mother's purse. And he had refused to confess, for he knew he was innocent, until the darkness had become thick and heavy and hot, like a strangler's blanket thrown around him, and he, unable to endure any longer the terror, the blackness, and the walls that seemed to be moving in on him to crush him, had screamed and screamed until his mother, thrusting his father aside, had opened the door and given him light and space and a broad, deep bosom upon which to weep and sob.

And since then. . . .

Keet's voice, somehow not so cold now, said, 'I could not get much from you other than that you were an electronics specialist, that you had been on the luxury liner *Calvin Coolidge*, that you were leaving your wife for a trial separation and going to live with your mother who resides upon a university campus. There you were going to take up the old, safe, academic life, teaching, and there you were going to spend the rest of your days with your mother until she died. But when I struck that thought, you suddenly reverted to the closet incident, and I could do nothing more with you. Unfortunately, I am equipped with only the lightest of drugs and cannot put you under deep hypnosis. If I could, I could penetrate past that episode or set it to one side. But every time I begin the questioning, I touch that particular territory of the past.'

Was it his imagination or did he detect a slightly querulous or plaintive note? It was possible. If the enemy had built in a modulator so it could imitate sympathy and kindness, he could also install circuits to mock other emotions. Or was it possible that the machine, which was, after all, a highly intelligent 'brain', could manipulate voice mechanism to reproduce desired effects?

He would probably never know. Yet there was no doubt that the voice contained at least a hint of emotion.

He was glad that he was intrigued by the potentialities of *Keet*. Otherwise, he would have been struggling like a thing out of its mind to loose himself from these bonds strapping him down to the cot. The walls were too close, too close. And while he could endure them now, as long as the light was on, he knew he would go mad if that light were to go out.

Keet must have known that by now, too, yet she had made no threat, no attempt to utilize the knowledge. Why? Why hadn't she tried to scare his knowledge from him? Such would have been the methods of the men who had made her, and she was, after all, only a reflection of them. Why hadn't she tried to terrify him?

The answer was not long in coming.

'You must understand that I am in trouble. At the same time, that means that you, Jones, are also in trouble. If I sink, you do, too.'

Jones tensed. Now would come the crux of it. He was surprised to hear the almost pleading tone in her voice. Then he remembered that her builders would have put the whole range of emotions in her voice for her to use whenever occasion required.

'While you were unconscious I was attacked by planes. They must have been carrying some device unknown to me, for I was a hundred fathoms deep, yet they spotted me,' *Keet* said.

Jones was sure now. There *was* emotion in her voice, and it was half-way between sullenness and hurt feelings. When *Keet* had been sent to sea, the stage, thought Jones, had lost a great actress.

Despite his situation, he could not help chuckling. *Keet* overheard, for she said, 'What is that noise, Jones?'

'Laughter.'

'Laughter?'

There was a pause. Jones could imagine *Keet* waiting while she searched through the channels of her electronic memory-banks for the definition of the thing called laughter.

'You mean like this?' *Keet* said.

The speaker burst out with a blood-chilling cackle.

Jones smiled tightly. Evidently the creators of *Keet* had included the definition of laughter and ability to reproduce such in her make-up. But the laughter they had given her was just what you would expect from them. It was designed to frighten their victims. There was nothing of amusement or gaiety in this. He told her so. Another pause. Then the speaker chuckled. But this expressed contempt and scorn.

'That is not what I mean,' he answered.

Keet's voice trembled. Jones wondered about that. Surely the enemy engineers had not meant for her to express her own emotions. Machines, he knew, could be frustrated, but they did not 'feel' such disappointments as human beings did. But it was possible that in their desire to make her emulate a human as much as possible, they had included this device. It would be carrying construction to a fantastic limit, but it could be so.

It was then that he received another slight shock. *Keet* had started telling him why she needed help, but she had suddenly switched to this discussion and this vain attempt to reproduce his laughter.

Keet could be sidetracked.

He filed away that information. Perhaps he could use it against her later on if he ever got in a position where he could use it. At present, with the bands locking him down, there did not seem to be much hope.

'What were you saying?' he asked.

'I said that I was in trouble, and that, therefore, we both are. If you want to survive, you must aid me.'

She paused as if searching her metal-celled brain for the psychologically right combination of words. He tensed, for he knew that this was his only chance, and listened carefully.

'While you were sleeping,' she said, 'these planes – which I suppose were bourgeois Yankee aircraft – somehow located me and dropped depth charges. They exploded quite close, but I am built rather strongly and compactly, and they did little external harm. But they did shake me up quite a bit.

'I dived at a slant and got away from them. But when I had come to the bottom, I stopped. My nose is in the abysmal ooze, and I cannot back away.'

Good Lord, thought Jones, how deep are we? Thousands of feet?'

The thought brough back his claustrophobia. Now the walls did indeed seem to crowd in on him. They bent beneath the mountain-heavy weight of the fathoms above him.

Black and crushing.

Keet had paused, as if to allow him time to dwell upon the terror that hovered beyond her thin skin. Now, as if she had gauged his reactions correctly, she continued.

'My walls are strong and they are flexible enough so they will not, even at this depth, collapse. But I have sprung a leak!

'It is a very small one, but it is filling a compartment between my outer wall and my inner. And, I must confess, a panel from my inner wall has been dislodged by the impact of the explosions. They were quite close.'

She spoke as if she were a woman telling her doctor that she had a diseased kidney.

'My pumps are working well enough so that I can keep this water from eventually filling up my interior,' she said. 'Unfortunately, the wetness has affected part of the circuits that direct my steering gear. I can direct myself in but one direction because my diving rudders are now locked.'

She paused dramatically and then said, 'That direction is downward.'

Her words brought terror. There would be no opening of this door. It would only bring in the blackness and the crushing, not light and air and his . . .

He clenched his fists and summoned the strength to hurl back the panic. She would know what effect her words were having; she'd be counting on them. The chances were very strong that the bonds around his arms contained instruments to measure his blood pressure and heart beats. She could tell when he was lying to her and also when he was in a state of fear.

'I have means with which to repair myself,' she continued, 'but this leak has, unfortunately, also put out of commission those circuits that direct the repairing arms. Most unfortunate.'

His voice was tight as his clenched fists. 'So?'

'So I wish to release you from your cell and allow you to stop the leak and to repair the circuits. The material for stopping the leak and the box containing the blueprints are in my engine room. You can read the circuits from these.'

'And if I do this?'

'I will take you back unharmed to the mother ship.'

'And if I don't?'

'I will shut off your air. But first, I will turn off your light.'

She might as well have struck him on the head and slammed the coffin lid shut in his face. He knew he couldn't stand against what she threatened. He didn't want to admit himself a coward; he wanted desperately to believe that he was strong. But he knew that there was something buried in him that would betray him.

When the darkness came, and the air grew hot and stuffy, he would be as a child again, a child shut up inside a closet that seemed to him to be sinking down towards the earth's centre, never to rise again. And above him would be the weight of the earth itself, its seas and mountains and the people walking far,

far overhead.

'Well?' Her voice was impatient.

He sighed. 'I'll do it.'

After all, as long as he lived, he had hopes of escaping. Perhaps of seizing this monstrosity. . . .

He shook his head wryly. Why try to fool himself? He was a coward and no good. If he hadn't been, he'd never have been running away from fear all his life, running home to his mother. He'd not have given up that prominent teaching job at a big midwestern university and come out to the coast to teach because he could be close to his mother there.

She had refused to leave her home, so he had come to her.

And afterwards, when he met Jane and allowed her to talk him into working at that big electronics laboratory in Hawaii, he had thought several times that he'd like to have his mother come and visit them. And when, after many bitter quarrels, Jane had refused to allow it because she said his mother was smothering the manhood out of him, he had walked out on her.

And now, here he was back in the closet sinking ever deeper into the crushing abyss, back in the closet because he had run away again. If he had had the guts to stay with Jane, he wouldn't be in this predicament.

The terrible part about it was that he recognized that Jane was right. He'd known his mother had her hold over him because of this curious twist in his brain. Yet he'd not been able to do anything about it except struggle feebly, just as he had been swept into the open maw of this monster and was now obeying her every word. And all because of a fear that he could not face.

Her sharp voice drove into his reverie.

'There is only one thing holding me back from releasing you.'

'What is that?'

'Can I trust you?'

'What can I do? I don't want to die, and only by staying with you can I live. Even if it is as a prisoner.'

'Oh, we treat our co-operative technicians very well.'

He did not miss the stress on co-operative. He shivered and wondered what was ahead for him and if, perhaps, it would not be as well to refuse her. He would at least go down with honour.

Honour was such a meaningless word, here so many solid fathoms under the seas, where nobody would ever know the sacrifice that he had made. He'd just be one of the missing, forgotten by all except his mother and Jane. And she – she was young and pretty and intelligent. She'd find somebody else, soon enough. The thought sent a wave of anger through him.

Keet said, 'Your blood pressure went up. What were you thinking?'

He wanted to tell her it was none of her business, but he knew that she might suspect he was devising some ways of tricking her. He confessed.

Indifferently, she said, 'You bourgeois Yankees should learn to control your emotions. Or, better yet, get rid of them. You will lose the war because of your stupidity and your sheep-like emotions.'

Under other circumstances, Jones would have laughed at the idea of a machine spouting off such patriotisms, but now he was only slightly interested to know that *Keet*'s builders had not neglected even the ideological side of the well-brought-up, mechanical brain.

Besides – and this was a thought that made him wince – she might be right.

'Before I let you loose, Jones,' she said, her voice taking on more of an edge, 'I must warn you that I am taking precautions against any sabotage on your part. I will be very frank with you and confess that, while you are in the engine room, I cannot keep as close a check on you as I can while you are here. But I have all sorts of means for following your movements. If you should touch any unauthorized parts – or even get near them – I will be warned.

'Now, I will admit that I have only one aggressive weapon against you. If you do not behave, I will at once release an anaesthetic gas. I will leave the cell door open so the gas will eventually flood the rest of me. As the corridors are very narrow – being designed solely for maintenance men who work on me when I am in port – these quarters will quickly fill up. You will be overcome.'

'And after that?' asked Jones.

'I will keep up the flow until you die. Then we both perish. But I will have the satisfaction of knowing that no capitalist boot-licker conquered me. And I am not afraid of death, as you are.'

Jones doubted that last statement. It was true she would not be afraid in the sense he was. But her makers must have built into her a striving for survival that would be as strong as his. Otherwise, she would not be the fighting machine the enemy wanted, and they might as well construct the more conventional type of sub manned with beings who would fight for their lives.

The main difference was that, being a machine, she was not neurotic. He was a man, much more highly organized. Therefore, he was much more capable of having something go wrong with him. The higher the creature, the greater the downfall.

His plastic bonds snapped back. He rose, rubbing his tingling arms and legs. At the same time, the cell door slid back into a hollow in the wall. He walked towards it and then peered down the passageway. He drew back.

'Go ahead!' said *Keet*, impatiently.

'It's so dark,' he said. 'And so low and narrow. I'll have to crawl.'

'I can't give you any light,' she snapped. 'There are flashlights for the maintenance men, but those are located in a locker in the engine room. You'll have to go get them.'

He could not. It was impossible to urge his legs into that solid blackness.

Keet swore an enemy oath. At least, he supposed it was an oath. It certainly sounded like one.

'Jones, you bourgeois coward! Get out of this room!'

He whimpered, 'I can't.'

'Ha! If all Yankee civilians are like you, you will surely lose the war.'

He could not explain to her that everybody was not like him. His weakness was special; it excused him. There was just no fighting against it.

'Jones, if you do not get out of here, I will flood this cell with the gas.'

'If you do, you will be lost, too,' he reminded her. 'You will stay here forever with your nose in the mud.'

'I know that. But I have a stronger directive than survival. If I have to take a choice between being captured or perishing, I accept the latter. Without the qualms that distinguish you bourgeois.'

She paused and then, with a contempt so strong he could

almost see the curl of the speaker's lip, she said 'Now, *get!*'

He had no doubt she meant what she said. Moreover, so burning had been the derision in her voice, he felt as if a flame had lashed out and burnt the back of his legs. He crouched down and plunged into the darkness and the narrowness.

Even then, he knew that she was not capable of any real contempt. It was just the makers had put into her electronic brain the directives that she treat the captured enemy in such and such a fashion. She was aware of his psychological states, and she automatically turned on contempt or whatever emotion was needed when the time came. Nevertheless, there had been a sting in her voice, and it had struck deep.

Bent over, knuckles almost touching the plastic floor, he walked like an ape in a strange forest. His eyes burned through the darkness as if they would furnish their own light. But he could see nothing. Several times he glanced nervously over his shoulder and was always comforted by the square of light that the cell globe threw out. As long as he had that in sight, he wouldn't be too lost.

The corridor took a little curve. When he looked behind him, there was only the faintest glow to show that all was not black, that he was not, after all, shut up in a closet. His heart beat fast, and something welled up from the lowest and deepest part of his being. It brought with it an oily, heavy, black scum of fear and reasonless panic. It filled his heart and crept up into his throat. It tried to choke him.

He stopped and put both hands out against the walls on either side. They were solid and cold to the touch and they were not shifting in towards him to crush him. He knew that. Yet, for just the flicker of a feeling, he had felt them *move*. And he had felt the air thicken, as if it were a snake about to coil around his neck.

'My name is Chris Jones,' he said aloud. His voice rang along the corridors. 'I am thirty years old. I am not a child of six. I am a specialist in electronics and capable of making my own living. I have a wife, whom I realize now, for the first time, dear God, I love more than anything else in the world. I am an American, and I am now at war with the enemy, and it is my duty and right and privilege, and should be my joy, if I were of the heroic mould, to do everything in my power to cripple or destroy that enemy. I have my two good hands and my knowledge. Yet God knows

I am not doing what I should. I am creeping along a tunnel like a small child, shivering in my boots, ready to run crying for mother, back to the light and the safety. And I am aiding and abetting the enemy so that I may have that light and safety and my mother's voice once again.'

His voice shook, but he firmed it. Its hardening was an indication of what was taking place within him. Now or never, he breathed to himself. Now or never. If he turned back, if his legs and heart failed him, it was all up with him. It would not matter at all that he might eventually reach safety as a prisoner of the enemy. Or even that he might be rescued and go home to his own people, free. If he did not break that fault in him, throw it down and march over it, he would always be a prisoner of the enemy. He had always been a captive of the enemy, he realized, and the enemy was himself. Now, deep under the sea, caught in this confined and lightless corridor, he must wrestle with that enemy whose face he couldn't see but knew well, and he must overthrow it. Or be thrown.

The question was, how?

The answer was, go ahead. Do not stop.

He moved slowly, feeling the wall with his right hand. *Keet* had given him directions; if he followed them he could locate the locker in the engine room. And he did. After what seemed hours of groping and fighting off the choking sensation around neck and breast, he felt an object whose dimensions answered *Keet's* description. The key was hanging by a chain from a staple; he inserted it and unlocked the door. Another minute, and he had turned on the flashlight.

He played it like a hose about him. Beside him was the huge cube of the atomic reactor. Its exterior consisted of newly invented alloy that blocked radiation, yet did not weigh nearly as much as the now obsolete lead shielding. Nevertheless, knowing that there was some radiation leaking through and that the maintenance men would wear anti-radiation suits, he felt uncomfortable. If, however, he did not linger long, he would be safe.

He located, easily enough, the dislodged panel. It was in itself evidence that *Keet*, though she may have been well-planned, had been hastily built.

He changed that conclusion. Perhaps one of the men who had helped build her had been a member of the underground, a saboteur. This weak part of *Keet* was his handiwork.

He turned his flashlight into the opening. It showed a fine spray of water spurting at intervals of several seconds through an invisible hole. This might be further evidence that there were hands among the enemy working for the so-called bourgeois swine. The sub was formed of parts welded together for greater strength, instead of being riveted. *Keet's* body should not leak unless a projectile had shattered a hole in the metal. That did not seem likely. So it was possible that this section had been deliberately flawed.

It did not matter, Jones thought. Whether on purpose or by accident, the deed had been done. It was up to him to take advantage of it.

He examined the compartment. The circuits inside were under water, but it was not because of their immersion that they were not working. Incased in plastic, they could operate inside a water-filled chamber. But due to a series of safety devices, this section of circuits had an automatic shut-off in case of emergencies such as the present. *Keet* could not turn them on until the leak was stopped up.

Jones returned to the locker and took out a spray gun. He squirted a semi-fluid over the spray which came through the wall rhythmically. The stuff congealed and dried. The spray was at once shut off.

Jones rose and turned to walk, stooped over, backed to the locker. There he would look for a dipper with which to remove the water faster, inasmuch as the pumps were not working swiftly enough. But he stopped, one foot ahead of the other, as if he had been frozen in mid-stride.

What a fool he was! Why hadn't he noticed this before? He must have been in a hell of a blue funk not to have thought at once of this!

Keet had said that her nose was buried in the mud and that she could not withdraw until the circuits governing the steering mechanism were turned on again.

Yet there was no evidence at all that the craft was tilted. He could walk without having to lean one way or the other to compensate for the supposed incline.

Keet, then, was lying for reasons of her own.

He forgot about the fear that was still pressing around him, kept back only by an effort of strong will. This problem demanded all of his attention, and he gave every bit of it.

He had taken her word for the true state of their situation because it had not occurred to him that a robot could lie. But now that he thought about it, it was only natural that the machine should be cast in the mould of the makers. They boasted that lying was a good thing if it got them what they desired. And they would, of course, have built a lie-fabricator into *Keet*. If the occasion demanded it, she would make up something contrary to reality.

The big, million-dollar question was – why should she feel it necessary to do so?

Answer: She must feel weak, exposed.

Question: Where did she feel weak?

Answer: He, Jones, was her tender spot.

Why?

Because he was a man. He could walk around, and he could think. He might get nerve enough to take action against her. If he did, he might overcome her.

Keet was not nearly as bold and strong as she pretended. She had had to play upon his own weakness, his fear of the dark and the narrow, of the awful weight of water supposedly hanging above him. She had relied on that to make him meekly repair the damage and then, like the sheep he was, return to the pen. And, he thought, probably to the slaughter. He doubted now that she would take him back to the mother ship.

She might be out to sea for a year or more until she found enough targets at which to shoot all of her forty torpedoes. In the meantime, she would have to be feeding him and giving him air. She was not built large enough for that; she did not have that much cargo space.

The cell in which he had lain must have been for the temporary keeping of prisoners who could be questioned. Also, it was probably meant for the cabins of spies and saboteurs who would be let out, some dark night, on America's coast. *Keet* had been lying to him from the beginning.

The irony of it was that, in forcing him to repair her damage, she had had to use his particular fault of character to get him to do so. Yet, in so doing, she had forced him to overcome his weakness; she had made him strong.

For the first time since he had left his wife, he smiled with sincerity.

At the same instant, his flashlight picked out the spray gun where he had laid it. His eyes narrowed. *Keet* had been correct in her fears. In essence, she was a machine with a machine's limitations, and he was a man. He was mobile, and he had an imagination. Therein lay the enemy's defeat.

He could hear her voice echoing down the corridors, asking where he was and threatening to release the gas if he did not report at once to her.

'I'm coming, *Keet*,' he called. His one hand held a screwdriver which he had taken from the locker, and the other held the spray gun.

Two days later, a Navy patrol boat dived towards the sub, which lay helpless upon the surface. The alert observer spotted the man standing upon the sleek back and waving a white shirt. The plane did not release its bombs, but, after a judicious scouting, landed and picked up the man, who turned out to be an American with the good old American name of Jones.

He told his story over the radio on his way back to Hawaii. A destroyer close by immediately set out to take over *Keet*. When Jones landed, he had to make an official report and repeat in greater detail what had happened. In reply to a question a naval officer put to him, he answered, 'Yes, I did take a chance, but I had to. I was sure that she – pardon me, the robot – was lying to me. If we'd had our nose stuck in the mud, I should have detected at once that the cell and the corridor were on a slant. Moreover, the water was not coming out steadily, as it would have if it had had great pressure behind it. It spurted through the fissure, true, but only at intervals. It didn't take much deduction to see that we were on the surface, and that every time a wave hit that side, it forced some of its water through.

Keet was depending on me not to notice this, to be so overwhelmed by our supposed situation that I would fix up the trouble and then creep back into the cell.'

And I would have, too, he thought grimly, if it had not been for that unutterable scorn in her voice and the fact that then was the moment in which I had to prove myself forever a man or a coward.

I'm still afraid of the dark and the narrow, but it is a fear that I can conquer. *Keet* did not think I could. But to make sure, she told me that I was at the bottom of the sea. She did not want me to know that her steering gear was set so that she could only go up, instead of down, as she told me, and that she was on the surface, an easy prey to the first American ship that came by. She calculated that if I knew that, I might get nerve enough to revolt. Unfortunately for her, she did not give me any credit for brains. Or else she banked on my fear neutralizing my intelligence. And she was *so* near to being correct.

'Now, just what did you do with the spray gun?' asked the Lieutenant-Commander.

'First, I held my breath and ran into the cell where I had been prisoner. I located the vent from which the gas was coming and sprayed the stop-leak cement on it. That blocked it. Then I retreated to the locker, read the blueprints there, and located *Keet's* "brain."

'It took me only a minute to disconnect her from her "body." '

He grinned. 'That did not stop her voice, which gave me an unladylike cussing. But, inasmuch as it was in the enemy's tongue, I didn't understand a word of it. Funny, isn't it, that she, like a human being, should revert to her native tongue in a moment of fury and frustration?'

'Yes, and then?'

'I stimulated the circuits that opened the deck hatch and let in air from the outside.'

'And you weren't sure whether or not air or water would come flooding in?'

He nodded. 'That is right.' He did not add that he had stood there, cold and shaking, while he waited.

'Very well,' said the Lieutenant-Commander with an admiring glance that warmed Jones and for the first time made him realize that he had, after all, done something in the heroic mould. 'You may go. We'll call you if we want to hear any more. Is there anything you wish before you go?'

'Yes,' he said looking around. 'Where's the telephone? I'd like to call my wife.'

THE sixth night on Mars, Lane wept.

He sobbed loudly while tears ran down his cheeks. He smacked his right fist into the palm of his left hand until the flesh burned. He howled with the anguish of loneliness. He swore the most obscene and blasphemous oaths he knew, and he knew quite a few after ten years in the UN's Space Arm.

After a while, he quit weeping. He dried his eyes, downed a shot of Scotch, and felt much better.

He wasn't ashamed because he had bawled like a woman. After all, there had been a Man who had not been ashamed to weep. Moreover, one of the reasons he had been chosen to be in the first party to land on Mars was this very ability to cry. No one could call him coward or weakling. A man with little courage could never have passed the battery of tests on Earth's space school, let alone have made the many thrusts to the Moon. But, though male and masculine, he had a woman's safety valve. He could dissolve in tears the grinding stones of tension within; he was the reed that bent before the wind, not the oak that toppled, roots and all.

Now, the weight and ache in his breast gone, feeling almost cheerful, he made his scheduled report over the transceiver to the circum-Martian vessel five hundred and eight miles overhead. Then he did what men must do any place in the universe. Afterwards, he lay down in the bunk and opened the one personal book he had been allowed to bring along, an anthology of the world's greatest poetry.

He read here and there, running, pausing for only a line or two, then completing in his head the thousand-times murmured lines. Here and there he read, like a bee tasting the best of the nectar. ...

It is the voice of my beloved that knocketh, saying,
Open to me, my sister, my love, my dove, my undefiled ...

We have a little sister,
And she hath no breasts;

What shall we do for our sister
In the day when she shall be spoken for?

Yea, though I walk through the valley of the shadow of death,
I will fear no evil: for Thou art with me ...

Come live with me and be my love
And we shall all the pleasures prove ...

It lies not in our power to love or hate
For will in us is over-ruled by fate ...

With thee conversing, I forget all time,
All seasons, and their change, all please alike ...

He read on about love and man and woman until he had almost
forgotten his troubles. His lids drooped; the book fell from his
hand. But he roused himself, climbed out of the bunk, got down
on his knees, and prayed that he be forgiven and that his blasphemy and despair be understood. And he prayed that his four
lost comrades be found safe and sound. Then he climbed back
into the bunk and fell asleep.

At dawn he woke reluctantly to the alarm clock's ringing.
Nevertheless, he did not fall back into sleep but rose, turned on
the transceiver, filled a cup with water and instant, and dropped
in a heat pill. Just as he finished the coffee, he heard Captain
Stroyansky's voice from the 'ceiver. Stroyansky spoke with
barely a trace of Slavic accent.

'Cardigan Lane? You awake?'

'More or less. How are you?'

'If we weren't worried about all of you down there, we'd be
fine.'

'I know. Well, what are the captain's orders?'

'There is only one thing to do, Lane. You must go look for the
others. Otherwise, you cannot get back up to us. It takes at least
two more men to pilot the rocket.'

'Theoretically, one man can pilot the beast,' replied Lane.

'But it's uncertain. However, that doesn't matter. I'm leaving
at once to look for the others. I'd do that even if you ordered
otherwise.'

Stroyansky chuckled. Then he barked like a seal. 'The success of the expedition is more important than the fate of four men. Theoretically, anyway. But if I were in your shoes, and I'm glad I am not, I would do the same. So, good luck, Lane.'

'Thanks,' said Lane. 'I'll need more than luck. I'll also need God's help. I suppose He's here, even if the place does look Godforsaken.'

He looked through the transparent double plastic walls of the dome.

'The wind's blowing about twenty-five miles an hour. The dust is covering the tractor tracks. I have to get going before they're covered up entirely. My supplies are all packed; I've enough food, air, and water to last me six days. It makes a big package, the air tanks and the sleeping tent bulk large. It's over a hundred Earth pounds, but here only about forty. I'm also taking a rope, a knife, a pickaxe, a flare pistol, half a dozen flares. And a walkie-talkie.

'It should take me two days to walk the thirty miles to the spot where the tracs last reported. Two days to look around. Two days to get back.'

'You be back in five days!' shouted Stroyansky. 'That's an order! It shouldn't take you more than one day to scout around. Don't take chances. Five days! Otherwise, court-martial for you, Lane!'

And then, in a softer voice, 'Good luck, and, if there is a God, may He help you!'

Lane tried to think of things to say, things that might perhaps go down with the *Doctor Livingstone, I presume*, category. But all he could say was, 'So long.'

Twenty minutes later, he closed behind him the door to the dome's pressure lock. He strapped on the towering pack and began to walk. But when he was about fifty yards from the base, he felt compelled to turn around for one long look at what he might never see again. There, on the yellow-red felsite plain, stood the pressurized bubble. That was to have been the home of the five men for a year. Nearby squatted the glider that had brought them down, its enormous wings spreading far, its skids covered with the forever-blowing dust.

Straight ahead of him was the rocket, standing on its fins, pointing towards the blue-black sky, glittering in the Martian sun, shining with promise of power, escape from Mars, and return to the orbital ship. It had come down to the surface of Mars on the back of the glider in a hundred and twenty mile an hour landing. After it had dropped the two six-ton caterpillar tractors it carried, it had been pulled off the glider and tilted on end by winches pulled by those very tractors. Now it waited for him and for the other four men.

'I'll be back,' he murmured to it. 'And if I have to, I'll take you up by myself.'

He began to walk, following the broad double tracks left by the tank. The tracks were faint, for they were two days old, and the blowing silicate dust had almost filled them. The tracks made by the first tank, which had left three days ago, were completely hidden.

The trail led north-west. It left the three-mile-wide plain between two hills of naked rock and entered the quarter-mile corridor between two rows of vegetation. The rows ran straight and parallel from horizon to horizon, for miles behind him and miles ahead. A person flying above them would have seen many such lines, marching side by side. To observers in the orbital ship the hundreds of rows looked like one solid line. That line was one of the so-called canals of Mars.

Lane, on the ground and close to one row, saw it for what it was. Its foundation was an endless three-foot high tube, most of whose bulk, like an iceberg's, lay buried in the ground. The curving sides were covered with blue-green lichenoids that grew on every rock or projection. From the spine of the tube, separated at regular intervals, grew the trunks of plants. The trunks were smooth shiny blue-green pillars two feet thick and six feet high. Out of their tops spread radially many pencil-thin branches, like bats' fingers. Between the fingers stretched a blue-green membrane, the single tremendous leaf of the umbrella tree.

When Lane had first seen them from the glider as it hurtled over them, he had thought they looked like an army of giant hands uplifted to catch the sun. Giant they were, for each rib-supported leaf measured fifty feet across. And hands they were, hands to beg for and catch the rare gold of the tiny sun. During the day, the ribs on the side nearest the moving sun dipped towards the ground, and the furthest ribs tilted upwards. Obviously, the daylong manoeuvre was designed to expose the complete area of the membrane to the light, to allow not an inch to remain in shadow.

It was to be expected that strange forms of plant life would be found here. But structures built by animal life were not expected. Especially when they were so large and covered an eighth of the planet.

These structures were the tubes from which rose the trunks of the umbrella trees. Lane had tried to drill through the rock-like side of the tube. So hard was it, it had blunted one drill and had done a second no good before he had chipped off a small piece. Contented for the moment with that, he had taken it to the dome, there to examine it under a microscope. After an amazed look, he had whistled. Embedded in the cement-like mass were plant cells. Some were partially destroyed; some, whole.

Further tests had shown him that the substance was composed of cellulose, a lignin-like stuff, various nucleic acids, and unknown materials.

He had reported his discovery and also his conjecture to the orbital ship. Some form of animal life had, at some time, chewed up and partially digested wood and then had regurgitated it as a cement. From the cement the tubes had been fashioned.

The following day he intended to go back to the tube and blast a hole in it. But two of the men had set out in a tractor on a field exploration. Lane, as radio operator for that day, had stayed in the dome. He was to keep in contact with the two, who were to report to him every fifteen minutes.

The tank had been gone about two hours and must have been about thirty miles away, when it had failed to report. Two hours later, the other tank, carrying two men, had followed the prints of the first party. They had gone about thirty miles from base and were maintaining continuous radio contact with Lane.

'There's a slight obstacle ahead,' Greenberg had said. 'It's a tube coming out at right angles from the one we've been paralleling. It has no plants growing from it. Not much of a rise, not much of a drop on the other side, either. We'll make it easy.'

Then he had yelled.

That was all.

Now, the day after, Lane was on foot, following the fading trail. Behind him lay the base camp, close to the junction of the two *canali* known as Avernus and Tartarus. He was between two of the rows of vegetation which formed Tartarus, and he was travelling north-eastward, towards the Sirenum Mare, the so-called Siren Sea. The Mare, he supposed, would be a much broader group of tree-bearing tubes.

He walked steadily while the sun rose higher and the air grew warmer. He had long ago turned off his suit-heater. This was summer and close to the equator. At noon the temperature would be around 70 degrees *Fahrenheit*.

But at dusk, when the temperature had plunged through the dry air to zero, Lane was in his sleeping tent. It looked like a cocoon, being sausage-shaped and not much larger than his body. It was inflated so he could remove his helmet and breathe while he warmed himself from the battery-operated heater and ate and drank. The tent was also very flexible; it changed its cocoon shape to a triangle while Lane sat on a folding chair from which hung a plastic bag and did that which every man must do.

During the daytime he did not have to enter the sleeping tent for this. His suit was ingeniously contrived so he could unflap the rear section and expose the necessary area without losing air or pressure from the rest of his suit. Naturally, there was no thought of tempting the teeth of the Martian night. Sixty seconds at midnight were enough to get a severe frostbite where one sat down.

Lane slept until half an hour after dawn, ate, deflated the tent, folded it, stowed it, the battery, heater, food-box, and folding chair into his pack, threw away the plastic sack, shouldered the pack, and resumed his walk.

By noon the tracks faded out completely. It made little difference, for there was only one route the tanks could have taken. That was the corridor between the tubes and the trees.

Now he saw what the two tanks had reported. The trees on his right began to look dead. The trunks and leaves were brown, and the ribs drooped.

He began walking faster, his heart beating hard. An hour passed, and still the line of dead trees stretched as far as he could see.

'It must be about here,' he said out loud to himself.

Then he stopped. Ahead was an obstacle.

It was the tube of which Greenberg had spoken, the one that ran at right angles to the other two and joined them.

Lane looked at it and thought that he could still hear Greenberg's despairing cry.

That thought seemed to turn a valve in him so that the immense pressure of loneliness, which he had succeeded in holding back until then, flooded in. The blue-black of the sky became the blackness and infinity of space itself, and he was a speck of flesh in an immensity as large as Earth's land area, a speck that knew no more of this world than a new-born baby knows of his.

Tiny and helpless, like a baby . . .

No, he murmured to himself, not a baby. Tiny, yes. Helpless, no. Baby, no. I am a man, a man, an Earthman . . .

Earthman: Cardigan Lane. Citizen of the U.S.A. Born in Hawaii, the fiftieth state. Of mingled German, Dutch, Chinese, Japanese, Negro, Cherokee, Polynesian, Portuguese, Russian-Jewish, Irish, Scotch, Norwegian, Finnish, Czech, English, and Welsh ancestry. Thirty-one years old. Five foot six. One hundred and forty pounds. Brown-haired. Blue-eyed. Hawkfeatured. M.D. and Ph.D. Married. Childless. Methodist. Sociable mesomorphic mesovert. Radio ham. Dog breeder. Deer hunter. Skin diver. Writer of first-rate but far from great poetry. All contained in his skin and his pressure suit, plus a love of companionship and life, an intense curiosity, and a courage. And now very much afraid of losing everything except his loneliness.

For some time he stood like a statue before the three-foot-high wall of the tube. Finally, he shook his head violently, shook off his fear like a dog shaking off water. Lightly, despite the towering pack on his back, he leaped up on to the top of the tube and looked on the other side, though there was nothing he had not seen before jumping.

The view before him differed from the one behind in only one respect. This was the number of small plants that covered the ground. Or rather, he thought, after taking a second look, he had never seen these plants this size before. They were foot high replicas of the huge umbrella trees that sprouted from the tubes. And they were not scattered at random, as might have been expected if they had grown from seeds blown by the wind. Instead, they grew in regular rows, the edges of the plants in one row separated from the other by about two feet.

His heart beat even faster. Such spacing must mean they were planted by intelligent life. Yet intelligent life seemed very improbable, given the Martian environment.

Possibly some natural condition might have caused the seeming artificiality of this garden. He would have to investigate.

Always with caution, though. So much depended on him:

the lives of the four men, the success of the expedition. If this one failed, it might be the last. Many people on Earth were groaning loudly because of the cost of Space Arm and crying wildly for results that would mean money and power.

The field, or garden, extended for about three hundred yards. At its far end there was another tube at right angles to the two parallel ones. And at this point the giant umbrella plants regained their living and shining blue-green colour.

The whole set-up looked to Lane very much like a sunken garden. The square formation of the high tubes kept out the wind and most of the felsite flakes. The walls held the heat within the square.

Lane searched the top of the tube for bare spots where the metal plates of the caterpillar tractor's treads would have scraped off the lichenoids. He found none but was not surprised. The lichenoids grew phenomenally fast under the summertime sun.

He looked down at the ground on the garden side of the tube, where the tractors had presumably descended. Here there were no signs of the tractors' passage, for the little umbrellas grew up to within two feet of the edge of the tube, and they were uncrushed. Nor did he find any tracks at the ends of the tube where it joined the parallel rows.

He paused to think about his next step and was surprised to find himself breathing hard. A quick check of his air gauge showed him that the trouble wasn't an almost empty tank. No it was the apprehension, the feeling of eeriness, of something *wrong*, that was causing his heart to beat so fast, to demand more oxygen.

Where could two tractors and four men have gone? And what could have caused them to disappear?

Could they have been attacked by some form of intelligent life? If that had happened, the unknown creatures had either carried off the six-ton tanks, or driven them away, or else forced the men to drive them off.

Where? How? By whom?

The hairs on the back of his neck stood up.

'Here is where it must have happened,' he muttered to himself. 'The first tank reported seeing this tube barring its way and said it would report again in another ten minutes. That was the last I heard from it. The second was cut off just as it was on top of the tube. Now, what happened? There are no cities on the surface of Mars, and no indications of underground civilization. The orbital ship would have seen openings to such a place through its telescope . . .'

He yelled so loudly that he was deafened as his voice bounced off the confines of his helmet. Then he fell silent, watching the line of basketball-size blue globes rise from the soil at the far end of the garden and swiftly soar into the sky.

He threw back his head until the back of it was stopped by the helmet and watched the rising globes as they left the ground, swelling until they seemed to be hundreds of feet across. Suddenly, like a soap bubble, the topmost one disappeared. The second in line, having reached the height of the first, also popped. And the others followed.

They were transparent. He could see some white cirrus clouds through the blue of the bubbles.

Lane did not move but watched the steady string of globes spurt from the soil. Though startled, he did not forget his training. He noted that the globes, besides being semi-transparent, rose at a rightangle to the ground and did not drift with the wind. He counted them and got to forty-nine when they ceased appearing.

He waited for fifteen minutes. When it looked as if nothing more would happen, he decided that he must investigate the spot where the globes seemed to have popped out of the ground. Taking a deep breath, he bent his knees and jumped out into the garden. He landed lightly about twelve feet out from the edge of the tube and between two rows of plants.

For a second he did not know what was happening, though he realized that something was wrong. Then he whirled around. Or tried to do so. One foot came up, but the other sank deeper.

He took one step forward, and the forward foot also disappeared into the thin stuff beneath the red-yellow dust. By now the other foot was too deep in to be pulled out.

Then he was hip-deep and grabbing at the stems of the plants to both sides of him. They uprooted easily, coming out of the soil, one clenched in each hand.

He dropped them and threw himself backwards in the hope he could free his legs and lie stretched out on the jelly-like stuff. Perhaps, if his body presented enough of an area, he could keep from sinking. And, after a while, he might be able to work his way to the ground near the tube. There, he hoped, it would be firm.

His violent effort succeeded. His legs came up out of the sticky semi-liquid. He lay spreadeagled on his back and looked up at the sky through the transparent dome of his helmet. The sun was to his left; when he turned his head inside the helmet he could see the sun sliding down the arc from the zenith. It was descending at a slightly slower pace than on Earth, for Mars' day was about forty minutes longer. He hoped that, if he couldn't regain solid ground, he could remain suspended until evening fell. By then this quagmire would be frozen enough for him to rise and walk up on it. Provided that he got up before he himself was frozen fast.

Meanwhile, he would follow the approved method of saving oneself when trapped in quicksand. He would roll over quickly, once, and then spreadeagle himself again. By repeating this manoeuvre, he might eventually reach that bare strip of soil at the tube.

The pack on his back prevented him from rolling. The straps around his shoulders would have to be loosened.

He did so, and at the same time felt his legs sinking. Their weight was pulling them under, whereas the air tanks in the pack, the air tanks strapped to his chest, and the bubble of his helmet gave buoyancy to the upper part of his body.

He turned over on his side, grabbed the pack, and pulled himself up on it. The pack, of course, went under. But his legs were free, though slimy with liquid and caked with dust. And he was standing on top of the narrow island of the pack.

The thick jelly rose up to his ankles while he considered two courses of action.

He could squat on the pack and hope that it would not sink too far before it was stopped by the permanently frozen layer that must exist . . .

How far? He had gone down hipdeep and felt nothing firm beneath his feet. And . . . He groaned. The tractors! Now he knew what had happened to them. They had gone over the tube and down into the garden, never suspecting that the solid-seeming surface covered this quagmire. And down they had plunged, and it had been Greenberg's horrified realization of what lay beneath the dust that had made him cry out, and then the stuff had closed over the tank and its antenna, and the transmitter, of course, had been cut off.

He must give up his second choice because it did not exist. To get to the bare strip of soil at the tube would be useless. It would be as unfirm as the rest of the garden. It was at that point that the tanks must have fallen in.

Another thought came to him: that the tanks must have disturbed the orderly arrangement of the little umbrellas close to the tube. Yet there was no sign of such a happening. Therefore, somebody must have rescued the plants and set them up again.

That meant that somebody might come along in time to rescue him.

Or to kill him, he thought.

In either event, his problem would be solved.

Meanwhile, he knew it was no use to make a jump from the pack to the strip at the tube. The only thing to do was to stay on top of the pack and hope it didn't sink too deeply.

However, the pack did sink. The jelly rose swiftly to his knee then his rate of descent began slowing. He prayed, not for a miracle but only that the buoyancy of the pack plus the tank on his chest would keep him from going completely under.

Before he had finished praying, he had stopped sinking. The sticky stuff had risen no higher than his breast and had left his arms free.

He gasped with relief but did not feel overwhelmed with joy. In less than four hours the air in his tank would be exhausted. Unless he could get another tank from the pack, he was done for.

He pushed down hard on the pack and threw his arms up in the air and back in the hope his legs would rise again and he could spreadeagle. If he could do that, then the pack, relieved of his weight, might rise to the surface. And he could get another tank from it.

But his legs, impeded by the stickiness, did not rise far enough, and his body, shooting off in reaction to the kick, moved a little distance from the pack. It was just far enough so that when the legs inevitably sank again, they found no platform on which to be supported. Now he had to depend entirely on the lift of his air tank.

It did not give him enough to hold him at his former level; this time he sank until his arms and shoulders were nearly under, and only his helmet stuck out.

He was helpless.

Several years from now the second expedition, if any, would perhaps see the sun glinting off his helmet and would find his body stuck like a fly in glue.

If that does happen, he thought, I will at least have been of some use; my death will warn them of this trap. But I doubt if they'll find me. I think that Somebody or Something will have removed me and hidden me.

Then, feeling an inrush of despair, he closed his eyes and murmured some of the words he had read that last night in the base, though he knew them so well it did not matter whether he had read them recently or not.

Yea, though I walk through the valley of the shadow of death, I will fear no evil; for Thou art with me.

Repeating that didn't lift the burden of hopelessness. He felt absolutely alone, deserted by everybody, even by his Creator. Such was the desolation of Mars.

But when he opened his eyes, he knew he was not alone. He saw a Martian.

A hole had appeared in the wall of the tube to his left. It was a round section about four feet across, and it had sunk in as if it were a plug being pulled inwards, as indeed it was.

A moment later a head popped out of the hole. The size of a Georgia watermelon, it was shaped like a football and was as pink as a baby's bottom. Its two eyes were as large as coffee cups and each was equipped with two vertical lids. It opened its two parrot-like beaks, ran out a very long tubular tongue, withdrew the tongue, and snapped the beak shut. Then it scuttled out from the hole to reveal a body also shaped like a football and only three times as large as its head. The pinkish body was supported three feet from the ground on ten spindly spidery legs, five on each side. Its legs ended in broad round pads on which it ran across the jellymire surface, sinking only slightly. Behind it streamed at least fifty others.

These picked up the little plants that Lane had upset in his struggles and licked them clean with narrow round tongues that shot out at least two feet. They also seemed to communicate by touching their tongues, as insects do with antennae.

As he was in the space between two rows, he was not involved in the setting up of the dislodged plants. Several of them ran their tongues over his helmet, but these were the only ones that paid him any attention. It was then that he began to stop dreading that they might attack him with their powerful looking beaks. Now he broke into a sweat at the idea that they might ignore him completely.

That was just what they did. After gently embedding the thin roots of the plantlets in the sticky stuff, they raced off towards the hole in the tube.

Lane, overwhelmed with despair, shouted after them, though he knew they couldn't hear him through his helmet and the thin air even if they had hearing organs.

'Don't leave me here to die!'

Nevertheless, that was what they were doing. The last one leaped through the hole, and the entrance stared at him like the round black eye of Death itself.

He struggled furiously to lift himself from the mire, not caring that he was only exhausting himself.

Abruptly, he stopped fighting and stared at the hole.

A figure had crawled out of it, a figure in a pressure-suit.

Now he shouted with joy. Whether the figure was Martian or not, it was built like a member of homo sapiens. It could be presumed to be intelligent and therefore curious.

He was not disappointed. The suited being stood up on two hemispheres of shiny red metal and began walking towards him in a sliding fashion. Reaching him, it handed him the end of a plastic rope it was carrying under its arm.

He almost dropped it. His rescuer's suit was transparent. It was enough of a shock to see clearly the details of the creature's body, but the sight of the two heads within the helmet caused him to turn pale.

The Martian slidewalked to the tube from which Lane had leaped. It jumped lightly from the two bowls on which it had stood, landed on the three-foot high top of the tube, and began hauling Lane out from the mess. He came out slowly but steadily and soon was scooting forward, gripping the rope. When he reached the foot of the tube, he was hauled on up until he could get his feet in the two bowls. It was easy to jump from them to a place beside the biped.

It unstrapped two more bowls from its back, gave them to Lane, then lowered itself on the two in the garden. Lane followed it across the mire.

Entering the hole, he found himself in a chamber so low he had to crouch. Evidently, it had been constructed by the dekapeds and not by his companion for it, too, had to bend its back and knees.

Lane was pushed to one side by some dekapeds. They picked up the thick plug, made of the same grey stuff as the tube walls, and sealed the entrance with it. Then they shot out of their mouths strand after strand of grey spiderwebby stuff to seal the plug.

The biped motioned Lane to follow, and it slid down a tunnel which plunged into the earth at a forty-five degree angle. It illuminated the passage with a flashlight which it took from its belt. They came into a large chamber which contained all of the fifty dekapeds. These were waiting motionless. The biped, as if sensing Lane's curiosity, pulled off its glove and held it before several small vents in the wall. Lane removed his glove and felt warm air flowing from the holes.

Evidently this was a pressure chamber, built by the ten-legged things. But such evidence of intelligent engineering did not mean that these things had the individual intelligence of a man. It could mean group intelligence such as Terrestrial insects possess.

After a while, the chamber was filled with air. Another plug was pulled; Lane followed the dekapeds and his rescuer up another forty-five degree tunnel. He estimated that he would find himself inside the tube from which the biped had first come. He was right. He crawled through another hole into it.

And a pair of beaks clicked as they bit down on his helmet!

Automatically, he shoved at the thing, and under the force of his blow the dekaped lost its bite and went rolling on the floor, a bundle of thrashing legs.

Lane did not worry about having hurt it. It did not weigh much, but its body must be tough to be able to plunge without damage from the heavy air inside the tube into the almost-stratospheric conditions outside.

However, he did reach for the knife at his belt. But the biped put its hand on his arm and shook one of its heads.

Later, he was to find out that the seeming bite must have been an accident. Always – with one exception – the leggers were to ignore him.

He was also to find that he was lucky. The leggers had come

out to inspect their garden because, through some unknown method of detection, they knew that the plantlets had been disturbed. The biped normally would not have accompanied them. However, today, its curiosity aroused because the leggers had gone out three times in three days, it had decided to investigate.

The biped turned out its flashlight and motioned to Lane to follow. Awkwardly, he obeyed. There was light, but it was dim, a twilight. Its source was the many creatures that hung from the ceiling of the tube. These were three feet long and six inches thick, cylindrical, pinkish-skinned, and eyeless. A dozen frond-like limbs waved continuously, and their motion kept air circulating in the tunnel.

Their cold firefly glow came from two globular pulsing organs which hung from both sides of the round loose-lipped mouth at the free end of the creature. Slime drooled from the mouth, and dripped on to the floor or into a narrow channel which ran along the lowest part of the sloping floor. Water ran in the six-inch deep channel, the first native water he had seen. The water picked up the slime and carried it a little way before it was gulped up by an animal that lay on the bottom of the channel.

Lanes's eyes adjusted to the dimness until he could make out the water-dweller. It was torpedo-shaped and without eyes or fins. It had two openings in its body; one obviously sucked in water, the other expelled it.

He saw at once what this meant. The water at the North Pole melted in the summertime and flowed into the far end of the tube system. Helped by gravity and by the pumping action of the line of animals in the channel, the water was passed from the edge of the Pole to the equator.

Leggers ran by him on mysterious errands. Several, however, halted beneath some of the downhanging organisms. They reared up on their hind five legs and their tongues shot out and into the open mouths by the glowing balls. At once the fire-worm – as Lane termed it – its cilia waving wildly, stretched itself to twice its former length. Its mouth met the beak of the legger, and there was an exchange of stuff between their mouths.

Impatiently, the biped tugged at Lane's arm. He followed it down the tube. Soon they entered a section where pale roots came down out of holes in the ceiling and spread along the curving walls, gripping them, then becoming a network of many thread-thin rootlets that crept across the floor and into the water of the channel.

Here and there a dekaped chewed at a root and then hurried off to offer a piece to the mouths of the fire-worms.

After walking for several minutes, the biped stepped across the stream. It then began walking as closely as possible to the wall, meanwhile looking apprehensively at the other side of the tunnel, where they had been walking.

Lane also looked but could see nothing at which to be alarmed. There was a large opening at the base of the wall which evidently led into a tunnel. This tunnel, he presumed, ran underground into a room, or rooms, for many leggers dashed in and out of it. And about a dozen, larger than average, paced back and forth like sentries before the hole.

When they had gone about fifty yards past the opening, the biped relaxed. After it had led Lane along for ten minutes, it stopped. Its naked hand touched the wall. He became aware that the hand was small and delicately shaped, like a woman's.

A section of the wall swung out. The biped turned and bent down to crawl into the hole, presenting buttocks and legs femininely rounded, well shaped. It was then that he began thinking of it as a female. Yet the hips, though padded with fatty tissue, were not broad. The bones were not widely separated to make room to carry a child. Despite their curving, the hips were relatively as narrow as a man's.

Behind them, the plug swung shut. The biped did not turn on her flashlight, for there was illumination at the end of the tunnel. The floor and walls were not of the hard grey stuff nor of packed earth. They seemed vitrified, as if glassed by heat.

She was waiting for him when he slid off a three-foot high ledge into a large room. For a minute he was blinded by the strong light. After his eyes adjusted, he searched for the source of light but could not find it. He did observe that there were no shadows in the room.

The biped took off her helmet and suit and hung them in a closet. The door slid open as she approached and closed when she walked away.

She signalled that he could remove his suit. He did not hesitate. Though the air might be poisonous, he had no choice. His tank would soon be empty. Moreover, it seemed likely that the atmosphere contained enough oxygen. Even then he had grasped the idea that the leaves of the umbrella plants, which grew out of the top of the tubes, absorbed sunlight and traces of carbon dioxide. Inside the tunnels, the roots drew up water from the channel and absorbed the great quantity of carbon dioxide released by the dekapeds. Energy of sunlight converted gas and liquid into glucose and oxygen, which were given off in the tunnels.

Even here, in this deep chamber which lay beneath and to one side of the tube, a thick root penetrated the ceiling and spread its thin white web over the walls. He stood directly beneath the fleshy growth as he removed his helmet and took his first breath of Martian air. Immediately afterwards, he jumped. Something wet had dropped on his forehead. Looking up, he saw that the root was excreting liquid from a large pore. He wiped the drop off with his finger and tasted it. It was sticky and sweet.

Well, he thought, the tree must normally drop sugar in water. But it seemed to be doing so abnormally fast, because another drop was forming.

Then it came to him that perhaps this was so because it was getting dark outside and therefore cold. The umbrella trees might be pumping the water in their trunks into the warm tunnels. Thus, during the bitter subzero night, they'd avoid freezing and swelling up and cracking wide open.

It seemed a reasonable theory.

He looked around. The place was half living quarters, half biological laboratory. There were beds and tables and chairs and several unidentifiable articles. One was a large black metal box in a corner. From it, at regular intervals, issued a stream of tiny blue bubbles. They rose to the ceiling, growing larger as they did so. On reaching the ceiling they did not stop or burst but simply penetrated the vitrification as if it did not exist.

Lane now knew the origin of the blue globes he had seen appear from the surface of the garden. But their purpose was still obscure.

He wasn't given much time to watch the globes. The biped took a large green ceramic bowl from a cupboard and set it on a table. Lane eyed her curiously, wondering what she was going to do. By now he had seen that the second head belonged to an entirely separate creature. Its slim four foot length of pinkish skin was coiled about her neck and torso; its tiny flat-faced head turned towards Lane; its snaky light blue eyes glittered.

Suddenly, its mouth opened and revealed toothless gums, and its bright red tongue, mammalian, not at all reptilian, thrust out at him.

The biped, paying no attention to the worm's actions, lifted it from her. Gently, cooing a few words in a soft many-vowelled language, she placed it in the bowl. It settled inside and looped around the curve, like a snake in a pit.

The biped took a pitcher from the top of a box of red plastic. Though the box was not connected to any visible power source, it seemed to be a stove. The pitcher contained warm water which she poured into the bowl, half filling it. Under the shower, the worm closed its eyes as if it were purring soundless ecstasy.

Then the biped did something that alarmed Lane.

She leaned over the bowl and vomited into it.

He stepped towards her. Forgetting the fact that she couldn't understand him, he said, 'Are you sick?'

She revealed human-looking teeth in a smile meant to reassure him, and she walked away from the bowl. He looked at the worm, which had its head dipped into the mess. Suddenly, he felt sick, for he was sure that it was feeding off the mixture. And he was equally certain that she fed the worm regularly with regurgitated food.

It didn't cancel his disgust to reflect that he shouldn't react to her as he would to a Terrestrial. He knew that she was totally alien and that it was inevitable that some of her ways would repel, perhaps even shock him. Rationally, he knew this. But if his brain told him to understand and forgive, his belly said to loathe and reject.

His aversion was not much lessened by a close scrutiny of her as she took a shower in a cubicle set in the wall. She was about five feet tall and slim as a woman should be slim, with delicate bones beneath rounded flesh. Her legs were human; in nylons and high heels they would have been exciting – other things being equal. However, if the shoes had been toeless, her feet would have caused much comment. They had four toes.

Her long beautiful hands had five fingers. These seemed nailless, like the toes, though a closer examination later showed him they did bear rudimentary nails.

She stepped from the cubicle and began towelling herself, though not before she motioned to him to remove his suit and also to shower. He stared intently back at her until she laughed a short embarrassed laugh. It was feminine, not at all deep. Then she spoke.

He closed his eyes and was hearing what he had thought he would not hear for years: a woman's voice. Hers was extra-ordinary: husky and honeyed at the same time.

But when he opened his eyes, he saw her for what she was. No woman. No man. What? It? No. The impulse to think *her, she,* was too strong.

This, despite her lack of mammaries. She had a chest, but no nipples, rudimentary or otherwise. Her chest was a man's, muscled under the layer of fat which subtly curved to give the impression that beneath it . . . budding breasts?

No, not this creature. She would never suckle her young. She did not even bear them alive, if she *did* bear. Her belly was smooth, undimpled with a navel.

Smooth also was the region between her legs, hairless, un-broken, as innocent of organ as if she were a nymph painted for some Victorian children's book.

It was that sexless joining of the legs that was so horrible. Like the white belly of a frog, thought Lane, shuddering.

At the same time, his curiosity became even stronger. How did this thing mate and reproduce?

Again she laughed and smiled with fleshy pale-red humanly everted lips and wrinkled a short, slightly uptilted nose and ran her hand through thick straight red-gold fur. It was fur, not hair, and it had a slightly oily sheen, like a water-dwelling animal's.

The face itself, though strange, could have passed for human, but only passed. Her cheekbones were very high and protruded upwards in an unhuman fashion. Her eyes were dark blue and quite human. This meant nothing. So were an octopus's eyes.

She walked to another closet, and as she went away from him he saw again that though the hips were curved like a woman's they did not sway with the pelvic displacement of the human female.

The door swung momentarily open, revealed the carcasses of several dekapeds, minus their legs, hanging on hooks. She re-moved one, placed it on a metal table, and out of the cupboard took a saw and several knives and began cutting.

Because he was eager to see the anatomy of the dekaped, he approached the table. She waved him to the shower. Lane re-moved his suit. When he came to the knife and axe he hesitated, but, afraid she might think him distrustful, he hung up the belt containing his weapons beside the suit. However, he did not take off his clothes because he was determined to view the inner organs of the animal. Later, he would shower.

The legger was not an insect, despite its spidery appearance. Not in the terrestrial sense, certainly. Neither was it a vertebrate. Its smooth hairless skin was an animal's, as lightly pigmented as a blond Swede's. But, though it had an endo-skeleton, it had no backbone. Instead, the body bones formed a round cage. Its thin ribs radiated from a cartilaginous collar which adjoined the back of the head. The ribs curved outwards, then in, almost meeting at the posterior. Inside the cage were ventral lung sacs, a relatively large heart, and liver-like and kidney-like organs. Three arteries, instead of the mammalian two, left the heart. He couldn't be sure with such a hurried examination, but it looked as if the dorsal aorta, like some terrestrial reptiles, carried both pure and impure blood.

There were other things to note. The most extraordinary was that, as far as he could discern, the legger had no digestive system. It seemed to lack both intestines and anus unless you would define as an intestine a sac which ran straight through from the throat half-way into the body. Further, there was nothing he could identify as reproductive organs, though this did not mean that it did not possess them. The creature's long tubular tongue, cut open by the biped, exposed a canal running down the length of tongue from its open tip to a bladder at its base. Apparently these formed part of the excretory system.

Lane wondered what enabled the legger to stand the great pressure differences between the interior of the tube and the Martian surface. At the same time he realized that this ability was no more wonderful than the biological mechanism which gave whales and seals the power to endure without harm the enormous pressures a half mile below the sea's surface.

The biped looked at him with round and very pretty blue eyes, laughed, and then reached into the chopped open skull and brought out the tiny brain.

'Hauaimi,' she said slowly. She pointed to her head, repeated. 'Hauaimi,' and then indicated his head. 'Hauaimi.'

Echoing her, he pointed at his own head. 'Hauaimi. Brain.'

'Brain,' she said, and she laughed again.

She proceeded to call out the organs of the legger which

corresponded to hers. Thus, the preparations for the meal passed swiftly as he proceeded from the carcass to other objects in the room. By the time she had fried the meat and boiled strips of the membranous leaf of the umbrella plant, and also added from cans various exotic foods, she had exchanged at least forty words with him. An hour later, he could remember twenty.

There was one thing yet to learn. He pointed to himself and said, 'Lane.'

Then he pointed to her and gave her a questioning look.

'Mahrseeya,' she said.

'Martia?' he repeated. She corrected him, but he was so struck by the resemblance that always afterwards he called her that. After a while, she would give up trying to teach him the exact pronunication.

Martia washed her hands and poured him a bowlful of water. He used the soap and towel she handed him, then walked to the table where she stood waiting. On it was a bowl of thick soup, a plate of fried brains, a salad of boiled leaves and some unidentifiable vegetables, a plate of ribs with thick dark legger meat, hard-boiled eggs and little loaves of bread.

Martia gestured for him to sit down. Evidently her code did not allow her to sit down before her guest did. He ignored his chair, went behind her, put his hand on her shoulder, pressed down, and with the other hand slid her chair under her. She turned her head to smile up at him. Her fur slid away to reveal one lobeless pointed ear. He scarcely noticed it, for he was too intent on the half-repulsive, half-heartquickening sensation he got when he touched her skin. It had not been the skin itself that caused that, for she was soft and warm as a young girl. It had been the *idea* of touching her.

Part of that, he thought as he seated himself, came from her nakedness. Not because it revealed her sex but because it revealed her lack of it. No breasts, no nipples, no navel, no pubic fold or projection. The absence of these seemed wrong, very wrong, unsettling. It was a shameful thing that she had nothing of which to be ashamed.

That's a queer thought, he said to himself. And for no reason, he became warm in the face.

Martia, unnoticing, poured from a tall bottle a glassful of dark wine. He tasted it. It was exquisite, no better than the best Earth had to offer but as good.

Martia took one of the loaves, broke it into two pieces, and handed him one. Holding the glass of wine in one hand and the bread in the other, she bowed her head, closed her eyes, and began chanting.

He stared at her. This was a prayer, a grace-saying. Was it the prelude to a sort of communion, one so like Earth's it was startling?

Yet, if it were, he needn't be surprised. Flesh and blood, bread and wine: the symbolism was simple, logical, and might even be universal.

However it was possible that he was creating parallels that did not exist. She might be enacting a ritual whose origin and meaning were like nothing of which he had ever dreamed.

If so, what she did next was equally capable of misinterpretation. She nibbled at the bread, sipped the wine and then plainly invited him to do the same. He did so. Martia took a third and empty cup, spat a piece of wine-moistened bread into the cup, and indicated that he was to imitate her.

After he did, he felt his stomach draw in on itself. For she mixed the stuff from their mouths with her finger and then offered it to him. Evidently, he was to put the finger in his mouth and eat from it.

So the action was both physical and metaphysical. The bread and the wine were the flesh and blood of whatever divinity she worshipped. More, she, being imbued with the body and the spirit of the god, now wanted to mingle hers and that of the god's with his.

What I eat of the god's, I become. What you eat of me, you become. What I eat of you, I become. Now we three are become one.

Lane, far from being repelled by the concept, was excited. He knew that there were probably many Christians who would have refused to share in the communion because the ritual did not have the same origins or conform to theirs. They might even have thought that by sharing they were subscribing to an alien god. Such an idea Lane considered to be not only narrow-minded and inflexible, but illogical, uncharitable, and ridiculous. There could be but one Creator; what names the creature gave to the Creator did not matter.

Lane believed sincerely in a personal god, one who took note of him as an individual. He also believed that mankind needed redeeming and that a redeemer had been sent to Earth. And if other worlds needed redeeming, then they too would have got or would get a redeemer. He went perhaps further than most of his fellow religionists, for he actually made an attempt to practice love for mankind. This had given him somewhat of a reputation as a fanatic among his acquaintances and friends. However, he had been restrained enough not to make himself too much of a nuisance, and his genuine warmheartedness had made him welcome in spite of his eccentricity.

Six years before, he had been an agnostic. His first trip into space had converted him. The overwhelming experience had made him realize shatteringly what an insignificant being·he was, how awe-inspiringly complicated and immense was the universe, and how much he needed a framework within which to be and to become.

The strangest feature about his conversion, he thought afterwards, was that one of his companions on that maiden trip had been a devout believer who, on returning to Earth, had renounced his own sect and faith and become a complete atheist.

He thought of this as he took her proffered finger in his mouth and sucked the paste off it.

Then obeying her gestures, he dipped his own finger into the bowl and put it between her lips.

She closed her eyes and gently mouthed the finger. When he began to withdraw it, he was stopped by her hand on his wrist. He did not insist on taking the finger out, for he wanted to avoid offending her. Perhaps a long time interval was part of the rite.

But her expression seemed so eager and at the same time so ecstatic, like a hungry baby just given the nipple, that he felt uneasy. After a minute, seeing no indication on her part that she meant to quit, he slowly but firmly pulled the finger loose. She opened her eyes and sighed, but she made no comment. Instead, she began serving his supper.

The hot thick soup was delicious and invigorating. Its texture was somewhat like the plankton soup that was becoming popular on hungry Earth, but it had no fishy flavour. The brown bread reminded him of rye. The legger meat was like wild rabbit, though it was sweeter and had an unidentifiable tang. He took only one bite of the leaf salad and then frantically poured wine down his throat to wash away the burn. Tears came to his eyes, and he coughed until she spoke to him in an alarmed tone. He smiled back at her but refused to touch the salad again. The wine not only cooled his mouth, it filled his veins with singing. He told himself he should take no more. Nevertheless, he finished his second cup before he remembered his resolve to be temperate.

By then it was too late. The strong liquor went straight to his head; he felt dizzy and wanted to laugh. The events of the day, his near-escape from death, the reaction to knowing his comrades were dead, his realization of his present situation, the tension caused by his encounters with the dekapeds, and his unsatisfied curiosity about Martia's origin and the location of others of her kind, all these combined to produce in him a half-stupor, half-exuberance.

He rose from the table and offered to help Martia with the dishes. She shook her head and put the dishes in a washer. In the meantime, he decided that he needed to wash off the sweat, stickiness, and body odour left by two days of travel. On opening the door to the shower cubicle, he found that there wasn't room enough to hang his clothes in it. So, uninhibited by fatigue and wine also mindful that Martia, after all, was *not* a female, he removed his clothes.

Martia watched him, and her eyes became wider with each garment shed. Finally, she gasped and stepped back and turned pale.

'It's not that bad,' he growled, wondering what had caused her reaction. 'After all, some of the things I've seen around here aren't too easy to swallow.'

She pointed with a trembling finger and asked him something in a shaky voice.

Perhaps it was his imagination, but he could swear she used the same inflection as would an English speaker.

'Are you sick? Are the growths malignant?'

He had no words with which to explain, nor did he intend to illustrate function through action. Instead, he closed the door of the cubicle after him and pressed the plate that turned on the water. The heat of the shower and the feel of the soap, of grime and sweat being washed away, soothed him somewhat, so that he could think about matters he had been too rushed to consider.

First, he would have to learn Martia's language or teach her his. Probably both would happen at the same time. Of one thing he was sure. That was that her intentions towards him were, at least at present, peaceful. When she had shared communion with him, she had been sincere. He did not get the impression that it was part of her cultural training to share bread and wine with a person she intended to kill.

Feeling better, though still tired and a little drunk, he left the cubicle. Reluctantly, he reached for his dirty shorts. Then he smiled. They had been cleaned while he was in the shower. Martia, however, paid no attention to his smile of pleased surprise but, grim-faced, she motioned to him to lie down on the bed and sleep. Instead of lying down herself, however, she picked up a bucket and began crawling up the tunnel. He decided to follow her, and, when she saw him, she only shrugged her shoulders.

On emerging into the tube, Martia turned on her flashlight. The tunnel was in absolute darkness. Her beam, playing on the ceiling, showed that the glowworms had turned out their lights. There were no leggers in sight.

She pointed the light at the channel so he could see that the jetfish were still taking in and expelling water. Before she could turn the beam aside, he put his hand on her wrist and with his other hand lifted a fish from the channel. He had to pull it loose with an effort, which was explained when he turned the torpedo-shaped creature over and saw the column of flesh hanging from its belly. Now he knew why the reaction of the propelled water did not shoot them backwards. The ventral-foot acted as a suction pad to hold them to the floor of the channel.

Somewhat impatiently, Martia pulled away from him and began walking swiftly back up the tunnel. He followed her until she came to the opening in the wall which had earlier made her so apprehensive. Crouching, she entered the opening, but before she had gone far she had to move a tangled heap of leggers to one side. There were the large great-beaked ones he had seen guarding the entrance. Now they were asleep at the post.

If so, he reasoned, then the thing they guarded against must also be asleep.

What about Martia? How did she fit into their picture? Perhaps she didn't fit into their picture at all. She was absolutely alien, something for which their instinctual intelligence was not prepared and which, therefore, they ignored. That would explain why they had paid no attention to him when he was mired in the garden.

Yet there must be an exception to that rule. Certainly Martia had not wanted to attract the sentinels' notice the first time she had passed the entrance.

A moment later he found out why. They stepped into a huge chamber which was at least two hundred feet square. It was as dark as the tube, but during the waking period it must have been very bright because the ceiling was jammed with glow-worms.

Martia's flash raced around the chamber, showing him the piles of sleeping leggers. Then, suddenly it stopped. He took one look, and his heart raced, and the hairs on the back of his neck rose.

Before him was a worm three feet high and twenty feet long.

Without thinking, he grabbed hold of Martia to keep her from coming closer to it. But even as he touched her, he dropped his hand. She must know what she was doing.

Martia pointed the flash at her own face and smiled as if to tell him not to be alarmed. And she touched his arm with a shyly affectionate gesture.

For a moment, he didn't know why. Then it came to him that she was glad because he had been thinking of her welfare. Moreover, her reaction showed she had recovered from her shock at seeing him unclothed.

He turned from her to examine the monster. It lay on the floor, asleep, its great eyes closed behind vertical slits. It had a huge head, football-shaped like those of the little leggers around it. Its mouth was big, but the beaks were very small, horny warts on its lips. The body, however, was that of a caterpillar worm's, minus the hair. Ten little useless legs stuck out of its side, too short even to reach the floor. Its sides bulged as if pumped full of gas.

Martia walked past the monster and paused by its posterior. Here she lifted up a fold of skin. Beneath it was a pile of a dozen leathery-skinned eggs, held together by a sticky secretion.

'Now I've got it,' muttered Lane. 'Of course. The egg-laying queen. She specializes in reproduction. That is why the others have no reproductive organs, or else they're so rudimentary I couldn't detect them. The leggers are animals, all right, but in some things they resemble terrestrial insects.

'Still, that doesn't explain the absence also of a digestive system.'

Martia put the eggs in her bucket and started to leave the room. He stopped her and indicated he wanted to look around some more. She shrugged and began to lead him around. Both had to be careful not to step on the dekapeds, which lay everywhere.

They came to an open bin made of the same grey stuff as the walls. Its interior held many shelves, on which lay hundreds of eggs. Strands of the spiderwebby stuff kept the eggs from rolling off.

Nearby was another bin that held water. At its bottom lay more eggs. Above them minnow-sized torpedo shapes flitted about in the water.

Lane's eyes widened at this. The fish were not members of another genus but were the larvae of the leggers. And they could be set in the channel not only to earn their keep by pumping water which came down from the North Pole but to grow until they were ready to metamorphose into the adult stage.

However, Martia showed him another bin which made him partially revise his first theory. This bin was dry, and the eggs were laid on the floor. Martia picked one up, cut its tough skin open with her knife, and emptied its contents into one hand.

Now his eyes did get wide. This creature had a tiny cylindrical body, a suction pad at one end, a round mouth at the other, and two globular organs hanging by the mouth. A young glowworm.

Martia looked at him to see if he comprehended. Lane held out his hands and hunched his shoulders with an I-don't-get-it air. Beckoning, she walked to another bin to show him more eggs. Some had been ripped from within, and the little fellows whose hard beaks had done it were staggering around weakly on ten legs.

Energetically, Martia went through a series of charades. Watching her, he began to understand.

The embryos that remained in the eggs until they fully developed went through three main metamorphoses: the jetfish stage, the glowworm stage, and finally the baby dekaped stage. If the eggs were torn open by the adult nurses in one of the first two stages, the embryo remained fixed in that form, though it did grow larger.

What about the queen? he asked her by pointing to the monstrously egg-swollen body.

For answer, Martia picked up one of the newly-hatched. It kicked its many legs but did not otherwise protest, being, like all its kind, mute. Martia turned it upside down and indicated a slight crease in its posterior. Then she showed him the same spot on one of the sleeping adults. The adult's rear was smooth, innocent of the crease.

Martia made eating gestures. He nodded. The creatures were born with rudimentary sexual organs, but these never developed. In fact, they atrophied completely unless the young were given a special diet, in which case they matured into egg-layers.

But the picture wasn't complete. If you had females, you had to have males. It was doubtful if such highly developed animals were self-fertilizing or reproduced parthenogenetically.

Then he remembered Martia and began doubting. She gave no evidence of reproductive organs. Could her kind be self-producing. Or was she a Martian, her natural fulfilment diverted by diet?

It didn't seem likely, but he couldn't be sure that such things were not possible in her scheme of Nature.

Lane wanted to satisfy his curiosity. Ignoring her desire to get out of the chamber, he examined each of the five baby dekapeds. All were potential females.

Suddenly Martia, who had been gravely watching him, smiled and took his hand, and led him to the rear of the room. Here, as they approached another structure, he smelled a strong odour which reminded him of clorox.

Closer to the structure, he saw that it was not a bin but a hemispherical cage. Its bars were of the hard grey stuff, and they curved up from the floor to meet at a central point. There was no door. Evidently the cage had been built around the thing in it, and its occupant must remain until he died.

Martia soon showed him why this thing was not allowed freedom. It – he – was sleeping, but Martia reached through the bars and struck it on the head with her fist. The thing did not respond until it had been hit five more times. Then, slowly, it opened its sidewise lids to reveal great staring eyes, bright as fresh arterial blood.

Martia threw one of the eggs at the thing's head. Its beak opened swiftly, the egg disappeared, the beak closed, and there was a noisy gulp.

Food brought it to life. It sprang up on its ten long legs, clacked its beak, and lunged against the bars again and again.

Though in no danger, Martia shrank back before the killer's lust in the scarlet eyes. Lane could understand her reaction. It was a giant, at least two feet higher than the sentinels. Its back was on a level with Martia's; its beaks could have taken her head in between them.

Lane walked around the cage to get a good look at its posterior. Puzzled he made another circuit without seeing anything of maleness about it except its wild fury like that of a stallion locked in a barn during mating season. Except for its size, red eyes, and a cloaca, it looked like one of the guards.

He tried to communicate to Martia his puzzlement. By now, she seemed to anticipate his desires. She went through another series of pantomimes, some of which were so energetic and comical that he had to smile.

First, she showed him two eggs on a nearby ledge. These were larger than the others and were speckled with red spots. Supposedly, they held male embryos.

Then she showed him what would happen if the adult male got loose. Making a face which was designed to be ferocious but only amused him, clicking her teeth and clawing with her hands, she imitated the male running amok. He would kill everybody in sight. Everybody, the whole colony, queen, workers, guards, larvae, eggs, bite off their heads, mangle them, eat them all up, all, all. And out of the slaughterhouse he would charge into the tube and kill every legger he met, devour the jetfish, drag down the glowworms from the ceiling, rip them apart, eat them, eat the roots of the trees. Kill, kill, kill, eat, eat, eat!

That was all very well, signed Lane. But how did. . . .?

Martia indicated that, once a day, the workers rolled, literally rolled the queen across the room to the cage. There they arranged her so that she presented her posterior some few inches from the bars and the enraged male. And the male, though he wanted to do nothing but get his beak into her flesh and tear her apart, was not master of himself. Nature took over; his will was betrayed by his nervous system.

Lane nodded to show he understood. In his mind was a picture of the legger that had been butchered. It had had one sac at the internal end of the tongue. Probably the male had two, one to hold excretory matter, the other to hold seminal fluid.

Suddenly Martia froze, her hands held out before her. She had laid the flashlight on the floor so she could act freely; the beam splashed on her paling skin.

'What is it?' said Lane, stepping towards her.

Martia retreated, holding out her hands before her. She looked horrified.

'I'm not going to harm you,' he said. However, he stopped so she could see he didn't mean to get any closer to her.

What was bothering her? Nothing was stirring in the chamber itself besides the male, and he was behind her.

Then she was pointing, first at him and then at the raging dekaped. Seeing this unmistakable signal of identification, he comprehended. She had perceived that he, like the thing in the cage, was male, and now she perceived structure and function in him.

What he didn't understand was why that should make her so frightened of him. Repelled, yes. Her body, its seeming lack of sex, had given him a feeling of distaste bordering on nausea. It was only natural that she should react similarly to his body. However, she had seemed to have got over her first shock.

Why this unexpected change, this horror of him?

Behind him, the beak of the male clicked as it lunged against the bars.

The click echoed in his mind.

Of course, the monster's lust to kill!

Until she had met him, she had known only one male creature. That was the caged thing. Now, suddenly, she had equated him with the monster. A male was a killer.

Desperately, because he was afraid that she was about to run in a panic out of the room, he made signs that he was not like this monster; he shook his head no, no, no. He wasn't, he wasn't, he wasn't!

Martia, watching him intently, began to relax. Her skin regained its pinkish hue. Her eyes became their normal size. She even managed a strained smile.

To get her mind off the subject, he indicated that he would like to know why the queen and her consort had digestive systems, though the workers did not. For answer, she reached up into the downhanging mouth of the worm suspended from the ceiling. Her hand, withdrawn, was covered with secretion. After smelling her fist, she gave it to him to sniff also. He took it, ignoring her slight and probably involuntary flinching when she felt his touch.

The stuff had an odour such as you would expect from pre-digested food.

Martia then went to another worm. The two light organs of this one were not coloured red, like the other, but had a greenish tint. Martia tickled its tongue with her finger and held out her cupped hands. Liquid trickled into the cup.

Lane smelled the stuff. No odour. When he drank the liquid, he discovered it to be a thick sugar water.

Martia pantomimed that the glowworms acted as the digestive systems for the workers. They also stored food away for them. The workers derived part of their energy from the glucose excreted by the roots of the trees. The proteins and vegetable matter in their diet originated from the eggs and from the leaves of the umbrella plant. Strips of the tough membranous leaf were brought into the tubes by harvesting parties which ventured forth in the daytime. The worms partially digested the eggs, dead leggers, and leaves and gave it back in the form of a soup. The soup, like the glucose, was swallowed by the workers and passed through the walls of their throats or into the long straight sac which connected the throat to the larger blood vessels. The waste products were excreted through the skin or emptied through the canal in the tongue.

Lane nodded and then walked out of the room. Seemingly relieved, Martia followed him. When they had crawled back into her quarters, she put the eggs in a refrigerator and poured two glasses of wine. She dipped her finger in both, then touched the finger to her lips and to his. Lightly, he touched the tip with his tongue. This, he gathered, was one more ritual, perhaps a bedtime one, which affirmed that they were at one and at peace. It might be that it had an even deeper meaning, but if so, it escaped him.

Martia checked on the safety and comfort of the worm in the bowl. By now it had eaten all its food. She removed the worm, washed it, washed the bowl, half-filled it with warm sugar water, placed it on a table by the bed, and put the creature back in. Then she lay down on the bed and closed her eyes. She did not cover herself and apparently did not expect him to expect a cover.

Lane, tired though he was, could not rest. Like a tiger in its cage, he paced back and forth. He could not keep out of his mind the enigma of Martia nor the problem of getting back to base and eventually to the orbital ship. Earth must know what had happened.

After half an hour of this, Martia sat up. She looked steadily at him as if trying to discover the cause of his sleeplessness. Then, apparently sensing what was wrong, she rose and opened a cabinet hanging down from the wall. Inside were a number of books.

Lane said, 'Ah, maybe I'll get some information now!' and he leafed through them all. Wild with eagerness, he chose three and piled them on the bed before sitting down to peruse them.

Naturally, he could not read the texts, but the three had many illustrations and photographs. The first volume seemed to be a child's world history.

Lane looked at the first few pictures. Then he said, hoarsely, 'My God, you're no more Martian than I am!'

Martia, startled by the wonder and urgency in his voice, came over to his bed and sat down by him. She watched while he turned the pages over until he reached a certain photo. Unexpectedly, she buried her face in her hands, and her body shook with deep sobs.

Lane was surprised. He wasn't sure why she was in such grief. The photo was an aerial view of a city on her home planet – or some planet on which her people lived. Perhaps it was the city in which she had – somehow – been born.

It wasn't long, however, before her sorrow began to stir a response in him. Without any warning he, too, was weeping.

Now he knew. It was loneliness, appalling loneliness, of the kind he had known when he had received no more word from the men in the tanks and he had believed himself the only human being on the face of this world.

After a while, the tears dried. He felt better and wished she would also be relieved. Apparently she perceived his sympathy, for she smiled at him through her tears. And in an irresistible gust of rapport and affection she kissed his hand and then stuck two of his fingers in her mouth. This, he thought, must be her way of expressing friendship. Or perhaps it was gratitude for his presence. Or just sheer joy. In any event, he thought, her society must have a high oral orientation.

'Poor Martia,' he murmured. 'It must be a terrible thing to have to turn to one as alien and weird as I must seem. Especially to one who, a little while ago, you weren't sure wasn't going to eat you up.'

He removed his fingers but, seeing her rejected look, he impulsively took hers in his mouth.

Strangely, this caused another burst of weeping. However, he quickly saw that it was happy weeping. After it was over, she laughed softly, as if pleased.

Lane took a towel and wiped her eyes and held it over her nose while she blew.

Now, strengthened, she was able to point out certain illustrations and by signs give him clues to what they meant.

This child's book started with an account of the dawn of life on her planet. The planet revolved around a star that, according to a simplified map, was in the centre of the Galaxy.

Life had begun there much as it had on Earth. It had developed in its early stages on somewhat the same lines. But there were some rather disturbing pictures of primitive fish life. Lane wasn't sure of his interpretation, however, for these took much for granted.

They did show plainly that evolution there had picked out biological mechanisms with which to advance different from those on Earth.

Fascinated, he traced the passage from fish to amphibian to reptile to warm-blooded but non-mammalian creature to an upright ground-dwelling apelike creature to beings like Martia.

Then the pictures depicted various aspects of this being's prehistoric life. Later, the invention of agriculture, working of metals and so on.

The history of civilization was a series of pictures whose meaning he could seldom grasp. One thing was unlike Earth's history. There was a relative absence of warfare. The Rameseses, Genghis Khans, Attilas, Caesars, Hitlers seemed to be missing.

But there was more, much more. Technology advanced much as it had on Earth, despite a lack of stimulation from war. Perhaps, he thought, it had started sooner than on his planet. He got the impression that Martia's people had evolved to their present state much earlier than homo sapiens.

Whether that was true or not, they now surpassed man. They could travel almost as fast as light, perhaps faster, and had mastered interstellar travel.

It was then that Martia pointed to a page which bore several photographs of Earth, obviously taken at various distances by a spaceship.

Behind them an artist had drawn a shadowy figure, half-ape, half-dragon.

'Earth means this to you?' Lane said. *Danger? Do not touch?*

He looked for other photos of Earth. There were many pages dealing with other planets but only one of his home. That was enough.

'Why are you keeping us under distant surveillance?' said Lane. 'You're so far ahead of us that, technologically speaking, we're Australian aborigines. What're you afraid of?'

Martia stood up, facing him. Suddenly, viciously, she snarled and clicked her teeth and hooked her hands into claws.

He felt a chill. This was the same pantomime she had used when demonstrating the mindless kill-craziness of the caged male legger.

He bowed his head. 'I can't really blame you. You're absolutely correct. If you contacted us, we'd steal your secrets. And then, look out! We'd infest all of space!'

He paused, bit his lip, and said, 'Yet we're showing some signs of progress. There's not been a war or a revolution for fifteen years; the UN has been settling problems that would once have resulted in world war; Russia and the U.S. are still armed but are not nearly as close to conflict as they were when I was born. Perhaps . . . ?

'Do you know, I bet you've never seen an Earthman in the flesh before. Perhaps you've never seen a picture of one, or if you did, they were clothed. There are no photos of Earth people in these books. Maybe you knew we were male and female, but that didn't mean much until you saw me taking a shower. And the suddenly revealed parallel between the male dekaped and myself horrified you. And you realized that this was the only thing in the world that you had for companionship. Almost as if I'd been shipwrecked on an island and found the other inhabitant was a tiger.

'But that doesn't explain what you are doing here, alone, living in these tubes among the indigenous Martians. Oh, how I wish I could talk to you!'

'*With thee conversing,*' he said, remembering those lines he had read the last night in the base.

She smiled at him, and he said. 'Well, at least you're getting over your scare. I'm not such a bad fellow, after all, heh?'

She smiled again and went to a cabinet and from it took paper and pen. With them, she made one simple sketch after another. Watching her agile pen, he began to see what had happened.

Her people had had a base for a long time – a long long time – on the side of the Moon the Terrestrials could not see. But when rockets from Earth had first penetrated into space, her people had obliterated all evidence of the base. A new one had been set up on Mars.

Then, as it became apparent that a terrestrial expedition would be sent to Mars, that base had been destroyed and another one set up on Ganymede.

However, five scientists had remained behind in these simple quarters to complete their studies of the dekapeds. Though Martia's people had studied these creatures for some time, they still had not found out how their bodies could endure the differences between tube pressure and that in the open air. The four believed that they were breathing hot on the neck of this secret and had got permission to stay until just before the Earthmen landed.

Martia actually was a native, in the sense that she had been born and raised here. She had been seven years here, she indicated, showing a sketch of Mars in its orbit around the sun and then holding up seven fingers.

That made her about fourteen Earth years old, Lane estimated. Perhaps these people reached maturity a little faster than his. That is, if she were mature. It was difficult to tell.

Horror twisted her face and widened her eyes as she showed him what had happened the night before they were to leave for Ganymede.

The sleeping party had been attacked by an uncaged male legger.

It was rare that a male got loose. But he occasionally managed to escape. When he did, he destroyed the entire colony, all life in the tube wherever he went. He even ate the roots of the trees so that they died, and oxygen ceased to flow into that section of the tunnel.

There was only one way a forewarned colony could fight a rogue male – a dangerous method. That was to release their own male. They selected a few who could stay behind and sacrifice their lives to dissolve the bar with an acid secretion from their bodies while the others fled. The queen, unable to move, also died. But enough of her eggs were taken to produce another queen and another consort elsewhere.

Meanwhile, it was hoped that the males would kill each other or that the victor would be so crippled that he could be finished off by the soldiers.

Lane nodded. The only natural enemy of the dekapeds was an escaped male. Left unchecked, they would soon crowd the tubes and exhaust food and air. Unkind as it seemed, the escape of a male now and then was the only thing that saved the Martians from starvation and perhaps extinction.

However that might be, the rogue had been no blessing in disguise for Martia's people. Three had been killed in their sleep before the other two awoke. One had thrown herself at the beast and shouted to Martia to escape.

Almost insane with fear, Martia had nevertheless not allowed panic to send her running. Instead, she had dived for a cabinet to get a weapon.

—A weapon, thought Lane. I'll have to find out about that.

Martia acted out what had happened. She had got the cabinet door open and reached in for the weapon when she felt the beak of the rogue fastening on her legs. Despite the shock, for the beak cut deeply into the blood vessels and muscles, she had managed to press the end of the weapon against the male's body. The weapon did its work, for the male dropped on the floor. Unfortunately, the beaks did not relax but held their terrible grip on her thigh, just above the knee.

Here Lane tried to interrupt so he could get a description of what the weapon looked like and of the principle of its operation. Martia, however, ignored his request. Seemingly, she did not care to reply. He was not entirely trusted, which was understandable. How could he blame her? She would be a fool to be at ease with such an unknown quantity as himself. That is, if he were unknown. After all, though she did not know him well personally she knew the kind of people from whom he came and what could be expected from them. It was surprising that she had not left him to die in the garden and it was amazing that she had shared that communion of bread and wine with him.

Perhaps, he thought, it is because she was so lonely and any company was better than nothing. Or it might be that she acted on a higher ethical plane than most Earthmen and could not endure the idea of leaving a fellow sentient being to die, even if she thought him a bloodthirsty savage.

Or she might have other plans for him, such as taking him prisoner.

Martia continued her story. She had fainted and some time later had awakened. The male was beginning to stir, so she had killed him this time.

One more item of information, thought Lane. The weapon is capable of inflicting degrees of damage.

Then, though she kept passing out, she had dragged herself to the medicine chest and treated herself. Within two days she was up and hobbling around, and the scars were beginning to fade.

They must be far ahead of us in everything, he thought. According to her some of her muscles had been cut. Yet they grew together in a day.

Martia indicated that the repair of her body had required an enormous amount of food during the healing. Most of her time had been spent in eating and sleeping. Reconstruction whether it took place at a normal or accelerated rate, still required the same amount of energy.

By then the bodies of the male and of her companions were stinking with decay. She had had to force herself to cut them up and dispose of them in the garbage burner.

Tears welled in her eyes as she recounted this, and she sobbed.

Lane wanted to ask her why she had not buried them, but he reconsidered. Though it might not be the custom among her kind to bury the dead, it was more probable that she wanted to destroy all evidence of their existence before Earthmen came to Mars.

Using signs, he asked her how the male had got into the room despite the gate across the tunnel. She indicated that the gate was ordinarily closed only when the dekapeds were awake or when her companions and she were sleeping. But it had been the turn of one of their number to collect eggs in the queen's chamber. As she reconstructed it, the rogue had appeared at that time and killed the scientist there. Then, after ravening among the still-sleeping colony, it had gone down the tube and there had seen the light shining from the open tunnel. The rest of the story he knew.

Why, he pantomimed, why didn't the escaped male sleep when all his fellows did? The one in the cage evidently slept at the same time as his companions. And the queen's guards also slept in the belief they were safe from attack.

Not so, replied Martia. A male who had got out of a cage knew no law but fatigue. When he had exhausted himself in his eating and killing he lay down to sleep. But it did not matter if it was the regular time for it or not. When he was rested he raged through the tubes and did not stop until he was again too tired to move.

So, then, thought Lane, that explains the area of dead umbrella plants on top of the tube by the garden. Another colony moved into the devastated area, built the garden on the outside, and planted the young umbrellas.

He wondered why neither he nor the others of his group had seen the dekapeds outside during their six days on Mars. There must be at least one pressure chamber and outlet for each colony, and there should be at least fifteen colonies in the tubes between this point and that near his base. Perhaps the answer was that the leaf-croppers only ventured out occasionally. Now that he remembered it, neither he nor anyone else had noticed any holes in the leaves. That meant that the trees must be cropped some time ago and were now ready for another harvesting. If the expedition had only waited several days before sending out men in tracs, it might have seen the dekapeds and investigated. And the story would have been different.

There were other questions he had for her. What about the vessel that was to take them to Ganymede? Was there one hidden on the outside, or was one to be sent to pick them up? If one was to be sent how would the Ganymedan base be contacted? Radio? Or some – to him – inconceivable method?

The blue globes! he thought. Could they be means of transmitting messages?

He did not know or think further about them because fatigue overwhelmed him and he fell asleep. His last memory was that of Martia leaning over him and smiling at him.

When he awoke reluctantly his muscles ached and his mouth was as dry as the Martian desert. He rose in time to see Martia drop out of the tunnel, a bucket of eggs in her hand. Seeing this, he groaned. That meant she had gone into the nursery again, and that he had slept the clock around.

He stumbled up and into the shower cubicle. Coming out much refreshed, he found breakfast hot on the table. Martia conducted the communion rite, and then they ate. He missed his coffee. The hot soup was good but did not make a satisfactory substitute. There was a bowl of mixed cereal and fruit, both of which came out of a can. It must have had a high energy content, for it brought him wide awake.

Afterwards, he did some setting-up exercises while she did the dishes. Though he kept his body busy he was thinking of things unconnected with what he was doing.

What was to be his next move?

His duty demanded that he return to the base and report. What news he would send to the orbital ship! The story would flash from the ship back to Earth. The whole planet would be in an uproar.

There was one objection to his plan to take Martia back with him.

She would not want to go.

Halfway in a deep knee-bend he stopped. What a fool he was! He had been too tired and confused to see it. But if she had revealed that the base of her people was on Ganymede she did not expect him to take the information back to his transmitter. It would be foolish on her part to tell him unless she were absolutely certain that he would be able to communicate with no one.

That must mean that a vessel was on its way and would arrive soon. And it would not only take her but him. If he was to be killed, he would be dead now.

Lane had not been chosen to be a member of the first Mars expedition because he lacked decision. Five minutes later he had made up his mind. His duty was clear. Therefore he would carry it out, even if it violated his personal feelings towards Martia and caused her injury.

First, he'd bind her. Then he would pack up their two pressure suits, the books, and any tools small enough to carry so they might later be examined on Earth. He would make her march ahead of him through the tube until they came to the point opposite his base. There they would don their suits and go out to the dome. And as soon as possible the two would rise on the rocket to the orbital ship. This step was the most hazardous, for it was extremely difficult for one man to pilot the rocket. Theoretically, it could be done. It had to be done.

Lane tightened his jaw and forced his muscles to quit quivering. The thought of violating Martia's hospitality upset him. Still, she had treated him so well for a purpose not altogether altruistic. For all he knew, she was plotting against him.

There was a rope in one of the cabinets, the same flexible rope with which she had pulled him from the mire. He opened the door of the cabinet and removed it. Martia stood in the middle of the room and watched him while she stroked the head of the blue-eyed worm coiled about her shoulders. He hoped she would stay there until he got close. Obviously, she carried no weapon on her nor indeed anything except the pet. Since she had removed her suit, she had worn nothing.

Seeing him approaching her, she spoke to him in an alarmed tone. It didn't take much sensitivity to know that she was asking him what he intended to do with the rope. He tried to smile reassuringly at her and failed. This was making him sick.

A moment later he was violently sick. Martia had spoken loudly one word, and it was as if it had struck him in the pit of his stomach. Nausea gripped him, his mouth began salivating, and it was only by dropping the rope and running into the shower that he avoided making a mess on the floor.

Ten minutes later, he felt thoroughly cleaned out. But when he tried to walk to the bed, his legs threatened to give way. Martia had to support him.

Inwardly, he cursed. To have a sudden reaction to the strange food at such a crucial moment! Luck was not on his side.

That is, if it was chance. There had been something so strange and forceful about the manner in which she pronounced that word. Was it possible that she had set up in him – hypnotically or otherwise – a reflex to that word? It would, under the conditions, be a weapon more powerful than a gun.

He wasn't sure, but it did seem strange that his body had accepted the alien food until that moment. Hypnotism did not really seem to be the answer. How could it be so easily used on him since he did not know more than twenty words of her language?

Language? Words? They weren't necessary. If she had given him a hypnotic drug in his food, and then had awakened him during his sleep, she could have dramatized how he was to react if she wanted him to do so. She could have given him the key word, then have allowed him to go to sleep again.

He knew enough hypnotism to know that that was possible. Whether his suspicions were true or not, it was a fact that he had been laid flat on his back. However, the day was not wasted.

He learned twenty more words and she drew many more sketches for him. He found out that when he had jumped into the mire of the garden he had literally fallen into the soup. The substance in which the young umbrella trees had been planted was a zoogloea, a glutinous mass of one-celled vegetables and somewhat larger anaerobic animal life that fed on the vegetables. The heat from the jam-packed water-swollen bodies kept the garden soil warm and prevented the tender plants from freezing even during the forty degrees below zero Fahrenheit of the midsummer nights.

After the trees were transplanted into the roof of the tube to replace the dead adults, the zoogloea would be taken piecemeal back into the tube and dumped into the channel. Here the jet-fish would strain out part and eat part as they pumped water from the polar end of the tube to the equatorial end.

Towards the end of the day, he tried some of the zoogloea soup and managed to keep it down. A little later, he ate some cereal.

Martia insisted on spooning the food for him. There was something so feminine and tender about her solicitude that he could not protest.

'Martia,' he said, 'I may be wrong. There can be good will and rapport between our two kinds. Look at us. Why, if you were a real woman, I'd be in love with you.

'Of course, you may have made me sick in the first place. But if you did, it was a matter of expediency, not malice. And now you are taking care of me, your enemy. Love thy enemy. Not because you have been told you should but because you do.'

She, of course, did not understand him. However, she replied in her own tongue, and it seemed to him that her voice had the same sense of sympático.

As he fell asleep, he was thinking that perhaps Martia and he would be the two ambassadors to bring their people together in peace. After all, both of them were highly civilized, essentially pacifistic, and devoutly religious. There was such a thing as the brotherhood, not only of man, but of all sentient beings throughout the cosmos, and . . .

Pressure on his bladder woke him up. He opened his eyes. The ceiling and walls expanded and contracted. His wristwatch was distorted. Only by extreme effort could he focus his eyes enough to straighten the arms on his watch. The piece, designed to measure the slightly longer Martian day, indicated midnight.

Groggily, he rose. He felt sure that he must have been drugged and that he would still be sleeping if the bladder pain hadn't been so sharp. If only he could take something to counteract the drug, he could carry out his plans now. But first he had to get to the toilet.

To do so, he had to pass close to Martia's bed. She did not move but lay on her back, her arms flung out and hanging over the sides of the bed, her mouth open wide.

He looked away, for it seemed indecent to watch when she was in such a position.

But something caught his eye – a movement, a flash of light like a gleaming jewel in her mouth.

He bent over her, looked, and recoiled in horror.

A head rose from between her teeth.

He raised his hand to snatch at the thing but froze in the posture as he recognized the tiny pouting round mouth and little blue eyes. It was the worm.

At first, he thought Martia was dead. The thing was not coiled in her mouth. Its body disappeared into her throat.

Then he saw her chest was rising easily and that she seemed to be in no difficulty.

Forcing himself to come close to the worm, though his stomach muscles writhed and his neck muscles quivered, he put his hand close to its lips.

Warm air touched his fingers, and he heard a faint whistling. Martia was breathing through it!

Hoarsely, he said, 'God!', and he shook her shoulder. He did not want to touch the worm because he was afraid that it might do something to injure her. In that moment of shock he had forgotten that he had an advantage over her, which he should use.

Martia's lids opened; her large grey-blue eyes stared blankly.

'Take it easy,' he said soothingly.

She shuddered. Her lids closed, her neck arched back, and her face contorted.

He could not tell if the grimace was caused by pain or something else.

'What is this – this monster?' he said 'Symbiote? Parasite?'

He thought of vampires, of worms creeping into one's sleeping body and there sucking blood.

Suddenly she sat up and held out her arms to him. He seized her hands, saying, 'What is it?'

Martia pulled him towards her at the same time lifting her face to his.

Out of her open mouth shot the worm, its head pointed towards his face, its little lips formed into an O.

It was reflex, the reflex of fear that made Lane drop her hands and spring back. He had not wanted to do that, but he could not help himself.

Abruptly, Martia came wide awake. The worm flopped its full length from her mouth and fell into a heap between her legs. There it thrashed for a moment before coiling itself like a snake, its head resting on Martia's thigh, its eyes turned upwards to Lane.

There was no doubt about it. Martia looked disappointed, frustrated.

Lane's knees, already weak, gave way. However, he managed to continue to his destination. When he came out, he walked as far as Martia's bed, where he had to sit down. His heart was thudding against his ribs and he was panting hard.

He sat behind her, for he did not want to be where the worm could touch him.

Martia made motions for him to go back to his bed and they would all sleep. Evidently, he thought, she found nothing alarming in the incident.

But he knew he could not rest until he had some kind of explanation. He handed her paper and pen from the bedside table and then gestured fiercely. Martia shrugged and began sketching while Lane watched over her shoulder. By the time she had used up five sheets of paper, she had communicated her message.

His eyes were wide, and he was even paler.

So – Martia *was* a female. Female at least in the sense that she carried eggs – and, at times, young – within her.

And there was the so-called worm. So called? What could he call it? It could not be designated under one category. It was many things in one. It was a larva. It was a phallus. It was also her offspring, of her flesh and blood.

But not of her genes. It was not descended from her.

She had given birth to it, yet she was not its mother. She was neither one of its mothers.

The dizziness and confusion he felt was not caused altogether by his sickness. Things were coming too fast. He was thinking furiously, trying to get this new information clear, but his thoughts kept going back and forth, getting nowhere.

'There's no reason to get upset,' he told himself. 'After all, the splitting of animals into two sexes is only one of the ways of reproduction tried on Earth. On Martia's planet Nature – God – has fashioned another method for the higher animals. And only He knows how many other designs for reproduction He has fashioned on how many other worlds.'

Nevertheless, he was upset.

This worm, no, this larva, this embryo outside its egg and its secondary mother . . . well, call it, once and for all, larva, because it did metamorphose later.

This particular larva was doomed to stay in its present form until it died of old age.

Unless Martia found another adult of the Eeltau.

And unless she and this other adult felt affection for each other.

Then, according to the sketch she'd drawn, Martia and her friend, or lover, would lie down or sit together. They would as lovers do on Earth speak to each other in endearing, flattering, and exciting terms. They would caress and kiss much as Terrestrial man and woman do, though on Earth it was not considered complimentary to call one's lover Big Mouth.

Then, unlike the Terran custom, a third would enter the union to form a highly desired and indeed indispensable and eternal triangle.

The larva, blindly, brainlessly obeying its instincts, aroused by mutual fondling by the two, would descend tail first into the throat of one of the two Eeltau. Inside the body of the lover a fleshy valve would open to admit the slim body of the larva. Its open tip would touch the ovary of the host. The larva, like an electric eel, would release a tiny current. The hostess would go into an ecstasy, its nerves stimulated electro-chemically. The ovary would release an egg no larger than a pencil dot. It would disappear into the open tip of the larva's tail, there to begin a journey up a canal towards the centre of its body, urged on by the contraction of muscle and whipping of cilia.

Then the larva slid out of the first hostess' mouth and went tail first into the other, there to repeat the process. Sometimes the larva garnered eggs, sometimes not, depending upon whether the ovary had a fully developed one to release.

When the process was successful, the two eggs moved towards each other but did not quite meet.

Not yet.

There must be other eggs collected in the dark incubator of the larva, collected by pairs, though not necessarily from the same couple of donors.

These would number anywhere from twenty to forty pairs.

Then, one day, the mysterious chemistry of the cells would tell the larva's body that it had gathered enough eggs.

A hormone was released, the metamorphosis begun. The larva swelled enormously, and the mother, seeing this, placed it tenderly in a warm place and fed it plenty of predigested food and sugar water.

Before the eyes of its mother, the larva then grew shorter and wider. Its tail contracted; its cartilaginous vertebrae, widely separated in its larval stage, shifted closer to each other and hardened. A skeleton formed, ribs, shoulders. Legs and arms budded and grew and took humanoid shape. Six months passed, and there lay in its crib something resembling a baby of homo sapiens.

From then until its fourteenth year, the Eeltau grew and developed much as its Terran counterpart.

Adulthood, however, initiated more strange changes. Hormone released hormone until the first pair of gametes, dormant these fourteen years, moved together.

The two fused, the chromatin of one uniting with the chromatin of the other. Out of the two – a single creature, wormlike, four inches long, released into the stomach of its hostess.

Then, nausea. Vomiting. And so, comparatively painlessly, the bringing forth of a genetically new being.

It was this worm that would be both foetus and phallus and would give ecstasy and draw into its own body the eggs of loving adults and would metamorphose and become infant, child, and adult.

And so on and so on.

He rose and shakily walked to his own bed. There he sat down, his head bowed, while he muttered to himself.

'Let's see now. Martia gave birth to, brought forth, or up, this larva. But the larva actually doesn't have any of Martia's genes. Martia was just the hostess for it.

'However if Martia has a lover, she will, by means of this worm pass on her heritable qualities. This worm will become an adult and bring forth, or up, Martia's child.'

He raised his hands in despair.

'How do the Eeltau reckon ancestry? How keep track of their relatives? Or do they care? Wouldn't it be easier to consider your foster mother, your hostess, your real mother? As, in the sense of having borne you, she is?

'And what kind of a sexual code do these people have? It can't, I would think, be much like ours. Nor is there any reason why it should be.

'But who is responsible for raising the larva and child? Its pseudo-mother? Or does the lover share in the duties? And what about property and inheritance laws? And, and ...'

Helplessly, he looked at Martia.

Fondly stroking the head of the larva, she returned his stare.

Lane shook his head.

'I was wrong. Eeltau and Terran couldn't meet on a friendly basis. My people would react to yours as to disgusting vermin. Their deepest prejudices would be aroused, their strongest taboos would be violated. They could not learn to live with you or consider you even faintly human.

'And as far as that goes, could you live with us? Wasn't the sight of me naked a shock? Is that reaction a part of why you don't make contact with us?'

Martia put the larva down and stood up and walked over to him and kissed the tips of his fingers. Lane, though he had to fight against visibly flinching, took her fingers and kissed them. Softly, he said to her, 'Yet ... individuals could learn to respect each other, to have affection for each other. And masses are made of individuals.'

He lay back on the bed. The grogginess, pushed aside for a while by excitement, was coming back. He couldn't fight off sleep much longer.

'Fine noble talk,' he murmured. 'But it means nothing. The Eeltau don't think they should deal with us. And we are, unknowingly, pushing out towards them. What will happen when we are ready to make the interstellar jump? War? Or will they be afraid to let us advance even to that point and destroy us before then? After all, one cobalt bomb.'

He looked again at Martia, at the not-quite-human yet

beautiful face, the smooth skin of the chest, abdomen, and loins, innocent of nipple, navel, or labia. From far off she had come, from a possibly terrifying place across terrifying distances. About her, however, there was little that was terrifying and much that was warm, generous, companionable, attractive.

As if they had waited for some key to turn, and the key had been turned, the lines he had read before falling asleep that last night in the base came again to him.

It is the voice of my beloved that knocketh, saying,
Open to me, my sister, my love, my dove, my undefiled .

We have a little sister,
And she hath no breasts:
What shall we do for our sister
In the day when she shall be spoken for?

With thee conversing, I forget all time,
All seasons, and their change, all please alike.

'With thee conversing,' he said aloud. He turned over so his back was to her, and he pounded his fist against the bed.

'Oh dear God why couldn't it be so?'

A long time he lay there, his face pressed into the mattress. Something had happened; the overpowering fatigue was gone; his body had drawn strength from some reservoir. Realizing this, he sat up and beckoned to Martia, smiling at the same time.

She rose slowly and started to walk to him, but he signalled that she should bring the larva with her. At first, she looked puzzled. Then her expression cleared, to be replaced by understanding. Smiling delightedly, she walked to him, and though he knew it must be a trick of his imagination, it seemed to him that she swayed her hips as a woman would.

She halted in front of him and then stooped to kiss him full on the lips. Her eyes were closed.

He hesitated for a fraction of a second. She – no, it, he told himself – looked so trusting, so loving, so womanly, that he could not do it.

'For Earth!' he said fiercely and brought the edge of his palm hard against the side of her neck.

She crumpled forward against him, her face sliding into his

chest. Lane caught her under the armpits and laid her face down on the bed. The larva, which had fallen from her hand on to the floor, was writhing about as if hurt. Lane picked it up by its tail and, in a frenzy that owed its violence to the fear he might not be able to do it, snapped it like a whip. There was a crack as the head smashed into the floor, and blood spurted from its eyes and mouth. Lane placed his heel on the head and stepped down until there was a flat mess beneath his foot.

Then, quickly, before she could come to her senses and speak any words that would render him sick and weak, he ran to a cabinet. Snatching a narrow towel out of it, he ran back and gagged her. After that he tied her hands behind her back with the rope.

'Now you bitch!' he panted. 'We'll see who comes out ahead! You would do that with me, would you! You deserve this; your monster deserves to die!'

Furiously he began packing. In fifteen minutes he had the suits, helmets, tanks, and food rolled into two bundles. He searched for the weapon she had talked about and found something that might conceivably be it. It had a butt that fitted to his hand, a dial that might be a rheostat for controlling degrees of intensity of whatever it shot, and a bulb at the end. The bulb, he hoped, expelled the stunning and killing energy. Of course, he might be wrong. It could be fashioned for an entirely different purpose.

Martia had regained consciousness. She sat on the edge of the bed, her shoulders hunched, her head drooping, tears running down her cheeks and into the towel around her mouth. Her wide eyes were focused on the smashed worm by her feet.

Roughly, Lane seized her shoulder and pulled her upright. She gazed wildly at him, and he gave her a little shove. He felt sick within him, knowing that he had killed the larva when he did not have to do so and that he was handling her so violently because he was afraid, not of her, but of himself. If he had been disgusted because she had fallen into the trap he set for her, he was so because he, too, beneath his disgust, had wanted to commit that act of love. Commit, he thought, was the right word. It contained criminal implications.

Martia whirled around, almost losing her balance because of her tied hands. Her face worked, and sounds burst from the gag.

'Shut up!' he howled, pushing her again. She went sprawling

and only saved herself from falling on her face by dropping on her knees. Once more, he pulled her to her feet, noting as he did so that her knees were skinned. The sight of the blood instead of softening him, enraged him even more.

'Behave yourself, or you'll get worse!' he snarled.

She gave him one more questioning look, threw back her head, and made a strange strangling sound. Immediately, her face took on a bluish tinge. A second later, she fell heavily on the floor.

Alarmed, he turned her over. She was choking to death.

He tore off the gag and reached into her mouth and grabbed the root of her tongue. It slipped away and he seized it again, only to have it slide away as if it were a live animal that defied him.

Then he had pulled her tongue out of her throat; she had swallowed it in an effort to kill herself.

Lane waited. When he was sure she was going to recover, he replaced the gag around her mouth. Just as he was about to tie the knot at the back of her neck, he stopped. What use would it be to continue this? If allowed to speak, she would say the word that would throw him into retching. If gagged, she would swallow her tongue again.

He could save her only so many times. Eventually, she would succeed in strangling herself.

The one way to solve his problem was the one way he could not take. If her tongue were cut off at the root, she could neither speak nor kill herself. Some men might do it; he could not.

The only other way to keep her silent was to kill her.

'I can't do it in cold blood,' he said aloud. 'So, if you want to die, Martia, then you must do it by committing suicide. That, I can't help. Up you go. I'll get your pack, and we'll leave.'

Martia turned blue and sagged to the floor.

'I'll not help you this time!' he shouted, but he found himself frantically trying to undo the knot.

At the same time, he told himself what a fool he was. Of course! The solution was to use her own gun on her. Turn the rheostat to a stunning degree of intensity and knock her out whenever she started to regain consciousness. Such a course would mean he'd have to carry her and her equipment, too, on the thirty mile walk down the tube to an exit near his base. But he could do it. He'd rig up some sort of travois. He'd do it!

Nothing could stop him. And Earth . . .

At that moment, hearing an unfamiliar noise, he looked up. There were two Eeltau in pressure suits standing there, and another crawling out of the tunnel. Each had a bulb-tipped handgun in her hand.

Desperately, Lane snatched at the weapon he carried in his belt. With his left hand he twisted the rheostat on the side of the barrel, hoping that this would turn it on full force. Then he raised the bulb towards the group . . .

He woke flat on his back, clad in his suit, except for the helmet, and strapped to a stretcher. His body was helpless, but he could turn his head. He did so, and saw many Eeltau dismantling the room. The one who had stunned him with her gun before he could fire was standing by him.

She spoke in English that held only a trace of foreign accent. 'Settle down, Mr. Lane. You're in for a long ride. You'll be more comfortably situated once we're in our ship.'

He opened his mouth to ask her how she knew his name but closed it when he realized she must have read the entries in the log at the base. And it was to be expected that some Eeltau would be trained in Earth languages. For over a century their sentinel spaceships had been tuning in to radio and TV.

It was then that Martia spoke to the captain. Her face was wild and reddened with weeping and marks where she had fallen.

The interpreter said to Lane, '*Mahrseeya* asks you to tell her why you killed her . . . baby. She cannot understand why you thought you had to do so.'

'I cannot answer,' said Lane. His head felt very light, almost as if it were a balloon expanding. And the room began slowly to turn around.

'I will tell her why,' answered the interpreter. 'I will tell her that it is the nature of the beast.'

'That is not so!' cried Lane. 'I am no vicious beast. I did what I did because I had to! I could not accept her love and still remain a man! Not the kind of man . . .'

'*Mahrseeya*,' said the interpreter, 'will pray that you be forgiven the murder of her child and that you will someday, under our teaching, be unable to do such a thing. She herself, though she is stricken with grief for her dead baby, forgives you. She hopes the time will come when you will regard her as a – sister. She thinks there is some good in you.'

Lane clenched his teeth together and bit the end of his tongue until it bled while they put his helmet on. He did not dare to try to talk, for that would have meant he would scream and scream. He felt as if something had been planted in him and had broken its shell and was growing into something like a worm. It was eating him, and what would happen before it devoured all of him he did not know.

Four pioneering novels by
JULES VERNE
the father of modern science fiction

'His imaginative power is dateless'
KENNETH ALLSOP in
THE DAILY MAIL

'. . . funny, prophetic, biting . . . None
of his novels date; good tale-telling
never does'
TRIBUNE

FIVE WEEKS IN A BALLOON
A classic tale of exploration and peril

BLACK DIAMONDS
A land of dark terror in the bowels
of the earth

PROPELLER ISLAND
They created a floating hell . . . and
called it Utopia

THE SECRET OF WILHELM
STORITZ
He harnessed a fundamental energy of
the Universe that was terrifying in its
implications. . . .

each 3/6

Tune in to

Panther Crimeband

**An all-star series
presenting the best in mystery,
detection, and suspense**

THE IPCRESS FILE
Len Deighton 3/6

Never before have you read a spy story like this – a novel of
terrifying originality by an ingenious and idiosyncratic
writer of great talent.

'Something entirely new in spy fiction'
EVENING STANDARD

FLORENTINE FINISH
Cornelius Hirschberg 3/6

A dazzling thriller involving three murders set against
the fascinating background of the New York diamond trade.

Winner of the Edgar Allan Poe Award of the Mystery Writers
of America.

'The best crime novel of 1964'
BOOKS AND BOOKMEN

THE RELUCTANT ASSASSIN
Alain Reynaud-Fourton 3/6

Five gangsters meticulously plot a final coup to make
them rich for life – a narcotics job worth a cool million dollars.
Things are going smoothly – to the point where each is getting
ready to pick up his million. Then one of them gets greedy.

DEATH THE SURE PHYSICIAN
John Wakefield 3/6

A hospital bed is a logical enough place to die; but not as Manuela, a wardmaid at St. Ethelburga's hospital, died. Not so murderously.

'Brilliant'
THE GUARDIAN

'Plenty of clues, passion and general information make this a first-class detective story'
BOOKS AND BOOKMEN

FLUSH AS MAY
P. M. Hubbard 3/6

A vanishing corpse, a sinister policeman, a famous TV personality, and a quiet English village – where a primitive cult engages in macabre rites!

'If any man ever had the art of making you read on, it is P. M. Hubbard'
TATLER

THE CHINESE BELL MURDERS
Robert van Gulik 5/–

'A rich new vein of detective fiction'
TIMES LITERARY SUPPLEMENT

'To the old Chinese, Judge Dee was as real as Sherlock Holmes and Mr. van Gulik has had the capital notion of turning three stories of Judge Dee into one long tale. Welcome, welcome, Judge Dee and Mr. van Gulik'
J. B. PRIESTLEY

THE CHINESE LAKE MURDERS
Robert van Gulik 5/–

'Judge Dee remains the happiest recent addition to detective fiction'
NEW YORK POST

'It is head and shoulders above the day-to-day stuff that comes roaring from the press'
TIME AND TIDE

Famous authors in
Panther Books

Henry Miller	Henry Williamson
Norman Mailer	Vladimir Nabokov
Maurice Procter	Fernando Henriques
Jean-Paul Sartre	John O'Hara
Jean Genet	Howard Fast
Alan Moorehead	Hubert Monteilhet
Nicholas Monsarrat	Julian Mitchell
Colin Willock	Agnar Mykle
James Jones	Simon Raven
Erich Maria Remarque	Marcel Proust
Len Deighton	John Rechy
Saki	Gore Vidal
Jack London	John Barth
James Hadley Chase	Alan Williams
Georgette Heyer	Bill Naughton
Rex Stout	John Horne Burns
Isaac Asimov	David Caute
Jules Verne	Ivan Turgenev
Hans Habe	Colin Wilson
Marquis de Sade	H.P. Lovecraft
Doris Lessing	Rachel Carson
Mary McCarthy	Jerzy Peterkiewicz
Edmund Wilson	Curzio Malaparte